AF603891

THE TASKS OF THE DEPARTED

Junaid Ashraf

JA

Copyright © 2022 Junaid Ashraf

All rights reserved

No part of this book may be reproduced, or stored in a retrieval system, or transmitted in any form or by any means, electronic, mechanical, photocopying, recording, or otherwise, without express written permission of the author.

For my mummy, Rafin, and baby brother, Yusuf.

1

Christmas Time

Edward and Helen Baba, and their teenage children Karen and Al, lived in a charming little town on the outskirts of Gloucestershire – and they all absolutely adored Christmas Time. Each year, without fail, that warm feeling of contentment which can only be summoned by the festive period flared up fervently in their hearts. There was a particular (quite magical!) reason as to why this was the case.

Like any other family, the Babas faced their fair share of problems, but the festive period always seemed to – quite miraculously – sweep away these problems; they just vanished like the leaves on the trees during that time of the year. Strange as it was, they had stopped questioning where this good fortune came from and simply accepted it.

Christmas Day was fast approaching, but the mood in the Baba household was not jolly – for the first time in many a year. Al had just informed his family that he was being bullied at school. They found this revelation hugely surprising: *how could this problem have endured during this unfailingly problem-free period?* Having established that Al was not joking for some reason, his mother, father and sister were advising him on what to do. All three were of the same opinion: perhaps this was not actually a major cause for concern. Perhaps nothing had changed after all.

"I don't think you should take it that seriously, darling," Helen told her son with a gentle smile. "I know you're trying to focus on your studies at the moment and this is the last thing you need, but ... it's normal to have a bit of name-calling and so on in school."

"Your mum's right, Al," said Edward. "Sounds like just a bit of banter. When I was your age, we even used to have full-blown fights in the playground. But it was just play-fighting. Things like that were just ... you know ... normal."

"Don't be so wimpy, Al," Karen said playfully to her younger brother.

Al half-heartedly mumbled that he agreed with them and excused himself.

As he made his way up to his bedroom, it was as though the house was trying to cheer him up in its own little way. It had been decorated for Christmas that very afternoon and looked enchanting. The Babas lived in a large Tudor house, which Edward had inherited from his father, Alfred, before his marriage to Helen. Al – who was named after him – had been told how fond Alfred had been of making the house come to life with festive decorations; it was partially in tribute to his late grandfather that it was so luxuriously decorated every year. Great garlands of holly and mistletoe bursting with berries had been draped over almost everything: from tree-trunk-like oak beams to the staircase balustrade. It was as though Nature had reclaimed the house from the Babas (maybe as a Christmas present) and given it a makeover. Al's misery was such, though, that it could not easily be remedied.

He did not bother switching on the light in his bedroom; it certainly would not have made a difference to the more profound darkness gradually becoming denser inside him. He sat on his bed, deep in thought.

Al had not revealed the full extent of his problem to his family – he was being *severely* bullied. It was far from just a simple case of name-calling. A new pupil called Bruce Blight had decided that he absolutely despised Al – maybe because Al was a little more enthusiastic in lessons than he deemed appropriate, or maybe because Al was less skilled at making friends than most of his classmates, or maybe for no particular reason at all. Bruce Blight would express his hatred verbally and physically at every opportunity.

Although Al was sure his parents would find a way to resolve this situation if they were made aware of the full horror of it, the feeling of shame had prevented him from revealing all. Edward had always encouraged his children to stand up for themselves, and although Helen had been less vocal about this matter, Al knew his mother felt the same. He could not bear the idea of his parents being disappointed with him for not being able to defend himself and allowing the situation to deteriorate this far; the idea of seeing even a flicker of disappointment on their faces filled him with dread.

Al could not help but question – again and again – just why Christmas Time had suddenly decided to stop being blissful for the first time in his life. What had *happened* to that inexplicable magic which vanquished all their problems? The desperation of his situation made him wish with all his might that he knew where it had come from and why his family had been blessed with it ... and how to make it return. He was a rational fourteen-year-old, though, and part of him had accepted that he may never find out.

Tap. Tap.

Al jumped up, his heart racing and his eyes fixed on his bedroom window. He could see with the light from a streetlamp that there was nothing out there. The sound had been so loud, though; he was sure he had not imagined it. He edged closer to the lattice window, opened it and looked down. Not a soul. The frost-covered gravel below, glowing eerily in the orange lamplight, was all he could make out.

Just as Al was about to close the window, the stillness beyond was broken by a gust of wind, which propelled something into his room. He quickly switched on his bedroom light and saw what looked like a strange, long leaf lying on the carpet. On closer inspection, he saw that it was actually – quite astonishingly – a green scroll. He picked it up and unfurled it. There were words written on it in old-fashioned calligraphy. Each one looked like an individual work of art:

All will be well.

Al stared at the scroll for at least a minute. And then his astonishment at the strangeness of this event slowly morphed into a feeling of ... *comfort*. The message on the scroll ignited a sense of real hope inside him – hope that everything *would* be well, even though he was still unsure as to how. Was it really a message intended for him? Al did not want to believe otherwise. He looked up at the open window: all seemed perfectly still again.

There was a knock on his bedroom door, and his father came in. Al quickly put the scroll into his pocket.

Edward was a middle-aged, bespectacled man with a distinctive bald patch in his jet-black hair but had a youthful, thin face that had retained its handsomeness. Although Al was not bespectacled and his neatly combed hair was dark brown like that of his mother and sister, he resembled his father a great deal: his face was almost a replica of Edward's, and their blue eyes were identical.

"Hope I'm not disturbing you ..." said Edward.

Al indicated that he was not, and Edward gestured that they should sit on the bed to talk.

"Your mum just wanted me to pop in and see how you were."

"Fine," Al said at once with an attempt at a reassuring smile.

"Al, you have told us the full story about what's going on, haven't you?"

"Yes," he said simply, avoiding his father's gaze.

"Definitely think it *is* just banter like I was saying before," said Edward, looking somewhat relieved. "Don't think it's malicious at all. You're very intelligent, so I'm sure you can come up with really good comebacks ... Might even be fun—"

"Dad, can I ask you something?"

"Of course."

"Where do you think our Christmas Time luck comes from?"

Al could not remember the last time he had discussed this with any member of his family. He suspected that the scroll had something to do with it. *Had* to. Edward had clearly not expected to be asked this and was unable to respond for a while. The topic seemed to make him very uncomfortable.

"Are you wondering about this because of what's going on in school?"

For a few moments, Al considered telling Edward about

the scroll but decided against it, being quite sure his father would not consider it to be of any importance.

Edward did not wait long for a reply. "I simply don't know where it comes from, Al." He sighed. "It's obviously very strange ... But we should be grateful ... wherever it comes from."

Al nodded.

"Anyway, it's getting late," said Edward, looking at his watch. "See you in the morning. Goodnight."

Al suspected that his father would not have left so abruptly if he had not asked him that question.

As he sat at his desk to look over the essay he had been working on, the scroll still tucked in his pocket, Al's new-found sense of hope still burned brightly. But the fear of what tomorrow (a school day) would bring had not been completely subdued.

◆ ◆ ◆

Meanwhile, Bruce Blight was also having a far from ordinary evening on the other side of town.

Bruce looked very much like a hyena that had had the misfortune of being transformed into a human teenager: he had an oval-shaped face with large, protruding ears, and though he was tall and well built, he was a little stooped. He lived with his mother, who *always* made sure he got exactly what he wanted; it was as though she thought the word 'No' was tantamount to a swear word and inappropriate to use in front of her son. But not anymore. Mrs Blight was having a heated argument with Bruce, and she was getting more and more impatient and hysterical with every word she spoke:

"Bruce – I said we're going right now, and I *mean* right now! Pack your things!"

"Have you gone mad? At least explain what's going on!"

Bruce genuinely thought madness was the only explanation for his mother's behaviour. He had been in the middle of watching his favourite television programme filled with all manner of violence and gore as he always did at this time, and instead of bringing him a snack, his mother had switched off the television and informed him that they were to leave town immediately and were not coming back.

"No! I don't have time to explain things!" snapped Mrs Blight, her eyes bulging and her face bright red. "They're *everywhere*!"

"What's everywhere?!"

"JUST GO AND GET YOUR THINGS, OR I'M LEAVING WITHOUT YOU!"

For the first time in his life, Bruce did as he was told. He was swearing ferociously as he gathered his belongings, but in little more than half an hour, his and Mrs Blight's luggage was stowed in the car, their house was shut up and they were driving away, never to return.

It was Christmas Eve in the Baba household and the day that Edward's mother, Margaret, would be arriving to join her family for the festivities.

Ever since Alfred had passed away Margaret had lived alone in a cottage in the village she had been brought up in: she had found it too painful to continue living in the same house without him. Although she was now nearly eighty years old, she had the energy and appearance of someone far younger and always looked impeccable. Al was very close to his grandmother; he loved listening to her stories about the past – especially those that featured his grandfather – and also greatly respected her wisdom, even though it was often expressed in a typically forthright manner. Now that the demonic presence of Bruce Blight had mysteriously disappeared from his life, Al was able to look forward to Margaret's visit and the festive time ahead without anything overshadowing his excitement.

As was always the case before Margaret visited, Helen had become even more determined than usual to ensure the house was dust-free and had given Al and Karen the task of making everything look absolutely spotless. Whilst she was busy baking her Christmas Eve cake, they were dusting all the old ceramic ornaments dotted about the sitting room for the second time that morning at their mother's insistence.

"Doing this once was bad enough," moaned Karen as she replaced a bird figurine on the mantelpiece after giving it a thorough clean. "Granny won't be inspecting the house for particles of dust with a magnifying glass!"

Karen was a very slender eighteen-year-old with a kind, pretty face, who always kept her long hair tied up in a ponytail.

"Thought you liked handling animals," Al said with a grin as she now carefully picked up a horse figurine.

"Yes ... *real* animals. I'm studying to be a vet, not an antique dealer!"

Al laughed, namely at the thought of his sister being stuck in a shop full of dusty, old things. Karen loved the great outdoors as much as she loved animals and was the sort of person who was determined to have a life that resembled a never-ending camping trip.

"Come to think of it," said Karen as she moved lazily over to a very large cabinet full of yet more decorative figurines, "don't think I've even finished wrapping all my presents. I'm going to tell Mum that's a much bigger priority right now. I'm sure you can manage the rest of these on your own. You're a lot quicker than I am!" She smiled at him imploringly.

"Yes, fine. I'll finish the rest off."

"Thanks, little brother. You're one in a million."

"Hope I get a nicer present from you this year ... Haven't worn those hiking boots I got last Christmas even once!"

"Well, I liked them. In fact, I sort of *borrowed* them without asking you. Sorry!"

Al feigned amazement before laughing as Karen skipped out of the room with her ponytail dancing behind her.

If merriment was a source of light, then the old house of the Babas would have lit up the whole town on that bitterly cold Christmas Eve. The warm, golden glow of the fire, the jewel-like radiance of the decorations, the abundance of delicious Christmas delicacies and the simple gift of spending time in each other's company without any worries whatsoever all had a part to play in their joy.

They were busy decorating the Christmas tree, which dominated one end of the sitting room and completely obscured the large oriel window and the darkness beyond. Everyone was picking out an ornate decoration in turn from an old wooden box that Alfred had made in his youth. Margaret – striving as ever for nothing short of perfection – was guiding her family as to where best to hang them, using her cane as a pointer. Much to the amusement of Al and Karen, she kept changing her mind about where on the tree Edward should place a pair of silver bells.

"A bit further up, dear."

"Here?"

"No, not there – that's far too close to the elf!"

"How about there?"

"Actually, put them on the other side again so they catch the firelight more."

It was Al's turn to pick a decoration. He rummaged in the box without looking – he had a knack for picking out his favourite piece every year without fail. And he brought it out by its green silk loop: an exquisitely enamelled robin with a lustre that Al was sure would remain eternally bright.

"Ah," Margaret said with an air of nostalgia, "this was a gift from me to Alfred. It was his particular favourite. You can place it right in the centre."

Al beamed with pride at the thought of having something in common with his grandfather. Having heard so much about him and realising how adored he had been by Margaret and Edward, he always wished he had had the opportunity to get to know him.

After a short while, the tree was fully encrusted with colour, and Helen decided it was about time they had helpings of her Christmas Eve cake.

She had baked a lemon drizzle, which happened to

be the one Margaret was fondest of. It was always evident how much Helen looked up to her mother-in-law. Margaret took her matriarchal duties extremely seriously, and Helen naturally saw herself as her eventual successor. She also, rather fittingly, resembled her somewhat: both had very rosy cheeks and big curly hair (though Margaret's was white instead of dark brown).

"So ... what does everybody think about the cake?" Helen asked with a hint of nervousness, glancing at Margaret.

"It's *very* tangy." The expression on Margaret's face was momentarily unreadable before she smiled warmly and said, "And, of course, that's what makes it so delicious."

"Glad you like it," said Helen, clearly delighted.

"*Our* opinions obviously don't really matter much," Karen muttered to Al, her large brown eyes glinting with mischief.

It seemed Edward was quite taken with the cake too: his slice had disappeared off the plate in a matter of seconds.

"During moments like these, Helen," he said, "I'm really grateful you came into my life. What a great day that was!"

The natural rosiness of Helen's cheeks deepened a touch, clearly not expecting her husband to be so openly affectionate. "Yes," she said, "you were lucky that confused old historian decided to attend the conference that day. Bless him."

"Can't argue with that," Edward chortled.

Edward and Helen were both historians. They had met at a conference after an elderly historian mistakenly informed Edward that Helen wanted to have a word with him. This gentleman had unknowingly played the role of

Cupid and become a figure forever held in high esteem by the Babas. Edward and Helen never saw him again, though.

"What's in that, dear?" Margaret was looking at a battered biscuit tin Helen had on her lap.

"Thought I'd take Karen and Al on a little trip down memory lane!" enthused Helen as she opened the tin with a clunk.

She took out some old envelopes with large colourful words written on each of them: they were all addressed to Father Christmas. Al and Karen got up at once and sat on either side of their mother, keen to become reacquainted with their long-forgotten desires.

"I suppose Father Christmas sent these back, did he?" asked Karen, grinning.

Helen laughed and retorted that there could be no other possible explanation.

"See, Al," said Karen, "there's nothing to worry about. He *is* real."

"Such a relief," Al said sarcastically.

As the siblings perused the letters they had penned so enthusiastically all those years ago, newly resurrected memories of their childhood brought much laughter and warmth with them. Al's favourite was the one in which he had asked for no less than a real dragon with real knights. He had gone to the trouble of illustrating the letter with a drawing of them having an epic battle on a castle.

"Look at how bad my handwriting is in this one!" said Al, laughing and showing it to his mother and sister. "It's all over the place!"

"Not as bad as mine," muttered Karen as she continued to decipher what looked like a rainbow of scrawls.

"Well, you both have beautiful handwriting now," said

Helen.

"I've managed to improve it even more lately," said Al. "I've been practising quite a lot."

Merriment sometimes seemed to unlock a little mischief in Al. He had just had an idea for a little prank to play on his family. He told them that he would show them an example of *exactly* how much his handwriting had improved and that they would all be amazed by its sheer beauty. Al was about to show his family the green scroll.

Although he had no idea exactly how the scroll was connected to Bruce Blight's sudden departure and the return of his usual Christmas bliss, Al was certain it *was* connected. It was not a mere coincidence that the reassuring words emblazoned on the scroll had proved to be prophetic the very next day. He was intrigued by the mystery behind it. The scroll reminded him never to lose hope, and Al vowed to treasure it. He had straightened it out and stuck it above his desk, and that same feeling of comfort he had experienced after first seeing the words written on it always soared through him whenever he glanced at it.

"That's beautiful!" Helen's eyes became wide with delightful surprise as Al handed her the scroll after bringing it down from his bedroom.

Karen leant over to have a look, then noticed the sheepish grin on Al's face.

"That's not your handwriting, is it?"

"I wish!" said Al, thinking it was futile to keep up the pretence.

"I knew it!" Karen laughed, looking extremely pleased with herself.

"I'm eager to see what all the fuss is about ..." said Margaret.

Helen handed over the scroll.

It seemed as though Margaret had suddenly transformed into a waxwork: she stared at the words on the scroll without blinking, her complexion now as white as her hair. She eventually looked up at Al.

"Where did you get this from? This is Alfred's handwriting."

2

The Unsighted Gate

The weak, wintry sunlight barely illuminated Al's bedroom when he woke up on Christmas morning. Although sleep had been extremely reluctant to come to him during the night, Al was now finding it quite difficult to slip out of its warm embrace and get out of bed on that cold morning.

He had not fully recovered from the shock of Margaret's revelation, nor had he fully digested the meaning of her words.

It had been a good few moments before he was able to explain to his family how he happened to have something that was written by someone who had died over twenty years ago – it was as though Margaret's words had temporarily turned his brain into a block of ice. After it eventually thawed, Al told them that he had simply found the scroll behind his wardrobe. He had then excused himself by pretending he was tired, desperate to be alone with his thoughts. Those thoughts were now swirling round inside his head again as he lay there staring at the ceiling –

Is there really such a thing as spirits? There's no other explanation. My dead grandfather sent the scroll. He made

Bruce Blight disappear from my life. This means he's the one who makes sure we have no problems during Christmas Time. How is this even possible?

Although Al had found the idea of a spirit watching over him and his family and intervening in their lives a little chilling at first, he now felt extremely comforted by it. He kept glancing at the frozen lattice window, almost expecting his grandfather to appear there at any moment. His bedroom remained spirit-free, though.

As the last remnants of drowsiness departed from his eyes, Al realised that it was unnaturally quiet for this time in the morning on Christmas Day: he had not heard a single creak of a floorboard or the sound of a familiar voice since he had woken up.

He then noticed something even stranger. His blanket and pillows as well as the uncovered parts of his pyjamas were dusted with what looked like a shimmering sand-like substance. It seemed as though handfuls of it had been thrown over his bed. And it was shining brighter and brighter. He simply could not work out where it had come from and was feeling a little alarmed. Touching the strange substance did not calm his nerves. His finger instantly became numb for a few moments before the effect wore off just as quickly.

Al threw aside his blanket and jumped out of bed. Slipping into his dressing gown and slippers as fast as he could, he set off to try and find out exactly what was going on.

His family had gone. Their beds had been slept in, but they were all still unmade. Panicking, Al shouted out the names of his loved ones, hoping as hard as he could that he would get a response. He was answered only by torturous silence. It was not long, though, before that silence *was* broken – by a loud screeching coming from the garden. Al ran towards it, even though it felt like the horrific sound was piercing his very soul.

The garden was Helen's pride and joy, as it had been Margaret and Alfred's once. It was substantial in size and home to a wide array of carefully selected plant life as well as a mixture of weathered stone sculptures of animals and urns. Its predominant feature, though, was an enormous oak tree at the very bottom. The winter months truly revealed this tree's ancientness as its age could no longer be disguised by foliage. Its gnarled branches looked like giant wrinkly fingers that had protruded from its plump trunk and formed a woody maze in the air. Ivy was draped around its thick, exposed roots and had started to climb up as though determined that it should be blessed with glorious greenery all year round.

The screeching sound was emanating from near the base of this tree. As Al ran into the garden, stumbling on the frosty lawn crunching beneath his slippers, he was met with a sight that generated such astonishment that he stopped in his tracks – transfixed.

The source of the dreadful noise was a huge, winged creature almost the size of a small car. Most of its plumage was charcoal coloured with blots of pure white here and there, but its head and extremely long tail were of a gleaming copper hue. It had a sabre-like beak and large yellow eyes, which shone a great deal more fiercely than the wintry sun. Although it looked other-worldly, Al thought that it must be closely related to a hawk.

It seemed like the creature was engaged in some sort of a battle with an invisible foe and was being shot at by invisible arrows: it kept staggering backwards with a jolt as it attempted to take flight by flapping its wings ferociously. Suddenly, something shiny and sand-like gushed out of its flapping wings and rose up as a mini tornado before vanishing; it was a counter-attack, and it had worked because the creature stopped screeching and staggering backwards. Al realised that the substance it had secreted was the very same that he had found in his bedroom.

And then absolute horror flooded him, the weight of it nearly making his legs buckle.

No less than four more of the hawk-like creatures were flying side by side towards the top branches of the oak tree, and in their talons were – unmistakably – *people*. Their limp limbs swayed gently as the creatures glided towards their destination, and their hair glinted vividly in the early morning sunlight. One had black hair, one had white hair and two had dark brown hair. The creatures were carrying Al's family. Just as it seemed as though they were about to collide with the branches, they disappeared.

Al stood there shivering in his slippers for what felt like an eternity, but he did not feel the cold; and although his eyes were still fixed on the point where his family had disappeared, they may as well have turned into glass.

He was soon roused by the creature near the base of the oak tree. With its huge head pointing squarely upwards in the direction of the branches, it had started to emanate a crescendo of screeches until the sound became almost unbearable … and then it fell silent. It lowered its head and proceeded to glare at Al across the frozen lawn. The noise it released had evidently been a call to its fellow creatures because they reappeared in the branches like the oak tree had regurgitated them.

They were no longer carrying Al's loved ones.

The creatures swooped downwards in unison as the one on the ground surged upwards to join them. They aligned themselves in an arrow formation – pointing directly at Al. A moment later, they were tearing through the air towards him, the strange sand-like substance streaming out of their mighty wings. Al screamed and fell backwards as he was hit with the full force of the golden gale. His subsequent scream was much louder. He had been lifted into the air by the collar of his dressing gown, which tightened round him like a harness. Not by any of the hawk-like creatures ... but something else.

Al could not help but writhe against the vice-like hold, not at all considering the consequences of being let go, but to no avail. He rose higher and higher as the frosty plants and sculptures beneath him became smaller and smaller, and screeches of fury rang in his ears. Whatever it was that was carrying him flew speedily towards the pinnacle of the oak tree to escape the predators behind them. With enormous difficulty, Al managed to crane his neck to catch a glimpse of his saviour: a sliver of fiery-red feathers was all he could make out before he realised with horror that they were about to collide with the branches ... But they did not. Instead, everything around him disappeared.

An intensely bright, golden light engulfed Al, blinding him. He was not at all warmed by it. Quite the contrary, it was as though he had been submerged into icy water. And then, as the light gradually became dimmer and dimmer, he passed out.

"... Robin has just brought him here. I have no idea who he is. In the two-and-a-half centuries I've been here, I've never known one of our kind to be so utterly unresponsive. Then again, these *are* strange times ..."

"Do you think Chief Alfred knows who he is and why Robin has brought him here, Sir?"

"I hope so, Frederick. I'm certain Robin is bringing him here as we speak; he flew away at once after placing this poor chap here and alerting me to his presence."

Al had drifted into consciousness mere seconds ago and been listening to the two speakers, though he hardly registered what they were saying. Opening his eyes was a hugely strenuous task, but he eventually managed to do so.

Al's first thought when he saw his surroundings and the light streaming through from every direction was that he had been placed inside some sort of empty greenhouse. He was in a tall, round tower made entirely of glass. What was even more astonishing was the elaborate chaise longue Al was lying on in the middle of the vast space; although it felt as comfortable as if it was stuffed full of feathers, it was as transparent as the structure – like it, *too*, was made of glass.

Mum! Dad! Karen! Granny!

Everything came flooding back. The image of the hawk-like creatures carrying the limp figures of his family burned into Al's mind as his eyes filled with stinging tears and he sniffed loudly.

The two speakers immediately came into view. Distressed as he was, Al could not help but be taken aback by the stark contrast between the two men.

One had a large face with droopy cheeks, and

was leaning on a knobbly, silver-topped cane; he was wearing an enormous powdered wig of fine curls and a sumptuous old-fashioned outfit, which comprised a knee-length coat of cobalt blue, a ruffled, crimson shirt with matching breeches, white silk stockings and black buckled shoes. The other was more muscular, younger and far less finely dressed. He had short, matted black hair and sideburns that travelled all the way down to the ends of his large moustache; *his* outfit comprised a dirty and heavily singed leather apron, an even dirtier yellow tunic, and thick, worn boots.

Both individuals smiled kindly at Al.

"Hello there, young Spirit!" said the older and more sumptuously dressed of the two in a booming voice. "I'm Ivar Havelock, Twelfth Viscount Havelock, and this is Mister Frederick Hancock. What's your name? And which Spirit-noble is your mentor?"

Al became convinced it was taking him a little longer than usual to process the meaning of the words being spoken to him.

"I'm ... I'm sorry. I don't understand what you mean. I-I'm not a spirit. My name is Al."

If Al was exhibiting some degree of perplexity, it was nothing compared to the looks of utter confusion that appeared on the faces of Ivar and Frederick. They seemed unsure of what to say.

"Not a Spirit?" Ivar said eventually. "In other words: you haven't yet *died*?!"

Hearing such an extraordinarily strange question being asked in a manner as though it was anything but made Al's heart pound fervently.

"No," he said with certainty, even though his head was full to the brim of so many other uncertainties. So many questions.

"Impossible!" Ivar and Frederick gasped in unison.

"I'm sorry, but where am I?" Al burst out as his desperation for answers became intolerable. "Where's my family?!"

"You were brought here on your own, young one," said Ivar, looking concerned.

"Al," said Frederick as he sat next to him, "think it's best if you tell us what happened in detail from the very beginning. Do you think you could do that?"

"I think so."

He recounted everything he could remember from the moment he had woken up in his bedroom that morning. Although at times both Ivar and Frederick looked horrified, confused and even a mixture of the two throughout Al's tale, neither interrupted him. When he finished, Al suspected from their expressions that they did have some idea of what was going on. Both looked worried.

"Could I just ask ..." said Frederick, unable to mask the graveness in his voice, "is your family name Baba?"

"Yes," Al said at once. "*Please* – tell me where I am."

"Sir ...?" Frederick had turned to Ivar, who was pacing back and forth and kept looking in the direction of a wide archway leading out of the tower as if he was expecting someone to walk through it at any moment.

"I don't believe he'd disapprove that much if we enlightened this young man somewhat," said Ivar.

Frederick hesitated before turning back to the boy slouching next to him, whose thirst for answers was finally about to be quenched.

"What I'm about to tell you, Al, will come as a bit of a surprise. Please don't be afraid, but it'll take you time to get used to the idea."

Al's concentration was now such that he was absorbing every word instantly.

"You have left the Domain of the Living through something called an Unsighted Gate and are now in Luxfons. This is a place where Spirits reside – we use our powers to secretly help the ones we love in the Domain of the Living."

It seemed the strangeness of what Al had seen and heard so far had made him immune to the shock of this revelation. Although Frederick's words sent a chill down his spine and made his hair stand on end, they were not akin to an earthquake shattering his sense of reality. In fact, Frederick's words took on the role of an invisible hand in his mind that started to piece together everything that had happened. The comforting and *extraordinary* conclusion he had reached after finding out that the message on the scroll was in his grandfather's handwriting had just been confirmed as true. But it was difficult to derive any sort of comfort from anything under such circumstances. He was determined to change them.

"Is my family still alive?" Al's voice was unwavering and clear.

Ivar and Frederick exchanged looks of amazement.

"I *know* they are," said Frederick, nodding and smiling.

"As do I!" interjected Ivar.

Something dark and heavy inside Al was expelled as a huge sigh of relief and tears of joy streamed from his eyes.

"But we don't know where they are," said Frederick.

"We know exactly *who* they're with, however!" Ivar said angrily.

Frederick looked very uncomfortable: it was obvious

he did not want to elaborate on Ivar's words. "It isn't up to us to give you any more information," he said emphatically but in a far from unkind manner. "This responsibility lies with someone else – someone more closely connected to you."

"And here they are!" Ivar chortled as Frederick stood up.

A very grand golden carriage – but with no wheels and no horses harnessed to it – flew through the archway into the tower. It was surmounted by a large, arched crown, which had enormous blue-and-green peacock feathers protruding from the top. Al stared at the carriage in astonishment as it glided closer and closer, sparkling like a jewel in the light-filled tower. It was not flying by itself as he had initially thought but – just as incredibly – was being carried by a tiny robin with a breast of familiar fiery-red feathers. The bird had its little claws gripped tightly around one of the arches of the crown and was carrying the carriage effortlessly. It placed the ornate vehicle soundlessly on the floor mere feet away from them.

Before Al was able to take a closer look at who was inside through its window, a figure stepped out.

He was elderly, bespectacled and wearing a tweed suit with a grey tie; and the few tufts of hair remaining on his shiny head were white and fluffy. His blue eyes became moist as he smiled warmly at Al, who recognised him instantly. He had seen him on countless occasions ... but only in old photographs. He felt he knew him ... but only through the memories of his father and grandmother.

Al was face to face with his deceased grandfather.

3

The Journey to Sundomum

"Hello, Al," said Alfred. "I think you know who I am."

Hearing his grandfather's voice for the first time in his life warmed Al in a way that a hot drink does on a cold day. Without saying a word, Al got up, and they hugged each other tearfully.

"Grandad – these bird creatures took our family!" Al said frantically when they eventually parted. "We need to find them and bring them back!"

"I know, my dear boy," Alfred sighed. "Robin has told me everything." He gestured towards the little bird on the carriage. "He's the one who rescued you from them. I don't know how much you've been told already ..."

Alfred looked at Ivar and Frederick in turn.

"He's only been made aware of where he is, old chap," Ivar said a little defensively.

"And that everyone is alive, Chief Sir," Frederick added with a bow.

"It would've been wiser to await my arrival before telling him anything," said Alfred.

There was no trace of anger in his voice, and yet it had the effect of making the two Spirits look like naughty schoolchildren. Although Al had no idea why his grandfather had expressed such a sentiment, even he was instantly convinced that it stemmed from wisdom.

Alfred turned to him again. "Al, I'm taking you to meet Her Nobleness Mistress Magistery. She's our leader, the Spirit-noblest of Luxfons. I was with her in Sundomum – her palace – when Robin came with the news. She's the only one who can help us get our family back."

Al nodded with fervour as Alfred opened the door of the carriage for him to climb inside.

"May Frederick and I have the quickest of words with you before you set off, Alfred?" asked Ivar before Al was able to take more than a couple of steps towards the carriage.

"Yes, of course," Alfred replied at once, as if he had expected to be asked such a question.

"Excellent. We can talk outside. It'll give us a decent view of the pond, which you haven't seen properly in a while. In fact, I believe you haven't either, Frederick."

"I'll return shortly, Al," said Alfred. "Robin will keep you company – and entertained too, I'm sure, with his musical abilities!"

With Ivar in the lead, the three Spirits walked past the carriage towards the archway.

A beacon of hope had been lit inside Al since he had been assured that his loved ones were alive; a beacon that seemed inextinguishable now that his grandfather was by his side. He was sure they would all be reunited. And as he digested the fact that he was in a different world to his own, full of *Spirits*, sheer fascination bubbled out of his fast-ebbing apprehension.

Al looked in all directions with enthusiasm, admiring the vastness of the transparent tower. His awe increased further when he noticed that the great see-through floor was resting on a bed of countless red-and-white roses, each one a perfect little masterpiece, beautified even more by the flood of glorious light. Distracted as he was by his surroundings, Al had forgotten he was not completely alone and was soon reminded of this as Robin flew down from the carriage and settled on the floor in front of him. With his beady black eyes fixed on Al, the little bird began to sing as Alfred had predicted. His pleasant whistle-like song went on for some time, amusing Al a great deal.

"Thank you for what you did for me today, Robin," he said as the bird, having finished his song, flew back to his original position on the carriage.

He tilted his feathery head in acknowledgement whilst the three Spirits came back inside to join them. Alfred and Ivar were in the middle of a debate.

"—I will be *quite* determined to accompany Her Nobleness to confront *that traitor* and aid her in seizing him!" Ivar's wig was almost in danger of falling off due to how animated he had become with rage.

"But I can't say with certainty that Her Nobleness *will* discover where he's hiding," retorted Alfred. "She merely said hearing Al's side of the story might give us a clue. I believe it would be wiser for you to remain here in Bloomturrim. He might try to contact you somehow."

"I'm certain he would've made contact already if that's what he desired. Or even attempted to take the boy! We're in one of the most exposed places in Luxfons: his Hawkanines would've seen that the boy is here by now, even if they cannot outfly Robin!"

"Something might have stopped him or his Spirit-creatures from coming here. Robin told me that when he was looking for a safe place to leave Al, he felt strangely drawn to Bloomturrim. But I think he *will* have a message for us and *will* attempt, somehow, to relay that message through you, Ivar."

"Could I make a suggestion with your permission, Sirs?"

It was Frederick who spoke as the three of them came to a halt by the carriage.

Alfred and Ivar turned round sharply, like they had momentarily forgotten he was there during their verbal battle.

"Of course, Frederick," said Alfred.

"I think he won't want to risk being captured by trying to communicate directly with Lord Havelock himself. I agree with you, Chief Sir, that he's bound to have a message for us, but I think he'll use one of his Hawkanines to deliver it. If Robin were to be sent back here from Sundomum and sat on the very top of the tower – as we're assuming the Hawkanine won't be able to enter it for whatever reason – I'm sure his message will be given to our little feathery friend."

Alfred and Ivar looked rather impressed. Evidently encouraged by their reaction, Frederick continued:

"Robin should not *actually* be sent back to Bloomturrim, though."

Alfred and Ivar now, unsurprisingly, looked quite perplexed.

"Morfox will be disguised as Robin, and it'll only *seem* like he was sent back," Frederick told them, smiling. "I'm sure my Spirit-creature can capture a Hawkanine. Lord Havelock and I can then bring it to you and Her Nobleness for questioning."

"That's a fine idea, and it'll be put into effect without any amendments," said Alfred, glancing at Ivar.

Ivar exclaimed that he was of the same opinion as Alfred, though, and shook Frederick's hand, congratulating him on his cunningness.

"I'm even more convinced, Frederick, that you'll be a great Spirit-noble one day when you succeed Ivar," said Alfred. "And now we really must leave for Sundomum. After you, Al."

Al was greeted by a pleasant cinnamon-like smell as he climbed into the carriage followed by Alfred, who sat opposite him. The seats were coated with peacock feathers, and large silver bells hung from each corner with sprigs of holly. The bells tinkled softly as the carriage was lifted up and they moved steadily towards the archway.

Al looked out of the window keenly as they left Bloomturrim. The tower was situated on a great mound, which was covered with red-and-white roses no less magnificent than those encased beneath its transparent floor. They flew over a large pond, which Al imagined was the one Ivar had referred to. It was surrounded by luscious greenery, and its water was of the brightest blue; many beautiful flowers floated on its surface, glittering like gemstones. The carriage sped up and everything beyond it became a blur, yet it felt like they were being flown quite leisurely – like they were floating in the air as gracefully as the flowers in the pond.

"You're taking all this rather well, my dear boy," Alfred said admiringly as he observed his grandson. "I'm sure anyone else would have run away screaming after being told they're amongst Spirits!"

They both chuckled.

"It's because of the scroll you sent me. Granny told me the handwriting on it was yours, and I sort of realised then that you were helping us. But I didn't know how."

"Margaret always had a good memory." Alfred became a little teary again. "I miss her very much. And your dad."

"How did you know about my bullying problem?" Al asked gingerly; he was intrigued but did not want to come across as nosey.

Alfred, however, had no qualms about satisfying his grandson's curiosity.

"The Spirits of Luxfons have a Connection with the minds of their living loved ones. It's through this Connection that we're able to see any difficulties they might be going through, and we then try to help with those difficulties.

"That's how I found out about Bruce Blight and the impact he was having on your life. I managed to create a set of circumstances that led to him leaving the town for good. However, I must apologise to you regarding that whole affair—"

"Apologise?" said Al, taken aback. "What for?"

"For the delay in sorting it out," said Alfred, looking ashamed. "Since Departing the Domain of the Living, I've tried my absolute best, in the time that I'm allowed, that you – my loved ones – never have any worries during Christmas Time. It was my favourite part of the year: full of joy that simply shouldn't be tarnished in any way at all. This year, however, I failed to carry out my task in good time. When I found out how badly your situation was affecting you, I immediately sent Robin to deliver that scroll, to let you know that you shouldn't lose hope."

"Thank you, Grandad," mumbled Al as fat tears leaked from his eyes.

Alfred patted him gently on the shoulder and said, "I think you deserve to hear an explanation as to why I had to leave it so late to help you."

Al straightened up a little to focus on the words that were about to follow.

"Let me first tell you about my position here in Luxfons: I'm a *Chief* Spirit-noble, the most senior Spirit here after Her Nobleness Mistress Magistery, outranking the ten Spirit-nobles and *Future* Spirit-nobles. My role is to help Her Nobleness with the task of upholding the Laws of Luxfons. The most important of these Laws, created by Her Nobleness herself, is to never harm a living being in any way – nor the beings of this world. Being dead does not, sadly, prevent us from being harmed. No Spirit in Luxfons has broken that Law for centuries – until quite recently.

"My fellow Chief Spirit-noble – Metanos – horrifically betrayed Her Nobleness by trying to steal the power that no Spirit or Spirit-creature possesses and is kept locked securely in Sundomum – *the Power to Kill.* Her Nobleness and I were able to prevent him from getting it with great difficulty. He then escaped, and we still don't know anything about his whereabouts *or* his motives. Although the special powers Metanos had as a Chief Spirit-noble have now been revoked, his other immense powers, coupled with his evil intentions, make him the most dangerous Spirit in Luxfons. We have tirelessly been trying to locate him. And that's why, for the first time ever, I was forced to neglect my task of helping those I love."

A few moments had gone by before Al – still gripped by Alfred's tale – was hit with a thunderbolt-like realisation.

"Is that who you were talking about with Ivar and Frederick?!" he asked, horrified. *"Was our family abducted by him?!"*

The look on his grandfather's lined face was confirmation enough.

"They won't be harmed," Alfred said firmly. "You'll get them back. Everything will be as it was. I promise."

Al's beacon of hope was dimming, though. "How can you be so sure?"

"Metanos has no reason whatsoever to harm them. Both Her Nobleness and I agree on the matter. His actions, however deplorable, will always be underpinned by firm logic."

"You said there's a Connection between you and us – could you not check they're definitely okay?" implored Al.

Alfred sighed. "I've tried, my dear boy. It looks like I can't once they've left the Domain of the Living. I'd never be so cruel as to give you false hope, though. They won't be harmed."

The conviction emanating from Alfred's repeated words bolstered Al with much-needed fuel for his beacon of hope. He nodded, half-smiling, to indicate that he had faith in what his grandfather said.

"What does he want with them?"

"I can only guess. I'm hoping Her Nobleness will be able to find some of the answers we're looking for after hearing your version of what happened this morning – namely where he's hiding. And if Frederick's plan works, and one of Metanos's Hawkanines is brought to us, then much-needed enlightenment is almost guaranteed."

"Is that what those bird creatures are called?" Al shuddered as he remembered how vicious they looked.

"Yes, they were created by Metanos, rather how Robin was created by me—"

A very loud chirping sound filled the carriage.

"Robin has forbidden me from comparing his

esteemed self to Metanos's Spirit-creatures!" Alfred chuckled.

Al could not help but also be tickled by the interruption as his grandfather continued:

"The Hawkanines were esteemed Spirit-creatures, too, not so very long ago. They're powerful enough to communicate with Metanos telepathically and also have the most superior sight in Luxfons. They can even see the Spirits-liminal: the Guardians of the Unsighted Gates, who, like the Gates themselves, are invisible to all other eyes in our world and yours. The Spirits-liminal ensure that only those who are meant to can cross the threshold into Luxfons. And they also prevent almost all Spirits and Spirit-creatures on this side of the divide from visiting the Domain of the Living more than twelve times a year – too much interference can lead to undesirable consequences that can't easily be remedied.

"It seemed, from what Robin told me, that the two Spirits-liminal flanking my personal Unsighted Gate in the oak tree tried their best to stop the Hawkanines ..."

"Yes, it looked like one of them was being attacked by something invisible, and then some sort of shiny sand stuff came out of its wings, and the attack stopped. The same stuff was on my bed." A question occurred to Al all of a sudden. "*What was that?*"

Alfred hesitated, as though he did not want this particular subject to be broached. "I believe it induces a deep sleep," he said finally, "and is obviously potent enough to do so in both Non-Spirits and Spirits alike. It seems the Hawkanines used it to make sure our family couldn't put up a fight before carrying them off."

"How come it didn't put me to sleep? Loads of it was on me when I woke up. I even touched it."

Alfred looked very uneasy now.

"I simply have no idea, Al," he said, staring unblinkingly into his grandson's blue eyes that so resembled his own. "I was really surprised when Robin told me that even when all five of the Hawkanines showered you with the substance, you were still unaffected. And so was Her Nobleness. Ivar and Frederick too; *that* is what they wanted to discuss with me."

"What does it mean?" asked Al, feeling as uneasy as his grandfather looked.

"That there's something ... something *special* about you, my dear boy. That's not necessarily a bad thing, though," Alfred added quickly. "I'm sorry for keeping this from you. I wasn't sure how you'd take it. That's why I disapproved of you being given information by Ivar and Frederick in my absence. But ... again – you've adapted to everything so far with extraordinary ease."

Although Al did not exactly despise the idea that he was a little different – or 'special' – he was sure he would have opted for normality if he had had a choice in the matter. *But then I wouldn't be in a position to help rescue my family.* He looked out of the window at the blur of colour whizzing past whilst contemplating all he had been told. Distinguishable shapes gradually started coming into view again.

The carriage eventually came to a complete halt and was lowered gently onto the ground. Al and Alfred stepped out.

They were standing on a carpet of peacock feathers in a large clearing in the middle of countless jagged rocks of all shapes and sizes. It was intensely bright, but Al did not see the sun nor, indeed, any other source of light when he looked up. What he did see took his breath away.

A palace made of lustrous, ochre-coloured stone was floating – in mid-air – high above the rocks. It had a squared central structure, topped with a gigantic dome and a silver spire, and each of the two wings adjoining this structure could have been palaces in their own right, such was their enormity; the extraordinary building had hundreds of round windows, which looked like hundreds of eyes surveying the rocky landscape.

Al stood there, open-mouthed, gaping at the marvel in the air for a few seconds before he started – he had felt something brush against his ankles. The peacock feathers on the ground were rising up collectively, and they had soon formed a bluey-green canopy above him and his grandfather. Without warning, it fell on them both like a veil. Al momentarily experienced a strange sensation of being scrutinised, as though he was being stared at in a spotlight. The feathers then dispersed and floated back down to their feet.

"Only those with good intentions can go up to Sundomum to see Her Nobleness," Alfred said in response to his grandson's questioning look, "and that's what the Oculus Plume was searching for. Chief Spirit-nobles are no longer excused from its scrutiny. Anyway, it looks like it's happy for us to go up."

The jagged rocks all around them started to rise, similar to the Oculus Plume, and were fitting together like a giant rocky jigsaw puzzle. In hardly any time at all, they had formed ancient-looking stairs, extending from the ground all the way up to the great golden doors of the palace.

Alfred started to climb them, with Robin hovering over his shoulder and Al close behind. Once their feet left a step, it dismantled and fell to the ground as rock fragments once more, and this continued to happen until they reached the very top. The golden doors were standing open to admit them.

4

Mistress Magistery

Alfred was about to step over the threshold into the palace when he stopped and turned round. Nudging his spectacles higher up his nose, he observed Al thoughtfully – namely what he was wearing. His grandson was still in his pyjamas, dressing gown and slippers.

"I think I should smarten you up a touch, my dear boy," he said in a tone indicating that Al did not have a choice in the matter. "You are, after all, about to meet the most powerful Spirit in Luxfons."

Robin chirped and nodded his little head.

A moment later, Al's grey pyjamas had transformed into a crisp black shirt and pair of trousers, his blue dressing gown into a jade-coloured cardigan and his slippers into shiny leather shoes.

"Thank you, Grandad!" enthused Al. "This is actually how I normally dress!"

"I had an inkling," Alfred said with a wink.

The open doors led them into a vast hall with monumental stone pillars and an ermine-patterned floor. In the very middle, stood a grand throne in the shape of a peacock tail. It was encrusted with countless emeralds and sapphires glittering in the light streaming through the windows and was flanked on either side by two smaller mahogany thrones carved with peacocks. As they made their way up to the stately seats, Al looked round with awe. He saw with a jolt that the two wide archways leading to each of the wings kept disappearing – turning into solid stone – and then reappearing, as though they were unsure whether or not they should remain in existence. This phenomenon carried on for a little while until the archway leading into the east wing decided to stay – just long enough to serve its purpose.

It had let an elderly female Spirit emerge from the darkness beyond before vanishing again. Al had somehow felt her presence before her entrance, and he was now unable to avert his eyes from her as she strode towards the grand throne. She had sleek, silver hair, which was plaited around her head like a crown, and she was wearing a sky-blue, hooded gown studded with yellow crystals, which seemed to be emitting light like little suns. Although her face was aged, it had a pearly – almost youthful – sheen. She sat on the throne and observed them silently and expressionlessly with her emerald-coloured eyes. They lingered very much on Al.

"Your Nobleness," Alfred said with a bow, "please allow me to introduce my grandson – Al Baba." He turned to Al. "And this is Her Nobleness Mistress Magistery."

Mistress Magistery nodded to acknowledge the introduction. Al felt as though he was in a spotlight again like he did in the clearing. This uncomfortable sensation certainly did not dissipate in any way when Alfred left his side and sat on the mahogany throne to the left of Mistress Magistery. Robin followed him and perched himself on the back of his master's grand seat.

Mistress Magistery then spoke. Her voice was monotonous – devoid of any emotion – but every word was uttered with flawless clarity.

"Welcome to Sundomum. Kindly tell me, in as much detail as you can, about the events leading up to your departure from the Domain of the Living."

Al found himself recounting the story once again.

"... and then when I touched the shiny sand stuff, my fingers went numb for a bit—"

"Did you notice anything else peculiar about this substance?" asked Mistress Magistery.

Al tried to visualise it. And then a little nugget of information remerged in his mind –

"It was becoming shinier."

Mistress Magistery flinched, and fear enveloped her face. It was as if the barrier that prevented any indication of her thoughts or feelings from rising to the surface had shattered. That barrier was immediately rebuilt, though, and her face became unreadable again. Her reaction had been noticed by Alfred, too, and he looked puzzled.

"And it had no other effect on you other than the one you've described?" she continued.

"No," said Al.

Mistress Magistery continued to gaze at him as silence ensued.

"It isn't necessary to hear anymore," she said after a few moments. "We're aware of what followed thanks to Robin" – she turned her head to look at the little bird – "who I cannot commend enough for not only spotting the Hawkanines hijacking Alfred's Unsighted Gate, but also preventing them from executing their plan successfully."

Robin chirped with delight as Alfred smiled and stroked the Spirit-creature's feathery head with his finger.

Al, too, could have been commended for his courage at that moment because he had mustered enough to ask the Spirit-noblest of Luxfons a question –

"Do you know where he's keeping my family?"

All three pairs of eyes were on Al once more; he commanded the full attention of the two Spirits and the Spirit-creature.

"I believe I do," said Mistress Magistery. "I'll travel to that place myself to confirm my suspicions."

"Thank you," said Al, beaming.

Alfred adjusted himself on his throne to face Mistress Magistery, looking inquisitive.

"From what this boy has just told me, Alfred," she said before he was able to say anything, "I believe your family is being kept in perhaps the most impenetrable place in Luxfons. I also believe that's where Metanos has been hiding all this time. The Orangery."

Alfred stared at her. "How did he get past Marshal?"

"I can only guess as to how initially," she replied, "but it's clear how he's been doing so subsequently: by using the same weapon his Hawkanines now possess. That sand-like substance isn't one of Metanos's creations as you thought, Alfred, and as I hoped. It's called Spiritsnuff and is much more ancient than he is and was created by a far more powerful Spirit – Queen Lamiobra."

"But she's entombed in stone in the Orangery with her followers – powerless," said Alfred, looking horrified.

"It seems Queen Lamiobra's powers were detached before she was entombed. That's how Metanos has managed to steal the power to create Spiritsnuff and equip his Spirit-creatures with it. Spiritsnuff should never be underestimated: it will grow more and more potent – appearing brighter and brighter – until it succeeds in contaminating the Spirit and putting it in the deepest of trances. It will simply not concede defeat. Hence the change in its appearance when the Spirit of this boy managed to resist it. The power to create it can only be derived from the Orangery, and this is also where Metanos is most likely to evade being captured."

"I wonder what other dark powers he's managed to salvage from that evil place ..." said Alfred, shuddering.

His attention was then captured by something behind Al.

"Ah, it seems Ivar and Frederick are on their way. Please allow me to explain, Your Nobleness ..."

As his grandfather began relaying Frederick's plan to Mistress Magistery, Al turned round. Two large flowers had just flown through the open doors into the hall: a red-and-white rose and a flame-orange lily. They fluttered towards them, their petals beating like little wings, and fell gracefully at Mistress Magistery's feet.

As soon as she, too, had commended Frederick's plan, the two Spirits looked as though they had been alerted by something that was not detected by any of Al's senses.

"We must stay here and wait for Lord Havelock and Mister Hancock," Mistress Magistery said to Alfred. "I dislike such unnaturalness as much as you do. However, the circumstances we find ourselves in leave us no choice."

Alfred nodded sadly, and then noticed the puzzlement on Al's face.

"When the Unsighted Gates open," he told him, "our Spirits-liminal let us know by a sound that can only be heard by us – it signals that we can return to the Domain of the Living to carry out our tasks. It's also at this time that the Spirits of some of those who have recently died are able to cross into Luxfons through Gates belonging to their Departed loved ones or ancestors.

"I've just heard the sound of bells being rung by my two Spirits-liminal: it looks like they've completely recovered from the Hawkanine attack! They will use a different sound to tell me when the Unsighted Gates have closed."

"But if we're all here now, in your world, why would you want to go back there?" asked Al.

Alfred smiled, looking impressed. "A Chief Spirit-noble has other tasks in the Domain of the Living in addition to helping their own family. Along with Her Nobleness, I help those who don't have loved ones residing in Luxfons. We also try to neutralise any negativity that has arisen due to the interference of Spirits in the matters of Non-Spirits. *We*, therefore, aren't limited to just twelve yearly visits.

"And now, my dear boy, I suggest you make yourself comfortable because the Noble Possessions are about to begin."

An old-fashioned, turquoise-coloured armchair appeared next to Alfred's throne. Al walked over to it and sat down, not having the faintest idea what he was about to witness as he stared across the hall at the great golden doors, which still stood open welcomingly.

No more fluttering flowers came into the hall this time but a stout male Spirit instead. He was wearing an oversized patchwork overcoat and carrying a top hat; although his head was completely hairless, he had an extremely bushy black beard. A red squirrel with a tail no less bushy than his beard was fast asleep on his shoulder. A phantom-like figure with indistinct features floated in after them – it looked like it was made of white smoke.

"Greetings to you all," the Spirit with the squirrel said

cheerfully as he came to a halt before them.

He grinned broadly, exhibiting a set of bright yellow teeth, and bowed to the two Spirits and Al in turn.

"Hello there, Hamelin," said Alfred. "I must thank you again for letting Fickle come to my aid. She carried out the task wonderfully. I'm glad to see she's having a well-earned rest."

"She finds my shoulder very comfortable!" said Hamelin, tilting his head towards the squirrel. "She's allowed to use it as a bed whenever she wants to. I really can't be accused of not spoiling my Spirit-creature!"

Hamelin had somehow managed to amuse himself, and his thunderous laugh echoed around the hall.

"Who's this Newly Departed Spirit you've brought to us?" asked Alfred, gesturing towards the phantom-like figure.

"Stephen Brown," said Hamelin. "I'm looking forward to mentoring him – he'll be a fine mentee. I hope!"

Hamelin began to roar with laughter again, but then stopped all of a sudden, and his large nose twitched like he was about to sneeze. At exactly the same time, much to Al's astonishment, the red squirrel on his shoulder morphed into a jet-black rat with thick fur, fast asleep like its predecessor.

"Oh dear," Alfred sighed.

Hamelin's cheery demeanour transformed in a dramatic fashion. His face contorted with anger, and his eyes widened unsettlingly as he looked directly at Al. He then turned to the two enthroned Spirits again.

"I'm deeply offended that you've appointed Metanos's replacement without consulting any of the Spirit-nobles and Future Spirit-nobles!" Hamelin's voice was shaking with rage. "Or was it *just* me who wasn't told?!"

Mistress Magistery did not answer: her attention had barely been captured by Hamelin since he had arrived. She was observing the figure of Stephen Brown hovering next to him.

"This isn't Metanos's replacement," Alfred laughed awkwardly. "This is my grandson."

"Recently Departed, has he?" asked Hamelin, still sounding offended.

"Yes ... in a way ..." said Alfred. "I needed Fickle to help *him* in the Domain of the Living."

This piece of enlightenment managed to fuel Hamelin's anger further. "I'm entitled to at least some gratitude for letting my Fickle be used by you in such a way and sacrificing my last yearly visit in the process!"

"I thanked you a few moments ago," implored Alfred.

"You couldn't have been that emphatic," Hamelin said with no less vigour. "Otherwise, I'd remember!" He turned to Al again. "I let my Fickle overexert herself by running round some poor woman terrified of rats, who was forced to leave town with her poor son – somehow for your benefit! Don't *you* think your grandfather should be more grateful?"

Al – realising just how Alfred had saved him from the unyielding cruelty of Bruce Blight – stared at his grandfather open-mouthed. Alfred winked at him, smiling mischievously.

Hamelin looked like he was ready to let many more grievances burst out of him and opened his mouth again, but he immediately swallowed his words. Mistress Magistery had risen from her grand throne. She still had her eyes on Stephen Brown.

"Welcome to Sundomum. You've been brought here for the Noble Possession, which every Newly Departed

Spirit in Luxfons must undergo. There are two possible outcomes of the Noble Possession: you'll be Accepted as a Spirit of Luxfons or you'll Depart Luxfons forever. Your fate will depend on what's hidden deep inside you. The Noble Possession will show us what we need to see. Are you willing to partake?"

A distinct "Yes" emanated from the mouthless figure.

Mistress Magistery turned round and nodded at Alfred. He also rose, and she offered him her hand, which he took into his own immediately. On forming this link between them, the elderly Spirits turned into a beam of white light. It permeated Stephen Brown and illuminated him from within, dazzling Al's awestruck eyes. After a few moments, the light departed from the smoky figure and morphed back into the figures of Alfred and Mistress Magistery. Alfred resumed his seat, whilst Mistress Magistery remained standing.

"Taurbrum," she said, looking round the hall, "kindly present me with the Sceptre."

Al gasped. An enormous black bull, crowned with a pair of golden horns, had materialised in their midst. Al felt the floor beneath him vibrate as the beast trudged towards Mistress Magistery. He came to a halt in front of her and gently lowered his head as if to bow. Mistress Magistery touched his horns with the tip of her forefinger, and in a flash of light, they had turned into an ornate golden rod firmly grasped in her hand. The bull, now hornless, melted into the air as quickly as he had emerged from it.

Mistress Magistery briefly placed the end of the Sceptre on each of Stephen Brown's barely distinguishable shoulders in turn like he was being knighted. The smoky figure was gone. In its place stood a handsome Spirit-youth with curly auburn hair in perfectly ordinary clothes. He raised both hands in front of his eyes, looking at them with awe before running them gently over his face and through his hair.

"You've been Accepted as a Spirit of Luxfons," said Mistress Magistery. "And you are, therefore, able to take your true form. During the Noble Possession, the Chief Spirit-noble and I saw the light inside you along with the darkness that resides there too. If that darkness was too monumental to be subdued by the light, you would've naturally Departed from this world, having not been Accepted. As you're now a Spirit of Luxfons, you have the ability to Depart whenever you see fit to do so."

"Where do we go when we leave this world?" Stephen Brown asked nervously.

This question had crossed Al's mind too.

"That I don't know," Mistress Magistery said at once. "The nature of that place is as mysterious to us as death is to those who are in the Domain of the Living – as it was to you not so very long ago."

Stephen Brown nodded meekly before Mistress Magistery continued:

"The Spirits of Luxfons have great powers – you can use them to help your loved ones with the difficulties they face in life. It's paramount that you learn to control these powers, however, and ensure their use doesn't harm a single living creature or the inhabitants of this world in any way. As the Spirit-noblest, I have a direct Connection with your powers and will be able to see how they're being used. Unfortunately, recent events have compelled me to suppress the powers of all Spirits in Luxfons, apart from a select few. I will lift that suppression as soon as circumstances permit me.

"Mister Hamelin Buck, having brought you to Sundomum, is your Spirit-noble and will be your mentor."

"You have a lot to learn," Hamelin snapped at Stephen Brown. "We should leave."

Hamelin's nose twitched again and, just as before, the Spirit-creature on his shoulder simultaneously changed form: the rat turned into a tiny harvest mouse. Hamelin's scowl vanished at once. He became fidgety and smiled uneasily, looking even more nervous than his newly Accepted mentee. Bowing quickly, he spun round and sprinted out of the hall, with Stephen Brown hurrying after him.

Al went on to witness the Noble Possessions of a dozen more Newly Departed Spirits, all of whom were Accepted. They had been brought to Sundomum by a Spirit-noble in a tattered naval uniform and bicorn hat called Admiral Keel, who was extremely old and pale and kept forgetting the names of those he had brought.

It was not long after this large group had left that Ivar and Frederick finally arrived. They were not alone. An enormous cage of raging flames was suspended in the air above them and drifted like a burning ship towards the centre of the hall. A winged creature was entrapped behind the bars and trying its utmost to avoid being scorched as it angrily clicked its sabre-like beak – a Hawkanine.

Alfred and Mistress Magistery did not wait for these latest visitors to finish processing up to the thrones. They had joined them in a flash, their gaze fixed on the fiery cage. Al got up and followed. He felt a tsunami of anger building up inside him, washing away any fragments of fear that had remerged at the sight of one of the vicious

Spirit-creatures again.

"You may step down now, Morfox," said Mistress Magistery.

The flames disintegrated into a shower of sparks. And then they were no longer sparks. They had taken the form of a handsome red fox, which leapt on to the floor next to Frederick.

The Hawkanine, now uncaged, lunged towards Mistress Magistery with a screech and a great flap of its wings. Mistress Magistery raised both hands in a defensive motion, and the Spirit-creature froze mid-attack. A tremor-like force had emanated from her, which almost made Al and the Spirits lose their balance and led to the Sceptre slipping out of her grasp. Al instinctively caught the heavy rod before it hit the floor and handed it back.

"You're no less wretched than your master!" spat Ivar, looking at the motionless Hawkanine with disgust.

"Did it have a message from Metanos?" asked Mistress Magistery.

"It did, Your Nobleness," Frederick said with a bow. "Morfox ..."

The fox began to speak in a low, growly voice. "Metanos wants Chief Alfred and his grandson to travel to his Unsighted Gate in Ancient Gates Wood to see him at the sounding of the Noble Trumpet."

A charged silence followed these words for a few moments. All eyes in the hall were on Alfred.

"I, of course, will go and see him," he said finally. "But —"

"I'm coming with you," Al interjected, envisaging what his grandfather was about to say. "I'll do anything he wants to get our family back. *Anything.*"

Alfred did not argue with his grandson but looked at him with uneasiness and also – Al thought – a hint of pride.

Mistress Magistery's eyes were back on the Hawkanine. "I give you the gift of speech," she said.

It opened its beak, but no screeching resonated from its depths this time.

"Release me immediately!" the Hawkanine said in a shrill voice.

"Unlike your master," said Mistress Magistery, "I have no desire to keep prisoners. He has left the path of righteousness, but you needn't do the same. You needn't lose your nobility. Help us defeat the darkness that has grown inside him and warped his senses. Tell us what intentions have sprung from that darkness. Why has Metanos had Alfred's family abducted?"

"How foolish of you to think I'd betray him so easily!" shrieked the Hawkanine. "Unlike you, they ... *he* is wise enough to know the true value of his powers and to use them as nature intended – not for the sole purpose of serving these lowly, powerless beings!"

The Hawkanine glared at Al with just as much contempt in its yellow eyes as there was in its speech. If it had expected him to cower with fear, it was mistaken. Al's eyes, too, were burning with hatred as he stared steadfastly back. Suddenly, the Hawkanine looked scared. It closed its eyes and became smoky and shapeless. And then it disappeared.

There were exclamations of shock from Alfred, Ivar and Frederick. Al looked round, perplexed, and thought he caught Mistress Magistery looking at him before quickly averting her eyes.

"The loyalty of Metanos's Hawkanines cannot be

faulted," she said to the others. "They'd rather Depart than betray their master." She turned to Ivar. "Lord Havelock, I'd like you to guide Alfred and his grandson to Metanos's Unsighted Gate when it's time, seeing as you know its exact location."

"Your Nobleness," Ivar said with a low bow, "I believe we should gather the remaining Spirit-nobles and Future Spirit-nobles as soon as the Noble Trumpet is sounded, and then attempt to capture that traitorous villain! Wouldn't that be wise?"

"He'll take measures to make it impossible to capture him," said Mistress Magistery. "Do you really imagine, Lord Havelock, that he would've revealed exactly where to meet him if he weren't able to do so? You know him better than most."

"No," said Ivar, shaking his head gravely. "I was hoping we'd learn at least *something* of value from his Hawkanine."

"We did," said Mistress Magistery. "His Hawkanine inadvertently referred to his master as 'they' during its tirade. Metanos has at least one accomplice."

5

The River

Alfred had decided it was about time his grandson focussed on those mundane activities which are a necessity for those who still happen to be alive: eating and sleeping. Al whole-heartedly agreed. And they had soon left Sundomum far behind as Robin piloted the carriage towards Alfred's abode. Al had been promised by his grandfather that he would be pleasantly surprised when they arrived, and he certainly was when they did.

Al stepped out of the carriage to find himself surrounded by swathes of pure, undisturbed snow in the shadow of a large timber-framed house with a steeply pitched roof, ornate redbrick chimneys and lattice windows. It was as though a giant, concluding that it would be lonely without its occupants, had scooped up the Babas' house and brought it to Luxfons.

"Welcome to the Spirit-twin of your home," said Alfred, smiling.

Al was lost for words. All he managed to say was "This is amazing" after a little while. Although it could not have been more than a few hours since he was in his actual house, it felt like it had been years and years in light of how much had changed in that time. Seeing it again (albeit as a replica) in this world of Spirits, which was so different to his own, was like seeing an old friend again, and he was comforted by its familiarity. But he could not help but feel saddened by the sight of it too: his yearning to return to the happy life he was so used to within the old walls was amplified greatly.

"Come inside into the warmth," said Alfred as Al began to shiver. "A roaring fire awaits us. It's even more luxurious when you've been out in the bitter cold!"

With Robin fluttering ahead of them, they carved their way through the thick snow until they reached the wreath-adorned front door. It creaked open to let them in. As Al stepped over the threshold into the house and he was greeted by the same cinnamon-like smell that perfumed the carriage, the wetness that had crept up to his ankles disappeared and he was bone-dry again.

This house, too, was luxuriously decorated for Christmas, but the likeness did not extend to the furniture, most of which Al did not recognise and which seemed very old-fashioned. And it contained no modern appliances at all. Al thought he understood why this was the case –

"Is this what the house looked like when you were young?" he asked his grandfather as they sat in green velvet armchairs by the large fireplace in the sitting room.

"Yes," Alfred said happily. He looked round at his surroundings with an air of nostalgia. "Everything you see reflects my memories of growing up there."

"Grandad – why didn't you come and visit us?"

Alfred did not respond immediately and looked as though he was gathering his thoughts. "Revealing myself to you all wouldn't have done you any good in the long run, my dear boy," he said eventually. "I'm just a spectre in the Domain of the Living as myself and can't take my true form there as I can in this world – where I belong now. Although I can take the form of anyone or anything in the Domain of the Living, that's not truly me. And even if all of you, somehow, wouldn't have cared about the form I took whilst communicating with you, my visits would always have been unpredictable and short-lived. The Unsighted Gates open when they please, and we're automatically drawn back into Luxfons when they close. And I will eventually Depart Luxfons itself, forever severing the connection between myself and the Domain of the Living.

"All I would have done, in short, is created the illusion that I *hadn't* died – this would've shattered sooner or later, leading to only pain."

"But now—" Al muttered more to himself.

"But now something previously unthinkable has happened," finished Alfred. "Metanos's villainy has not only exposed the fact that we Spirits exist, but has also led to your presence in our world. I can only hope the others are as resilient to such a surreal reality as you are."

"They will be," Al said confidently.

"That's the kind of attitude I like to see, my dear boy. Now what would you like to eat? Turkey sandwiches? Having spent a great deal of time peering into your mind all these years, I'm aware of your fondness for them."

Al laughed, nodding enthusiastically. A table laden with a tiered stand of turkey sandwiches and mince pies along with a large glass of orange juice appeared between them. Every bite and sip Al took was heavenly.

"Thank you, Grandad," he said after he had had his fill, stifling a yawn. "That was absolutely delicious."

"Time for bed, I think," said Alfred. "It's quite late in

your part of the Domain of the Living, but night never falls in Luxfons. Come, Robin and I will show you what your bedroom looked like seventy-five years ago!"

◆ ◆ ◆

Al was woken by the fanfare of a trumpet – one which, it felt like, had been blown directly into his ear.

Although the brightness in the Spirit version of his bedroom had not diminished at all since his grandfather and Robin had left him to slumber, Al had slept soundly. He was wearing pyjamas similar to those he usually wore. They had been housed in an antique chest of drawers that was in the exact spot where his desk stood in his actual bedroom. Although there were numerous such differences in the décor, they did not detract from the fact that the bedroom – indeed, the whole house – fulfilled every need of a Non-Spirit wanting to lead a life of comfort in this world of Spirits.

With the ghost of the fanfare still ringing in his ears, Al got out of bed and started to get ready to go downstairs. He chose to wear the thickest cardigan he could find in the wardrobe next to his bed; it contained an array of clothes similar to the ones his grandfather had gifted him before the golden doors of Sundomum.

When Al finally stepped into the sitting room, he saw Alfred pacing back and forth, lost in thought.

"That was the sound of the Noble Trumpet," he said after noticing that his grandson had joined him with a start. "Ivar will be here soon."

Any trace of apprehension on Alfred's face was fully masked by the time he sat in his armchair by the fire with

Al sitting opposite him. A table laden with buttered toast and tea appeared between them.

As Al tucked in, Alfred began to tell him about the Noble Trumpet: how it had been made hundreds of years ago by Mistress Magistery's predecessor and the first Spirit-noblest of Luxfons, Raja Nawab; how Mistress Magistery had honoured Metanos with the task of using it to summon the Spirit-nobles and Future Spirit-nobles to Sundomum; how Metanos always proudly carried it with him in a quiver and had fled with it after his betrayal.

As soon as Alfred finished the tale, he became restless again: he kept removing and replacing his spectacles for no apparent reason. Even Robin seemed unable to make up his mind whether he wanted to fly round the room or settle down in one particular spot. Al, on the other hand, had never felt calmer, now that the chance to free his loved ones from Metanos's clutches was in sight. He wanted to set off as quickly as possible and was hoping their journey to Ancient Gates Wood would be a short one. He was about to ask his grandfather what was worrying him when there was a knock on the front door.

"That must be Ivar," said Alfred, getting to his feet. "It's time to go, my dear boy."

Ivar had brought Frederick with him. They were standing at the end of an extremely wide, grassy path, which stretched behind them in the snow as far as the eye could see. The carver of this path was hovering between them at their feet: an enormous ball of flame.

"I hope you're not displeased with the idea of Frederick and Morfox accompanying us to Ancient Gates Wood, old chap ..." Ivar said to Alfred after everyone finished greeting each other. "I thought I'd take this opportunity to show Frederick exactly where my Unsighted Gate is in the Wood."

"Not at all," said Alfred.

"I'd like him to pay particular attention to my Gate when he has succeeded me as a Spirit-noble, so he can take any of my descendants appearing there under his wing immediately," Ivar explained proudly.

"That's very commendable," said Alfred. "But not *so* commendable that I'll overlook the unforgivable act of scarring my beautiful surroundings." He pointed at the path.

"Oh ... but ... but ..." began Ivar, pointing his cane at the trail of footsteps made by Al and Alfred from the carriage to the house.

Before he could utter another word, Alfred smiled mischievously, and the snow vanished to reveal a bright green lawn underneath, ornamented with daisies, dandelions and buttercups.

"You're permitted to change my landscape at will in future (within reason!) instead of using poor Morfox as a portable fireplace," Alfred chuckled.

The fireball turned into the handsome red fox.

"Ah, this is so much better!" enthused Ivar, looking round before bending down to pick a buttercup. "Don't you think so, Frederick?"

Fredrick chuckled nervously.

Ivar, though, did not seem to care that his views had not been validated by his future successor: "I've never understood the attraction of being surrounded by such bleakness!"

"Even the bleakest surroundings are not without beauty," retorted Alfred. "A lone house in the snow is as beautiful to me as a see-through tower surrounded by roses is to you."

"The transparency of Bloomturrim serves an important purpose in that I'm immediately able to see the Communicative Flowers—"

"We'd better get going," Alfred interrupted with a highly dramatic tone of urgency. "Lead on, Ivar!"

They walked and walked *and* walked, with Robin fluttering sometimes in front of them and sometimes behind them and sometimes above them. The expanse of luscious lawn seemed never-ending but was complemented perfectly by the cloudless blue sky.

The scene finally changed when the ground started to dramatically slope downwards, and a great river emerged before them. It was flowing serenely and silently, and its banks were lined with meadowsweet flowers. Floating on it in the very middle, unaffected by its current, was an oarless longship. It had numerous colourful shields, embossed with all kinds of flowers, mounted on top of the hull and a solitary square sail emblazoned with a red-and-white rose. As Al, the Spirits and the Spirit-creatures drew nearer to it, the sleek vessel began to rotate on the spot, and the golden head of what looked like a dragon carved on the bow was soon facing them. The longship then propelled forward, and when it reached the bank, they all climbed aboard.

"Welcome!" said Ivar, beaming. "The largest part of our journey will be spent on the Ragnarsson. She's been my companion for many a year and has always taken pride in ensuring that her passengers have a smooth voyage. I'm certain she won't make any exceptions on this occasion!"

"The River is far worthier of your adulation than I am, Master," said a high-pitched voice, which had emanated from the golden head on the bow.

"You're far too modest," said Ivar, waving his hand

dismissively. "Let's be on our way – the Fallen Tree is our destination!"

The Ragnarsson sailed back to her original position, but this time, she let the gentle flow of the current take her onwards.

"We have a long way to go, Al," said Alfred. "It's a good idea to take the weight off your feet."

He gestured towards the large wooden chests littered on the deck, upon one of which Frederick was already sitting. All were ornately carved, and Al sat on one etched with large sunflowers. Robin settled high up on the rigging and then chirped loudly, which caught the attention of Morfox, who looked up.

"Does he want you to join him, my friend?" Frederick asked him.

"Yes," growled the Spirit-creature.

"You should join him then!" Frederick looked amused. "The views will definitely be a lot better from up there."

The red fox was gone, and in its place hovered another little robin. It flew up and perched itself on the rigging beside its twin, with whom it started conversing in chirps.

"Did you create Morfox how Grandad created Robin?" Al asked Frederick, impressed with the fox's abilities.

"Yes, a long, long time ago," said Frederick, leaning towards Al. "He can take the form of anything that shares his hue – from autumn leaves to ... hot fires in my forge."

"As well as fireballs that ruin your front garden!" Alfred laughed. "Actually, that reminds me ..."

The side of the River from which they had approached it was suddenly blanketed in snow. The other side remained as it was: a wild and dismal-looking grassland.

"Ah ... well ... it's actually quite scenic ... I suppose,"

said Ivar, taking in the snowy landscape drifting by. “And it gives me an excuse to have a steaming beverage.”

A highly decorative porcelain teacup and saucer appeared in his outstretched hand. Placing his cane against the chest he was sitting on, Ivar proceeded to take a sip and purred with satisfaction. Al looked at his grandfather in surprise.

“The Spirits of Luxfons eat and drink solely for pleasure,” said Alfred. “And in this world, there’s no harm in overindulgence!”

“Here, warm yourself up with this, young one,” Ivar said kindly, getting up and giving Al a newly conjured teacup and saucer.

The hot liquid inside the teacup looked very much like milky tea, and the steam issuing from it in curly wisps had a pleasant aroma; it tasted very sweet and was incredibly filling. In fact, by the time Al finished drinking it, he felt like he had just consumed a rich three-course meal and would never feel hungry again. He placed the empty teacup and saucer down next to him on the chest, and it disappeared into thin air.

The snow was soon left behind as the Ragnarsson continued to sail steadfastly on. The River now snaked its way through grassland that was becoming wilder; long, tentacle-like blades of vegetation had crawled into the water on either side as though determined to escape from their unkempt surroundings. Soon after the Ragnarsson had navigated a series of meanders, Al saw an arched bridge in the distance. As they got closer to the simple stone structure, it became apparent that it was actually a busy thoroughfare: a great many Spirits wearing fashions from different eras were going about their business. A small group of Spirit-children in Victorian clothes were leaning over the low wall of the bridge and leisurely dropping pebbles into the River. They waved as the Ragnarsson and her passengers passed under them.

The banks eventually became dominated by tall, thick shrubs, which tangled together to form impenetrable walls of leaf and wood leaning over the River. Occasionally, Al would see the tops of gigantic trees poking out from behind them in the distance. Alfred pointed one of these out to him – a barely distinguishable outline of leafless branches – as being the Spirit-twin of the oak tree in their garden and the site of his Unsighted Gate in Luxfons. It was here, Al was told, that he had emerged with Robin after the little bird had rescued him from the Hawkanines.

As the Ragnarsson followed the River round yet another meander, it seemed like the three Spirits had been alerted by something.

"The Spirits-liminal call us forth to carry out our tasks," Ivar declared with a determined look on his old, droopy face. "I humbly beseech the Guardians of my Unsighted Gate to bring my Gate to me – it's beyond my reach at the present time."

He rose to his feet, looking round, and a moment later, he vanished.

"I'll make sure I'm back from the Domain of the Living before the Ragnarsson reaches the Fallen Tree," Alfred told Al, also rising to his feet. "And I'll also make sure Ivar, too, is back before then: we won't be able to reach our destination without his guidance. Frederick and Morfox will remain here with you."

Al was getting used to fantastical sights by now, but his eyes could not help but widen with astonishment when his grandfather replicated Morfox's metamorphosis at the start of their journey and ... turned into a robin. Out of the three identical robins now onboard, two of them flew away. The one left behind landed beside Frederick as a red fox.

"I'm not allowed any more visits to the Domain of the Living until next year," Frederick told Al. "I'm luckier than most Spirits in Luxfons, though. Her Nobleness Mistress Magistery hasn't suppressed my powers because I'm a Future Spirit-noble. All five Future Spirit-nobles are allowed to keep them, along with the five Spirit-nobles and Chief Alfred.

"Why were the powers of the other Spirits suppressed?"

"As a precaution. After Metanos failed to steal the Power to Kill, Her Nobleness thought he was bound to recruit other Spirits to his cause, whatever that is. She feared that if he gathered many followers, their combined powers could destroy Sundomum, easily allowing him to get the Power to Kill. It was decided that the suppression of powers was necessary because of that risk." A look of uneasiness flashed across Frederick's hairy face.

"Did you agree with that decision?" probed Al.

Frederick hesitated. "I understand the reasoning behind it. But the Spirits affected by the decision are being forced to make an enormous sacrifice: they can't carry out the task of helping their loved ones. I'm sure most think it's a necessary sacrifice, but others may not be so understanding.

"You'd have seen a completely different sight during peacetime when the Unsighted Gates opened – hundreds and hundreds of Spirits flocking to the Domain of the Living. It was quite something to see and be a part of," he added nostalgically.

"Why doesn't Mistress Magistery suppress Metanos's powers too?" demanded Al, frowning.

"He's too powerful," Frederick sighed. "So much so, that he was obviously able to hoodwink Her Nobleness and her old Chief Spirit-nobles during his Noble Possession. The nature of the darkness inside him remained hidden from them, and so Metanos was Accepted as a Spirit of Luxfons.

"Lord Havelock used to be his Spirit-noble; he's the one who found him wondering in Ancient Gates Wood and brought him to Sundomum. He always says how Metanos is the only one out of all his mentees so far who managed to teach *him* one or two things. But Metanos can't use his powers as the other Spirits in Luxfons do – to help their loved ones in the Domain of the Living. For some strange reason, the Spirits-liminal let him into our world even though he'd left no loved ones behind. According to Lord Havelock, having no task frustrated him a lot, and because he was capable of doing a lot of good in the role, Her Nobleness made him a Chief Spirit-noble."

There was a loud clatter on the deck. Ivar had left his cane leaning against the chest, and it had fallen down. Al got up and picked it up. On closer inspection, he saw that its silver finial was in the shape of a rose and heavily scratched and dented. He placed the cane more securely behind two smaller chests.

Al had barely resumed his seat when the River departed from a state of serenity into one of utter *chaos*. Wave upon wave collided into the Ragnarsson from all directions, and she became nothing more than a spinning top. The golden head was screaming and Morfox was whining – both clearly terrified. And so was Al. He yelled out in both fear and pain as he was thrust onto the polished surface of the now extremely wet deck.

"HOLD ON!" bellowed Frederick, clinging onto the chest he had been sitting on mere moments ago. "I'LL TRY TO LIFT HER UP INTO THE AIR!"

With great difficulty, Al clambered up to his own chest and embraced it as tightly as he could. He sighed with relief as Frederick managed to get the longship airborne. But only fleetingly. She plummeted back into the wild water and spun and swayed more and more dangerously as the River boiled and bubbled and frothed more and more fervently. As she rose unsteadily once more, Al hoped as hard as he could that, this time, Frederick would succeed in saving them from almost guaranteed submersion ... And they stayed safely in the air. But the River was not going to let them escape *that* easily –

Large droplets shot up towards them like bullets and battered the hull. These were soon followed by actual creatures made of water – seahorses, swordfishes, rays and even dolphins. All collided with the Ragnarsson and dispersed on impact – apart from one. The exception – a swordfish – targeted the terrified passengers themselves, exploding above Al's head and soaking him from head to toe.

It was at this very moment that the River became as peaceful as it was before.

"*What – why – it ...*" was all Al managed to utter as he struggled to his feet, panting and shivering.

"It's only ever behaved like *that* in the stories I've heard about the era of Raja Nawab, which was an extremely long time ago!" said Frederick, getting up and leaning over the dripping shields to look at the serene scene below. "Legend has it that once a Spirit is below its surface, they're very lucky to re-emerge."

"I implore you to lower me down now, Frederick," requested the golden head. "It's now safe to resume our journey."

"With pleasure," replied Frederick as his black eyes swept the deck and everything became bone-dry again. "I don't think I'm able to keep you suspended like this for much longer anyway."

Although Al momentarily felt alarmed at the idea of the Ragnarsson being back on the River, his increasing impatience to get to Metanos as soon as possible quickly made what had just happened seem quite trivial. The River, however, showed no sign of straying from its state of serenity again as the Ragnarsson was lowered onto its surface, and they began to sail forth once more.

It was a while before Alfred, Ivar and Robin joined them again. No sooner had the sumptuously dressed figure of Ivar reappeared than the two little robins whizzed back onboard, with one perching itself on the rigging and the other turning into the true form of Alfred Baba.

"Ah, I'm glad to see you're back, Ivar," said Alfred. "Otherwise, Robin and I would've had to go to your estate – well, your descendant's estate now – to politely request that you return to Luxfons. How did it go on this occasion?"

Ivar looked crestfallen as he picked up his cane from behind the small chests. "Not at all well, old chap," he sighed. "I took on the form of one of his spaniels and literally led him to the valuable painting in the dining room, but it was a futile exercise. The Twentieth Viscount Havelock isn't very bright, unfortunately. I'm now convinced that the estate cannot be saved."

"Oh, come now," Alfred said reassuringly, "you'll think

of something else before long. Try turning into a person next time!" he added with a chuckle.

"Perhaps I ought to take on the guise of a confused old man like you normally do," Ivar said thoughtfully.

"That's not a bad idea," said Alfred, smiling. "*He* started off as a matchmaker initially." He turned to Al. "Have your parents ever told you how they first met?"

It took Al a few seconds to realise what his grandfather was implying.

"That confused historian in the conference was you!"

"It certainly was," said Alfred, beaming. "Your father was going through a rough patch at the time, and I thought someone like Helen might be able to remedy that. And she did."

"Why are you two looking so dishevelled?" Ivar asked Al and Frederick, frowning with curiosity.

"Well ..." began Frederick ...

Alfred and Ivar both looked shocked after being told about the strange event that had occurred in their absence, and neither of them could explain why the River behaved as it did. They were still discussing it when a high-pitched voice announced that they had arrived at the Fallen Tree.

6

A Villainous Vision

The Ragnarsson had come to a halt next to what looked like an enormous tunnel. It was cutting through the base of the thick wall of shrubs and was crowned with gnarled, leafless branches, which were mingling with the surrounding vegetation in all directions. As Al took in its strange appearance, he realised that it was an actual – colossal – fallen tree with a hollow trunk. They disembarked and stumbled through the mesh of wood on the ground to get inside. It was pitch black, but pleasantly warm, and the air was carrying the cosy scent of old books. Al could just make out a tiny sliver of light ahead.

"Morfox, light the way, my friend," said Frederick.

A few moments later, the darkness was gone. It had been replaced by a bright orangey glow – a swarm of fireflies had risen from near their feet in a fine spiral, which had uncoiled and stretched ahead of them into the distance. The floor of the Fallen Tree was covered with green moss, twinkling like a carpet of emeralds in the light, and its walls had countless channels and crevices. There was enough space for them to walk comfortably in pairs. Alfred (with Robin on his shoulder) and Ivar lead the way whilst Al and Frederick followed closely behind.

"Now then, Frederick," said Ivar, looking over his shoulder, "I'd like you to pay close attention to the paths we take after we've left the Fallen Tree behind. There'll be quite a few to remember, unfortunately. But I'm not aware of a simpler way to reach my Unsighted Gate."

"Very well, Sir," said Frederick.

"Is Metanos's Unsighted Gate in the same thicket as yours?" Alfred asked Ivar.

"No, no – it's in the thicket of winter trees beyond. I found him floating there not long after the Gates had opened. It must be nearly a century ago now."

After what seemed like a very long time to Al, they emerged from the root-end, and the fireflies turned back into the red fox. They were now in a silent woodland, which was bathing in golden light. The closely growing trees were more like mountains in stature and looked as though they had decided to join forces to create a brand-new sky far, far above – one constructed with golden-brown branches and leaves of every shade of green imaginable. Directly in front of Al, amongst the low-growing wild vegetation, was a huge disc made of worn cobblestones, which had a number of paths leading off it.

Ivar stepped onto the disc and pointed at the path directly opposite the Fallen Tree with his cane.

"We're to take this one," he declared.

And so they did. It would be the first of twelve paths they would follow without stopping. Each one led to a similar cobblestone disc with a set of paths to choose from. Every so often, as he chose the one they were to take, Ivar would emphatically point out any of its memorable features to Frederick – namely the shapes or colours of particular cobblestones.

"Here we are!" boomed Ivar at the end of the twelfth

path. "This is the grand location of my Unsighted Gate!"

They were surrounded by trees that reflected the beauty of not one, but two seasons: spring and autumn. Richly coloured leaves were intertwined with equally as colourful blossoms, and together, they looked sublime in the golden light. Ivar directed their attention to a particularly grand tree with red-and-white roses encircling its trunk; his Unsighted Gate was in its branches. Although he endlessly praised the beauty of this place, which was so closely connected to him, none of the others fully reciprocated his enthusiasm.

Al felt frustrated at having to stop: his thoughts were now focussed entirely on their final destination and what he could *not* fail to do when he got there. *We're so close.*

"Shall we proceed, Ivar?" asked Alfred.

"Yes, yes – of course."

They set off on a path with quite a few stones missing, and the ones remaining were jagged and rough. As they followed its course, the colour and quantity of leaves around them began to diminish. Soon, they were amongst ancient-looking trees, which were completely leafless and grey. The golden light, too, had waned in this part of the Wood, and a kind of twilight had descended upon them.

Al and Ivar were walking on either side of Alfred, who was deep in thought. Al could not help but notice the return of the shadow of apprehension on his lined face. And Robin, once again, was flying a little erratically.

"I have no intention of letting Metanos evade capture any longer," Ivar told Alfred. "After much deliberation, I'm certain I can use this opportunity to bring the whole matter to an abrupt end."

"But you know Her Nobleness Mistress Magistery's

thoughts on the matter," said Alfred. "He will have ensured that it's impossible to capture him. It would be futile, therefore, to even consider capturing him on this occasion."

"Neither he nor his Spirit-creatures dared to cross the threshold of Bloomturrim," Ivar persisted in a manner like he had not paid much attention to what Alfred had just said. "I can only conclude he fears me somewhat."

Alfred sighed and remained silent for a few moments.

"Presently, I'm only concerned with restoring the freedom of my family," he said finally. "I don't want you to do anything which may hinder that."

Ivar tutted and strode ahead. He soon came to a complete stop, though.

"I first saw him over there by that rock," he told the others after they had caught up with him, pointing his cane at a large, mossy rock trapped between two very wrinkly tree trunks in the distance.

"Thank you, Ivar," Alfred said with a tone of unmistakable sincerity.

"Am I correct in assuming that you'd like those of us not expected by Metanos to remain here?" asked Ivar.

"I hope you understand," said Alfred. "Al, Robin – come."

The three of them left the path and headed towards the mossy rock. They navigated their way through the dead-looking trees in silence. The only sound that could be heard was the soft rustle of the vegetation being trodden on. Al's heart began to pound as they got closer and closer. And then – they were there.

"I was beginning to fear that you weren't going to show up," said a deep voice from behind the rock.

Al and Alfred exchanged startled looks before walking

briskly round the huge screen of stone and wood obscuring their view, Robin fluttering after them. Their startlement did not become any less profound when they saw what was on the other side.

Rather like the mossy rock, one of the Hawkanines was wedged between two tree trunks, and a tall Spirit with a taut, square face, bloodshot eyes and thinning black hair was sitting on its back. He was wearing a scarlet chainmail robe, and a leather quiver – which had the end of an archaic-looking golden trumpet pointing out of it – was hanging limply from his shoulder. His countenance was brimming with pride.

Before any of them could say anything, Al noticed movement a few feet away from where they were standing. An overgrown butterfly, the size of a small child, was trying to flap its colourfully patterned wings without much success in the grass. Suddenly, the wings turned into the colour of lead. In fact, it looked as though they had turned *to* lead, becoming rigid and moving no longer. Alfred scooped up the butterfly into his arms and stared fixedly at the Spirit on the Hawkanine, looking horrified.

"What have you done to her, Metanos?"

"Oh, something that was definitely not undeserved," Metanos said indifferently. "I simply don't appreciate being persistently spied on. As skilful as Io is at camouflaging herself, she can't hide from the eyes of my Hawkanines – nothing can. Mistress Magistery surely ought to consider that before endeavouring to send any more of her Spirit-creatures after me."

"Why did you have my loved ones abducted?" asked Alfred, unable to hide the contempt in his voice. "And why did you summon us here?"

Metanos smiled eagerly and said, "Well, you see—"

"WHERE'S MY FAMILY?!" bellowed Al.

The smile on Metanos's face disappeared as he turned his eyes towards Al and pierced him with his chilling gaze.

"I'LL DO ANYTHING YOU WANT! JUST LET THEM GO!"

"That's *exactly* what I wanted to hear," Metanos said calmly, his smile returning. "Now I need your grandfather to declare the same."

Al looked at Alfred expectantly, not at all doubting he would echo his own words. But he did not.

"What do you want us to do?" The apprehension that Al had caught glimpses of had now infiltrated Alfred's voice.

"Right, I think I'll start by revealing your task first, Alfred ... *If* you succeed in carrying it out, I'll happily release your loved ones. Your task is very simple: persuade Mistress Magistery to restore the powers of all Spirits."

Alfred remained silent for a few moments. The graveness etched on his face made him look older than ever.

"So ... you're definitely not acting alone," he said finally.

"Whether I am or am not, your task remains the same. By completing it, you'll become part of a truly historic plan, which will culminate in a glorious revolution," Metanos added with passion and earnestness.

"And what role will the Power to – to Kill play in this plan of yours?" Alfred asked fearfully.

"You speak of this power as though it's terrible." Metanos sounded almost offended. "Death hasn't really done us much harm. It's only because of death that you're one of the most powerful Spirits in Luxfons."

"Many of us would gladly sacrifice our powers and reunite with our families if there was a choice in the matter," said Alfred. "Many of us wouldn't think twice about becoming a part of their lives again like we used to be – basking in their love and facing whatever troubles lay ahead together. The power you seek snatches loved ones away and destroys lives. It *is* terrible!"

"Ah, but you see the Spirits of Luxfons will be able to remain in the Domain of the Living permanently after the revolution, should they choose to! There's no better way to alleviate the sadness of Departure. *And* they'll be able to retain their powers!"

"What?" Alfred blurted out. "*How?*"

The look of demented excitement on Metanos's face at being asked to elaborate sent a shiver down Al's spine.

"I have recently discovered a way to trick the Unsighted Gates into staying open – indefinitely. It's only mass death that can achieve such a feat. That's why I need that power hidden away in Sundomum. Not everyone in the Domain of the Living has to die, but quite a few will have to."

"What gives you the right to even entertain such an idea?!"

It was the first time Al had seen his grandfather lose his temper.

"*I* give myself that right. Me: Metanos. I possess the powers to give myself that right. And I'll ensure that idea becomes a reality."

"As you very well know, only a fraction of those who die end up in Luxfons!" cried Alfred. "Even if the Gates remained open, that wouldn't help the Spirits who go elsewhere. They'd never see their loved ones again!"

"A necessary sacrifice," Metanos said without a hint of

remorse.

"The Spirits of Luxfons would never be able to take their true forms," persisted Alfred. "It would never be the same ..."

"Non-Spirits would simply have to get used to slightly altered versions of their dead family members," Metanos said in a similar vein, shrugging.

"You truly believe this so-called utopia of yours justifies taking the lives of individuals against their will?"

"Of course," Metanos said at once. "Those that end up becoming Spirits of Luxfons as a result will feel indebted to me, having become better beings. They'll be just like us. But *unlike* us, they'll carry out their tasks openly and without the insulting restrictions imposed upon their powers by Unsighted Gates and Mistress Magistery." Metanos's voice was becoming increasingly passionate. "I will insist that no Spirit of Luxfons ever curtails their powers again after the revolution has taken place. Our powers will no longer be smothered just because Mistress Magistery fears they may cause what she perceives as 'harm.'"

"There'd be chaos everywhere," lamented Alfred. "Utter chaos."

"You can scarcely imagine what kind of benefits that 'chaos' as you call it can give rise to, but it'll be my noble task to control it across the divide when *I* see fit. Before it gets too out of hand. My experiences as a Chief Spirit-noble for all these years should help me a great deal. I'll finally be able to use my great powers to their full potential – as they're meant to be used."

"So this is your ultimate desire," said Alfred. "This is what has poisoned your senses. You want to use your powers to rule both Luxfons and the Domain of the

Living. And you're willing to murder millions in order to do so."

"Your task remains the same," repeated Metanos. "It doesn't matter what your views are. *It will remain the same.*"

The next moment, Metanos's eyes were back on Al.

"I'm glad to see that you're now much calmer," he said mockingly, "but if I were in your position, I'd look a little cheerier. You have an opportunity to get exactly what you want."

Al's anger had turned into horror whilst listening to Metanos reveal his heinous intentions with such relish, and this was reflected on his thin face. His resolution to get his family back – whatever the cost – remained as strong as ever, though.

"What do you want me to do?" he asked Metanos, unfalteringly meeting his gaze.

"Your task is very simple too: make sure your grandfather carries out *his* task. Make him see sense. Otherwise, I fear his reluctance to do as I say will mean that you never see your family again. You're already an extraordinary young man, Al, having inexplicably resisted Spiritsnuff. You'll be considered no less than heroic when, because of you, your family returns to the Domain of the Living and carries on from where they left off – like nothing happened."

Al did not require any persuasion to do what Metanos wanted. His mind was already firmly made up. He could sense his grandfather looking at him intently, but he kept his eyes on the proudly smiling Spirit opposite him.

Al nodded rigidly.

"Very wise, indeed!" exclaimed Metanos. "And let me assure you that none of my remaining Hawkanines will attempt to take you again. I've forbidden them from doing so. There's no need for you to be in my custody, and I very much hope I'm able to say that about your family before long."

"I'd like you to stop with this despicable foolishness immediately, Metanos!" rang out an indignant voice behind Al.

It belonged to Ivar. Frederick and Morfox were with him.

Metanos tilted his head back and let out a cackle. It sounded grotesque: brimming with pride, mockery and anger in equal measure.

"Is there anything else you'd like me to do for you, Ivar?"

Al expected Ivar to explode with rage at how disrespectful Metanos's demeanour was towards him. He did no such thing, though. Much to Al's surprise, Ivar looked scared and like he would rather be anywhere else but there – facing the sinister Spirit sitting on his scowling Spirit-creature.

"I would ... I would like you to come with us to S-Sundomum and ... and face the consequences of your actions," bleated Ivar.

Another horrific cackle burst out of Metanos.

"Did you really imagine, Ivar, that you would be able to intimidate *me*?" he spat. "I find that rather insulting."

He raised one of his bony forefingers and pointed it directly at his former Spirit-noble. What looked like reddish energy shot out from the end of his long, yellowy fingernail and took on the form of a dagger, which sped towards Ivar like a bullet. He did not have time to move out of the way, but it did not matter: the dagger suddenly changed its trajectory and sped off over the mossy rock and out of sight. Ivar struggled to maintain the grip on his cane as he began to tremble.

Metanos looked shocked for a moment before a look of what Al thought was gleeful realisation spread over his taut face. He raised the same finger once more, but this time, Frederick and Morfox stepped in front of Ivar.

"Oh, feel free to stand between your spineless Spirit-noble, who is full of so much pretence, and me, young blacksmith," Metanos said without lowering his finger. "Admirable as it is, it'll not make much difference. If you seek to attack me, on the other hand ... That would be very unwise. You see, I have the ability to form a union with my Unsighted Gate – I'm currently embedded into its very fabric. Attack me, and you'll be attacking the most integral part of Luxfons itself, and who knows what that could potentially lead to ...?"

"You won't gain anything by harming them, Metanos," implored Alfred. "Leave them be!"

Metanos ignored him. Another spurt of the same reddish energy erupted from his fingernail and took on the form of a spear. It headed rapidly towards Frederick's broad chest.

"No!" Al yelled instinctively.

And the spear stopped in mid-air. It rotated on the spot until the spearhead was facing Al and then continued to hover without moving – as though awaiting further instructions.

"Go back!" said Al.

He did not know why he did so, but it felt like the natural thing to do. He was not entirely sure the spear would listen to him once again, though.

It did.

The spear turned round at once and whizzed back

in the direction of Metanos, who collapsed onto his Hawkanine. The weapon collided loudly with something invisible between the two tree trunks. It then faded into nothingness. A great rumbling sound, like that of an avalanche, filled the air, and Metanos and his screeching Spirit-creature were thrown onto the ground. At the same time, vast cracks began to appear all around them on the woodland floor – like it was about to hatch open like an egg. And then – a wide chasm materialised mere inches from Al's feet, making him lose his balance –

"Robin – *Al!*" cried Alfred.

In a flash, Al had been rescued by the little bird for the second time, in a similar fashion to the first. Robin placed him next to Alfred, who was still cradling Io in his arms.

As they all tried with all their might to put as much distance between themselves and the rapidly expanding chaos, a beam of white light arrived in their midst and illuminated the exact spot where the spear had struck Metanos's Unsighted Gate. The rumbling stopped, and the cracks and the chasm disappeared. The glorious light then morphed into the stately figure of Mistress Magistery. She looked at each of them in turn, her pearly face as unreadable as ever. As soon as she turned her head towards Metanos, he and his Hawkanine morphed into reddish mist and drifted away above the treetops like a veil caught in a gust of wind.

"I've just averted nothing less than the destruction of our world," Mistress Magistery said in her monotonous voice. "What happened?"

There was silence. Al was looking at his shoes in a kind of haze. He, once again, had the feeling of being stared at in a spotlight, and it had never been more intense. He could not understand how he managed to repel Metanos's attack, and a horrible mixture of remorse and terror was swirling round in the pit of his stomach at the thought of what his actions very nearly led to. He wanted to own up, to somehow explain – confused as he was – and apologise. He looked up.

But Mistress Magistery was no longer waiting to be enlightened. She was striding towards Alfred, her eyes fixed on the Spirit-creature in his arms. Io was moving her delicate-looking antennae back and forth and side to side, undoubtedly communicating something to the powerful Spirit whose attention she had fully captured. Al noticed that the Spirit-creature's plum-sized black eyes suddenly became very moist.

"It was Metanos," said Alfred, placing Io into Mistress Magistery's arms. "It was too late for me to do anything, Your Nobleness."

Mistress Magistery spent a while examining her wings from every possible angle. When she finished her scrutiny, Al was surprised to see that her eyes, too, were moist.

"I need to get her back to Sundomum," she said. "A concoction I procured from Hermit may help her to recover to some extent. Her wings, however, will never be the same again.

"I want you all to kindly accompany me and would then like you, Alfred, to summon the remaining Spirit-nobles and Future Spirit-nobles. I have been to the Orangery and seen Marshal, and I'll reveal what I've discovered once all are gathered. And you can all reveal the details of what took place here. We'll then collectively decide what needs to be done."

"Very well, Your Nobleness," Alfred said with a bow.

"Your Nobleness," piped up Ivar, bowing deeply, "may I

have a moment to inform the Ragnarsson that there's no need to wait for us before we leave?" He was no longer trembling but sounded uncharacteristically deflated.

Mistress Magistery nodded. A dozen or so red-and-white roses in the shape of a large arrow appeared in the air in front of Ivar and, like Metanos's reddish dagger, zoomed off over the mossy rock.

Mistress Magistery and Io turned into a sphere of dazzling white light, which grew larger and larger until it encompassed them all. Al was blinded by it but felt pleasantly warm and weightless and then – like he was on the most thrilling rollercoaster he had ever been on. A few moments later, he found himself standing in the hall of Sundomum with the others.

7

Decisions

Mistress Magistery sprinted towards her throne, the yellow crystals on her gown shimmering spectacularly. Before she reached it, though, she suddenly stopped and then continued with a slight limp. After carefully placing Io on the throne, she removed a large sapphire from one of its jewelled arms. Gripping it between her thumb and forefinger, she shook it vigorously. Al then realised that what he had thought was a sapphire was actually a bright blue vial disguised as one. It was unstopped, and a single drop of the concoction it contained was administered to each of Io's wings. They immediately turned from the colour of lead to a much healthier-looking colour of rust, but a small, eye-like patch of grey still remained in the very middle of each wing.

"You need to rest, Io," said Mistress Magistery, replacing the vial in the throne's arm. She lifted the enormous butterfly up in her hands. "Go to the Meadow, and make sure you're not disturbed."

With her wings now flapping as they ought to – though they noticeably twitched now and again – Io fluttered out of Mistress Magistery's hands, across the hall and out of the open doors.

"Is Your Nobleness in need of recuperation?" Alfred asked worriedly. "Should I delay summoning the rest of the Spirit-nobles and Future Spirit-nobles?"

Mistress Magistery had collapsed onto the throne; her hands were trembling, and she was leaning her head back longingly.

"For a little while, yes – that would be much appreciated." She could not hide how weak she sounded and added even more faintly, "Saving Luxfons from the brink of destruction wasn't an easy task."

Al could not remember feeling guiltier than he did at this very moment: the one Spirit in Luxfons who, above all others, needed to remain strong during this time of crisis was too weak to carry out her duties. Because of him.

"It's all my fault," he said timidly. "I'm really sorry."

Mistress Magistery raised her head slowly to look at him. She did not seem surprised in the slightest. Every eye in the hall was now on Al. He felt as though they wanted him to continue, to explain in detail *how* he had managed to do what he had done. As much as he wanted to, he could not. He resumed the study of his shoes, avoiding their questioning eyes as he had done in Ancient Gates Wood.

A voice finally came to his aid by drawing the focus away from him; it was Frederick's:

"Al saved me from being seriously harmed by repelling Metanos's attack. Morfox and I were ... We were—"

"They were protecting me, Your Nobleness," said Ivar, unable to look at Mistress Magistery for more than a split second. "I was – somehow – unable to defend myself on this occasion."

"Metanos had lodged himself into his Unsighted

Gate to prevent any of us from trying to capture him," continued Frederick. "The dark force he generated wouldn't have hit the Gate if *he* hadn't ducked."

Morfox nodded his handsome head.

"How is it, Your Nobleness, that my grandson has the power to repel such a powerful attack?" Alfred's voice was heavy with dread and confusion. "He's certainly not a Spirit ... He can't be ... can he?"

"No," said Mistress Magistery. "His Spirit is still encased in flesh and bone as it was in the Domain of the Living. But the powers it possesses are no longer encased. They've not been fully unlocked because his Spirit hasn't left his body and, more importantly, because I've not Accepted it as a Spirit of Luxfons. These powers are so immense, however, that your grandson's mere presence in this world has allowed them to fractionally seep through."

On hearing these words, Al was convinced for a second or two that they could not possibly be referring to him. *Surely not.* When this state of disbelief passed, he found himself happily accepting the extraordinary idea that he was in possession of immense powers, and he could actually use some of them. He had no idea what lay ahead or how much longer he would have to stay in this world of Spirits, so it was comforting to know he was in a far better position to face any difficulties he may encounter than he had realised. So *this* was why he was 'special' as his grandfather had put it.

"Hence the Spiritsnuff was unable to have any effect on him whatsoever ..." Alfred said more to himself after a few moments of absolute silence.

"Indeed," said Mistress Magistery. She sounded markedly less weak and more like herself already. "I first began to suspect how powerful this boy's Spirit is when it was confirmed that the substance he was immune to was Spiritsnuff. And I became even more convinced when the Hawkanine decided to Depart after seeing him so closely for the first time here in Luxfons. Metanos's Spirit-creatures are able to see what we cannot, and it undoubtedly saw the powers this boy's Spirit possesses – the kind it wouldn't have been able to resist. And rather than risk betraying its master, the Hawkanine decided to sacrifice its remaining time in this world."

Alfred turned to his grandson. His old face was aglow with relief.

"I had started to fear that you had truly Departed from the Domain of the Living," he said, his voice full of emotion. "Your parents, your sister and your grandmother would have all been devastated. You have no idea how much you mean to them. But I do."

The two beamed at each other, and Robin, who had been sitting quietly on Alfred's shoulder, now chirped cheerily.

"It's time, Alfred," said Mistress Magistery. She seemed to be fully recovered: her hands were no longer trembling, and she was sitting bolt upright on her throne, looking as majestic as ever. "Kindly be seated, everyone."

As Alfred and Robin took their places on their mahogany throne, the same turquoise armchair Al had sat on during the Noble Possessions reappeared, and he dashed over to it at once.

A backless, semi-circular bench materialised directly behind Ivar, Frederick and Morfox. It, too, was made of mahogany and carved with peacocks like the two thrones flanking Mistress Magistery's. Ivar and Frederick took their places on it in the very centre, whilst Morfox remained sitting on the ermine-patterned floor close to his master. Alfred then withdrew a tiny silver bell from an inside pocket of his tweed jacket. It looked so delicate that Al expected it to produce nothing more than a tinkle when it was rung. He was quite taken aback, therefore, when the hall was filled with the deafening sound of heavy bells being rung collectively.

The peal did not die down until Alfred replaced it in his pocket, just as a familiar figure walked through the open doors: Hamelin Buck. He was followed by a young, mousy-faced male Spirit in full academic dress. They marched up to the bench, walked round it, bowed, announced their names and titles ("Hamelin Buck, Spirit-noble" and "Kerr Weston, Future Spirit-noble") and sat down next to Frederick. A snowy-white mouse was lounging on the rim of Hamelin's top hat, which he had been carrying upside down under his arm and which now rested on his lap; the tiny, red-eyed Spirit-creature was feasting on a juicy blackberry, which did not diminish in size in the slightest in spite of how fervently it was being gnawed.

Hamelin and Kerr were followed by three pairs of Spirits in quick succession: Admiral Keel, Spirit-noble and Polemus Tallow, Future Spirit-noble; Lady Tyto, Spirit-noble and Virginia Walsingham, Future Spirit-noble; Hexa Parr, Spirit-noble and Cloelia Iceni, Future Spirit-noble. The semi-circular bench was now fully occupied. The ten Spirits sitting on it were observing Mistress Magistery, who had risen to her feet to address them. Some of the new arrivals who Al had never seen before did, however, glance at him curiously once or twice.

"Greetings to you all," Mistress Magistery said without so much as a hint of a smile on her face. "I've summoned you all here so Alfred and I can enlighten you on recent developments concerning Metanos, namely the location of his hideout."

A buzz of excitement rose round the bench as each of the ten Spirits turned to those sitting next to them to share their immediate thoughts – it was as though they had collectively turned into a giant bumblebee.

"Where is he?" asked Polemus Tallow, an extremely fat Spirit in a scarlet frock coat, who had a permanent frown carved on his sweaty face. "*Where is he?*"

"I will impart that information in good time, Mister Tallow," said Mistress Magistery. "First, kindly allow me to explain how I came to be aware of the location. As a result, you will find out about the extraordinary step Metanos has recently taken: a step that has led to Non-Spirits being present in Luxfons." She gestured towards Al.

Al was still not used to being scanned and became rather interested in his shoes once more. He did not look up until he was sure that all eyes in the hall were on the stately figure of Mistress Magistery again. Apart from Ivar and Frederick, every Spirit on the bench looked stunned as she continued ...

Al had no choice but to relive the events of Christmas Day as Mistress Magistery narrated them in fine detail. It was strange to hear himself being depicted like a character in a book, and he wished what he was hearing was, indeed, fictitious.

At last, Mistress Magistery moved on to events which did not feature Al. Her revelations would make his heart skip a beat on more than occasion:

"And as soon as I was able, I set off for the Orangery to see the one who guards it: Marshal. It would've been unwise to question him undisguised, so I took on the form of a little Spirit-girl. He seemed quite dazed. I told him how fond I was of shiny objects and how much I admired his sword. To which he replied that he, on the other hand, was beginning to despise objects which shimmer even more than the evil ones he guards. He told me that shimmering sandstorms keep ravaging his surroundings, somehow causing him to enter into a momentary state of slumber and that if circumstances don't change, he might consider taking the Orangery elsewhere.

"I enquired whether he would let me have a peek inside, in case any of its legendary plants still remained ... This question naturally fanned the flames of his paranoia, and I received a fury-laden 'No' in response. He then told me that no Spirit has set foot in the Orangery for hundreds and hundreds of years – apart from one: 'a Spirit in a red chainmail robe,' who'd implored him for permission to merely satisfy his curiosity and that he'd only granted his wish reluctantly after this Spirit had detached all his powers from himself in front of his very eyes. This had convinced him that he wasn't being deceived by a Spirit who wanted to free his prisoners.

"I can now say with certainty that Metanos has made the Orangery his lair, and that's where he's keeping Alfred's family. We now know how he first got inside to get the power to create Spiritsnuff, and it's been confirmed that he has subsequently been getting past Marshal by using that very Spiritsnuff to subdue him."

Mistress Magistery sat down as Alfred rose to his feet; those on the bench remained as attentive as ever. He began recounting exactly what Metanos had said in Ancient Gates Wood ...

Every single one of the ten faces in the semi-circle was enveloped with terror-infused disbelief when he finally resumed his seat. The barrier which concealed Mistress Magistery's emotions had also shattered again. She did not only look horrified, but hurt too, and struggled to change her expression back to one of rigid neutrality. What she said when she finally succeeded made Al's heart sink:

"Most of you will agree that, in spite of his assurance that he'll release Alfred's family as a result, we cannot give Metanos what he wants – that restoring the powers of all Spirits is out of the question at the moment."

"Couldn't agree more, Your Nobleness," said Virginia Walsingham, a young, red-haired Spirit wearing a thick layer of white makeup, a lace ruff and a reddish-brown gown with trumpet-like sleeves. "Your Nobleness is as wise as she's graceful. We can all be confident that every decision you make will be the right one."

"We cannot say with absolute surety that Metanos has accomplices," said the grey-haired Spirit sitting next to Virginia: Lady Tyto. She was small and plump, and her large, round eyes and feathery cardigan made her look quite like an owl.

"No, but there's increasing evidence *indicating* that he does," said Hamelin as Kerr nodded vigorously. "If we think about the following as a whole: the captured Hawkanine's slip up, Metanos's desire to have the powers of all Spirits restored and the fact that his so-called revolution may seem appealing to those who are currently powerless, we can safely assume he has accomplices. Because of this, the powers of the vast majority of Spirits need to remain suppressed."

"I disagree," Admiral Keel wheezed with assertiveness.

"We should pay no heed to his demand. We should not let ... um ... this upstart bully us in this way!" The ancient-looking Spirit seemed taken aback as he looked round at the puzzled faces surrounding him.

With some difficulty, Polemus leant over to whisper something in his ear ...

"I do beg your pardon, Mister Buck," muttered Admiral Keel, doffing his frayed bicorn hat. "I misheard your remarks and wholeheartedly agree with what you *actually* said."

Many of the Spirits on the bench expressed the same sentiment. Al looked at his grandfather in desperation – his heart now felt as though it weighed a ton. Alfred was looking very grave again and did not seem to sense his grandson staring at him: his blue eyes remained fixed on the semi-circle in front of him. And Al's almost identical eyes turned back towards it, too, as Frederick began to speak:

"If all powers were to be restored, I believe Metanos would have fewer Spirits joining his cause. His idea of using powers unchecked to help your loved ones is, like Mister Buck implied, bound to be really attractive to those becoming impatient to resume their task. They'll be less willing to support him if they have use of their powers again. And Chief Alfred's family will finally be free."

Al's affection for the young blacksmith soared.

"But if Metanos already has many followers, it's going to be almost impossible to stop an *army* of Spirits with restored powers from taking the Power to Kill!" Hexa Parr blurted out like she was stating the obvious. She was exceedingly pretty and was wearing a far grander version of Virginia's gown, ornamented with a jewelled French hood. "Her Nobleness wouldn't be able to suppress their powers again – because he will have shared his personal immunity against the suppression of powers with them! I don't think you've given this situation much thought, Mister Hancock!"

"Our beautiful, peaceful world would be engulfed by war," lamented Cloelia Iceni, on the brink of tears. Out of all the Spirits Al had seen so far, she looked the most corpse-like: a white garment was draped around her skeletal form like a shroud, she had very little hair on her head and her eyes were sunken and dead-looking. Clinging tightly to her bony neck was a golden necklace in the shape of a horseshoe.

"If my Chief Spirit-noble concurs with the vast majority of us," said Mistress Magistery, "my final decision will be to continue suppressing the powers of all Spirits apart from ours until Metanos and his accomplices, however many of them there are, have been captured." She turned to her enthroned deputy, whose eyes were still glued to those sitting before him. "Alfred?"

Al's heart began to drum frantically. After what felt like a lifetime, his grandfather finally turned to look at Mistress Magistery. *He has to oppose them – for the sake of his family. He has to.*

"I concur," said Alfred.

"Then it's decided," Mistress Magistery declared at once.

In the moments that followed, Al lost all awareness of where he was – and who he was with, except for that one individual whose utterance of two simple words had snuffed out any hope he had of seeing his family again.

"YOU PROMISED I WOULD GET THEM BACK! YOU PROMISED EVERYTHING WOULD BE AS IT WAS! YOU PROMISED!"

"That promise still stands, my dear boy," Alfred said lovingly. "But we can't give Metanos what he wants. You heard what he means to do with the Power to Kill: so many lives will be destroyed. His savage tyranny will know no end."

"I ONLY CARE ABOUT MY FAMILY RIGHT NOW!" Al's tears were flowing as readily as his anger. "WHATEVER HAPPENS NEXT CAN BE DEALT WITH LATER!"

"Al, please listen to me ..."

Frederick's voice sounded to him like it was coming from a distance.

"We know where your family's being kept and – forgive me if I'm mistaken, Your Nobleness – our next step will be to plan how to rescue them."

"That's correct," said Mistress Magistery.

"I feared Metanos would present me with a torturous dilemma," Alfred sighed, his eyes becoming dewy, "and that fear was truly realised. Choosing to prevent catastrophe by prolonging the imprisonment of those I love was not an easy decision to make, my dear boy. But I'm determined that they should return to a world exactly like the one they left behind, in spite of its flaws – not one being terrorised by Metanos. We *will* get our family back from him, and we'll do it on our own terms. Not his."

"When, Grandad?" said Al, his thin face glistening with tears.

"Infiltrating the Orangery will be a momentous task," said Alfred. "Everyone in this hall will help, but such a task needs careful planning" – he hesitated – "and so it will take some time to come up with a sound plan. All I ask for is just a little more patience."

"OK," Al said resignedly. "I need a bit of a break from all this, though. I'm ... I'm tired. Really tired."

"Right ... well ..." muttered Alfred. He seemed unsure of what to say next and glanced at Mistress Magistery.

But Al was already on his feet. His hands were clenched up tightly into fists, which he stuffed into his pockets.

"I can take him to Vulcanest, Chief Sir, with your permission ..." said Frederick, also getting up. "Morfox can remain here and tell me about the decisions taken."

"Thank you, Frederick," said Alfred, clearly touched. "It's very noble of you to sacrifice your contribution for my sake. Very noble, indeed." He turned to Al. "Are you happy to go with Frederick to his abode for a little while?"

"Yes," Al said almost robotically without looking at his grandfather.

With the Spirits on the bench also praising him heartily – especially Ivar, now back to his usual energetic self – Frederick left their midst to join Al, who was making his way briskly towards the great golden doors. By the time they reached the threshold, the barely audible discussion behind them had already been diverted towards the subject of the rescue plan. ("Which of the routes leading to the Orangery would be ideal to take?" queried Kerr.)

The stairs to Sundomum finished reassembling just as they stepped outside, allowing Al and Frederick to start descending without delay. Al could not help but admire the view that his elevated position afforded him: a jumble of houses of all sizes and architectural styles imaginable dotted all around the rolling greenery beyond the litter of surplus jagged rocks. He could also make out the River in the far distance and the outlines of some of the bridges between its emerald banks.

"My house, Vulcanest, will only be a short way away after we've crossed that iron bridge," said Frederick, pointing it out. "Only Her Nobleness Mistress Magistery is skilled enough to travel as a beam of light, I'm afraid. Don't worry, though – we won't be going on foot!"

The stairs began to dismantle immediately as they stepped off them onto the carpet of Oculus Plume, and they stood extremely still until the shower of jagged rocks finished falling all round them.

Cupping his hands round his mouth, Frederick cried, "Kiang – my young friend and I need a little assistance from your good self!"

Al looked round in anticipation, but he had no idea what he was looking out for. A little while later, the sound of creaking metal filled his ears, and he looked up. A very large, winged donkey made of bronze was hurtling towards them at a speed tantamount to that of a rocket. Before Al could do little more than jump back in alarm, it crashed into the clearing mere feet away from them.

"Oh dear," said Frederick, looking at the heap of bronze lying on the Oculus Plume. "He's not used to flying, having only just been given his wings."

Kiang got to his feet and clunked over to Frederick with his wings spread like an angel.

"Are we going to *fly* to your house on him?" asked Al, dreading the answer.

"No, I don't think that's a good idea," Frederick chortled. "He definitely needs a little more practice before carrying anyone off into the air!" He looked at the Spirit-creature affectionately. "We can pretend you still don't have wings during this particular journey, my friend."

Al subtly sighed with relief as Kiang lowered his great wings and then the rest of himself too. Frederick climbed onto his back and invited Al to do the same, which he gingerly did so, trying his best not to kick the folded wings. He was surprised by how stable and comfortable he felt sitting on the smooth bronze surface – even when Kiang raised himself up again and started trotting away from Sundomum towards the jagged rocks realigning themselves to form a path out of the clearing.

They followed its extremely long and sloping course until they reached a village comprising pretty timber-framed cottages and cobbled streets. As the jagged rocks were left behind, they moved back to their original position, and the scar-like path ceased to exist.

The little village was brimming with activity. Kiang wove his way past individuals occupied with pursuits such as gardening, painting, crafting, reading or simply conversing with their neighbours. Although Al thought a handful of the villagers looked quite melancholy, the vast majority seemed perfectly content. Frederick was recognised by many of them, and they waved at him cheerily.

A couple of them stopped what they were doing and came over to greet him. One of these was a mature female Spirit wearing a bottle-green gable hood, who had been busy shearing a mini forest of brambles in front of her cottage; she showered the blacksmith with praise and complemented him on his skills because the shears he had made for her were "Absolutely delightful!" The other was a bearded, odorous Spirit wearing rags, who was in earnest need of a new chisel to finish off the marble statue he was carving. Kiang also managed to attract some attention in the village: a very small spaniel yapped uncontrollably as it ran round him in circles before being chased away by a fat black-and-white cat.

"They're just like a normal cat and dog," observed Al, feeling a little disappointed that he had not witnessed either of them display any supernatural abilities.

"Only for the moment," said Frederick, smiling. "To put it simply, Spirit-creatures are part of their creators in a way. Because of this, suppressing a Spirit's powers will suppress their Spirit-creature's powers too, sadly."

The cottages became scarcer as they journeyed on – traversing fields and heaths buzzing with Spirits and Spirit-creatures – until they reached the riverbank and the iron bridge that led to Vulcanest. The bridge was occupied by a group of merry Spirit-youths in tailcoats racing each other back and forth on penny-farthings. They did not become any less merry at having to stop this leisurely activity and allow Kiang to take Al and Frederick across the River. Al was glad when they reached the other side: the sound of heavy bronze hooves on iron was certainly not a pleasant one.

"That's Vulcanest – my humble abode." Frederick was pointing at a brick house with a red door, flanked by outbuildings, near a hillock. "Hope you'll find it comfortable enough to have a much-needed rest."

But Al had no intention of resting. He had made an important decision in Sundomum before excusing himself. It was a decision inspired by what he now knew he had at his disposal: powers. He did not yet know how he was going to get there, but he had decided to go to the Orangery on his own to rescue his family. He was not prepared to wait any longer.

8

The Guard of the Orangery

Al looked round curiously as he and Frederick dismounted in front of Vulcanest. The smaller of the two doorless outbuildings flanking it looked like it was being used for storage: carriage wheels, tools and pots and pans were amongst a huge array of metal goods piled up inside. The large one was undoubtedly the forge itself; it housed a huge anvil sitting in front of a hearth of raging fire. Countless iron chain links were littered about on the earthy floor around the anvil like confetti.

Vulcanest's red door flew open. A Spirit-boy with jet-black hair ran out to greet them. He could not have been more than eight years old and was clothed in a much smaller version of the tunic and leather apron Frederick was wearing. Standing on tiptoe, he put his little arms round Kiang's neck to embrace him.

"He hasn't been away for that long!" Frederick chuckled as the boy continued to embrace the Spirit-creature. "This is my son – Silvester. He helped me make Kiang, who I'm starting to think has the highest position in his affections now!"

"Hello Silvester," said Al, extending his hand, when the boy finally relinquished his gentle hold on Kiang's neck.

"Nice to meet you."

Silvester smiled shyly and shook Al's hand without saying a word.

"He's never been able to speak, I'm afraid," Frederick said sadly.

Silvester, on the other hand, was a picture of pure joviality; he ran off towards the hillock whilst Kiang spread his wings and trotted after him.

"Ah, you're back, my love. Was just about to—oh ... you've brought a guest."

A moon-faced female Spirit had emerged from Vulcanest. She looked embarrassed as she hastily removed the singed and dirty leather apron she, too, was wearing. She folded it up and tucked it under her arm to reveal a shabby, old-fashioned dress – a stark contrast to the gleaming gold stars decorating her dark, curly hair.

"This is Chief Alfred's grandson, Al," Frederick told her. "He's come here to rest for a short while."

"And I'm Alcea Hancock – Frederick's wife and mistress of Vulcanest," said the female Spirit, coming over and shaking Al's hand. "You're welcome to stay for as long as you like. My husband has told me about your circumstances already – a miracle in itself because he rarely tells me anything of importance."

Frederick chuckled sheepishly and said, "It's the duty of all the Spirits in my position to be discreet about what's discussed in Sundomum because of the present situation."

"I know, I know!" Alcea laughed, waving her hand dismissively. "Just trying to be humorous." She gazed at her husband lovingly and added, "I know how important your duties are to you, my love."

"What were you about to tell me?" he asked her with an

air of someone who wanted to change the subject.

"Oh, only that I was about to help you with your chain a little. Thought you might appreciate it. It's a momentous task – forging it by hand."

"You don't need to, dearest. I can manage by myself—"

"Nonsense!" snapped Alcea. "I don't mind at all. I *am* an ironmaster's daughter after all. We can work on it together. I promise I won't ask why Mistress Magistery has asked for it to be made this time!"

Frederick smiled awkwardly and said, "I'll just show Al in first and then join you in the forge."

Alcea gave Al a curt nod, slipped back into her apron and started making her way towards the forge.

As Al followed Frederick into Vulcanest, he immediately became aware of how cold it was inside and felt glad he was wearing a cardigan. They had stepped into a candlelit sitting room with bare brick walls, a dusty stone floor and a coarse ceiling. The furniture dotted about the room was all made of wrought iron and very dull, but Al's eye was also caught by small pieces of ornamental silverware glinting here and there. Frederick led him to an uncomfortable-looking settee with little tin models of knights and dragons strewn on it.

"Silvester's not known for tidying away his toys after playing with them," said Frederick before quickly scooping up the models and stowing them in a small toy chest under the settee. "Make yourself comfortable, Al."

The settee was instantly covered in colourful, bulbous cushions, which almost seemed to be inviting Al to sink into them.

"Thanks for everything, Frederick." He meant it whole-heartedly; the young blacksmith had won Al's everlasting gratitude for the unfaltering kindness he had shown him so far in Luxfons.

"Not at all, my friend. Have a good rest – you've been through a lot. And ... try not to worry too much. Believe me when I say, your grandad *will* fulfil his promise."

With a reassuring smile, Frederick left, closing the door behind him.

And Al was finally on his own.

He now had a clear idea of what steps he was going to take, but he suddenly felt nervous. He was about to test whether he could utilise his powers at will. Avoiding the temptation of sitting on the cushion-laden settee, Al went over to a large round table in the centre of the room. He was quite peckish and wanted to make something edible materialise in front of him – something simple ... *like an apple.* As soon as the image of the fruit flashed across his mind's eye, there it was – a juicy red apple. It was as though it had popped straight out of his head onto the table. Smiling, he picked it up and started eating it. He barely savoured its deliciousness, though, being quite eager to conjure something more substantial –

And that, too, appeared: a chestnut-brown pony squeezed between the table and a suite of sturdy chairs. But it looked rather sickly, like it had been starved, and was not at all like the strong, stocky one Al had wished for. He, nevertheless, felt a tremendous amount of affection for the Spirit-creature, being *his* creation. The pony turned its bony head towards him. Al's heart sank: its black eyes looked incredibly sad. He reached out to stroke its sparse mane, and it made a low snorting sound approvingly.

Al leant closer to its ear and whispered, "Um ... are you able to take me to the Orangery?"

He received no response. Al thought perhaps it lacked

the ability to understand him ... but it had just been contemplating his question: it shook its head. Al's face fell, succumbing to the feeling of disappointment flooding through him. All of a sudden, the pony started to whinny loudly and stamp its hooves on the dusty floor. Feeling somewhat alarmed, Al recommenced the stroking of its mane, and this gradually had the effect of calming it down. But then ... it became smoky and shapeless and began to fade ...

"No, no, *no*!" cried Al.

The pony had gone, though, and he was on his own again. He stood there looking aimlessly round the room with a lump in his throat. *What do I do now?!* Almost miraculously, the answer presented itself to him as his eyes fell on a small silver figure of a donkey on top of a tatty coffer. *That's the only option.*

He darted out of the room, closed the red door noiselessly behind him, sprinted past the forge, which was bursting with the deafening sound of metal hammering metal, and headed straight for the hillock – not stopping until he reached its grassy foot. Although substantial in size, the hillock was not too steep and was very flat-topped; it looked rather like an enormous tortoise shell. Silvester was standing on top of it all alone and was looking fixedly up at something in the blue sky.

Al tore up the hillock as the sound of creaking metal above him got louder and louder. Panting, he reached the top just in time to see Kiang land – surprisingly gracefully – next to Silvester, who stood on tiptoe and patted his bronze head. It was clear that Silvester had been actively encouraging the Spirit-creature to practise that particular manoeuvre.

Silvester looked taken aback when he saw Al

approaching him.

"Hello again," said Al after taking a few seconds to get his breath back. "I sort of need to borrow Kiang for a while. Need him to take me to the Orangery because my family is locked up in that place. Need to get them out of there right now. *Please*."

The Spirit-boy's little mouth had fallen open. He pointed at the forge.

"No one else can know," Al asserted at once, shaking his head. "They won't let me go."

Silvester gulped and stepped away from Kiang.

"Thank you," said Al, sighing with relief.

He expected the Spirit-creature to lower his outstretched wings and then himself as he had done earlier, but Kiang did no such thing. Al's eyes darted desperately towards Silvester, who did not seem surprised by Kiang's indifference and returned to his friend's side. Kiang turned his head to look at him, and Silvester smiled and nodded approvingly before stepping back once more. In a noisy flash, the huge wings were down and the Spirit-creature they graced was crouching on the grass. Al climbed onto his back and patted his neck in gratitude. But, yet again, he refused to move and Silvester, *yet again*, was compelled to intervene.

This time, his intervention proved to be fruitless, much to Al's dismay.

"Really sorry, Silvester, but could you come with us?"

Al had realised why Kiang was refusing to take him – the Spirit-creature had not been created to transport him: Al, unlike Silvester, was not one of his masters. Asking Frederick's power-deprived little boy to put himself in harm's way for the sake of his own family made Al feel incredibly selfish and dislike himself a great deal. But the thought of not helping his family when he had the means to was unbearable.

Silvester's innocent face lit up with excitement at being asked to accompany him, though, and he bounced onto Kiang's back behind Al. Kiang raised himself up, and then spread his wings.

"Oh, you're going to fly us there?" Al flung his arms round the bronze neck. "Hold on to me tightly, Silvester," he implored, looking back.

The little Spirit-boy seemed unable to hear him and was leaning side to side with his arms raised like he, too, had wings and was floating freely in the air. Unlike Silvester's imaginary ones, the actual wings in their midst were far from soundless as they began to beat. Kiang shot off the hillock up towards the vast blueness.

◆ ◆ ◆

They had been flying for a long time when Kiang finally began to glide towards the ground. The sea of colour that had been flowing beneath them had now taken on a less aesthetic hue: murky grey. Al's thin nostrils singed with the odour of rotting vegetation as they got closer and closer to what looked like a diseased meadow. Kiang landed on it with a great squelch and lowered his wings, and the two boys – Non-Spirit and Spirit – dismounted.

"Are we there?" asked Al, looking from Silvester to Kiang in confusion.

Although he had no idea what the Orangery actually looked like, he imagined it to be some sort of guarded building. But he could see nothing apart from swathes and swathes of sludge.

Silvester shook his tiny head and pointed at something he could clearly see in the distance. And sure enough, with squinting eyes, Al was just able to make out a structure far, far away, which looked little more than a dark speck. Silvester then pointed it out to Kiang, too, and nodded encouragingly as he had done on the hillock. This made the Spirit-creature jump back as though he had received an electric shock, and with a clattering sound that Al found almost unbearable to hear, he began to tremble. Silvester looked at Al helplessly, and then started making his way towards the dark structure.

Al did not budge.

"I think I should go up there on my own, Silvester!" he shouted over the clattering. "Don't exactly know what we'll find there! Might be really dangerous ... even for a Spirit!"

Silvester quickened his pace, undeterred by the slippery sludge beneath his little feet. Al sighed defeatedly. After patting Kiang on the head in an attempt to comfort him, he staggered after Silvester as quickly as he could, only managing to catch up with great difficulty. On they went side by side. Al soon felt sickened by the pungent smell of rot. It was becoming more and more potent as they got closer and closer to their destination. He did not find the thick grey haze suddenly rising up from the ground like hundreds of ghostly serpents and swirling round him very endearing either. But neither he nor his companion slowed down, cutting through the haze until it was finally left behind.

And then – they were there.

Al felt uneasy as he beheld the building in front of them. Its glassless windows were all choked with tangles of thorny black vines, which, he was sure, made it impossible for the tiniest sliver of light to enter or, indeed, leave the place. It seemed like the deadly-looking vines were unsatisfied with merely starving the wretched place of light: they were clinging to the entire structure and the ground around it as though determined to keep it shackled too. A heavy wooden door with dozens of bolts, chains and padlocks – untouched by the vines – was embedded into the stonework.

Is this the Orangery? If so, where's this Marshal, who guards it? Is my family on the other side of that door?! As these tormenting questions sprang up in his mind, Al stepped closer to the locked door until it was within touching distance. He wanted it to open.

One of the padlocks fell to the ground with a sound that was a cross between a splash and a thud – a sound that was tantamount to a siren. It had alerted something on the other side of the building.

The sludgy ground shook as the unseen being thundered across it. Silvester pulled Al away from the door as a Spirit-creature of two distinct halves rose up from behind the building, flew over it and landed in front of them. It had the head, torso and arms of a fully armoured knight and the wings, belly, hind legs and tail of a ruby-red dragon. Its gauntleted hands were grasping a gigantic golden sword with a lustrous copper tip – it was pointing this in the air as though it was about to strike down its enemies.

"Do you know who I am?!" the Spirit-creature asked in a grating, icy voice, which rang out of its silver helmet.

"M-Marshal." It had taken Al a while to get the word out as the surge of fear had snatched his breath away.

Silvester was trembling from head to toe.

"I am *the* Marshal!" cried the Spirit-creature. "And do

you know what my task is? What it's been for hundreds and hundreds of years since the time of the exalted Raja Nawab? Do you?!"

"G-guarding the Orangery."

"Correct!" Marshal replied proudly. "My entire existence is defined by that task. My – entire – existence! Do you think I'm not going to take it seriously? HOW DARE YOU ASSUME THAT YOU CAN SIMPLY UNLOCK THE DOOR OF THE ORANGERY AND WALK IN?! *How dare you?!*"

Al lost the ability to speak again.

"Those imprisoned inside will never be freed!" Marshal continued, stomping his great clawed feet in the sludge. "NEVER! It's futile and foolish for you to even try and free them! Attempt to do so again, and you'll suffer a fate far, far worse than the evil Spirits behind that door!"

Al and Silvester nodded emphatically and stepped back.

Not everyone behind that door is evil, though. With an enormous effort, Al found his voice once more –

"Please ... my family's in there. They're not Spirits. *I'm* not a Spirit. They were brought here by Metanos. They haven't done anything wrong, and I want them back. *Please.*"

"Who's this Metanos you speak of, and how can you *not* be a Spirit?!" Marshal's aggression had not at all dampened. "Are you trying to trick me to gain access? Me? I – can – never – be – tricked. Never!"

"No!" Al said pacifyingly. "Metanos is the reason my family and I ended up here! He's the one who tricked you!"

"I – can – never – be – tricked!"

Marshal let out a blood-curdling scream and brandished his sword towards Al and Silvester. They gasped and fell onto the ground, their eyes glued to the blade hovering above their heads like that of a guillotine. The idea of seeing his family again, embracing them all lovingly and going home together suddenly encapsulated Al's mind and reinforced his determination to tell the truth ... no matter how sickeningly scared he felt about further antagonising the Spirit-creature towering above them. *There's a chance that he might believe me.*

"Really, *really* don't mean to offend you, but Metanos *has* taken over the Orangery and imprisoned my innocent family in there. The shiny sandstorms that have been putting you to sleep ... That's how he's been getting past you. It's Spiritsnuff! He stole it from the Orangery. Just have a look inside yourself – please."

"You – have – just – doomed yourself." The earnestness with which Marshal uttered these words left Al in no doubt that he was, indeed, doomed. "I can see right through your skilfully spun story. I don't know how you found out about the sandstorms, but it matters not. This little factual nugget will not convince me that your story is in any way credible. Ha - no! I've never before witnessed such zeal that the door behind me be opened. I'm absolutely positive that the sole desire of you and your accomplice is to free the evil ones I guard. And *this* I cannot ALLOW!"

With all the strength he could muster, Al scrambled out of the way as the sword slashed through the air to strike him. He got to his feet and ran clumsily across the decaying meadow, Marshal charging after him.

"RUN, SILVESTER!" he shouted, though he had now lost all sense of where the Spirit-boy was or what he was doing.

But Al soon found that running was a futile exercise.

Marshal was not only incredibly agile, but could also fly. As he almost boastfully glided down to block Al's path, his red wings spread like a cape and his sword poised for another attack, Al stopped running. *I have to – somehow – fight back.* A split second later, Al was grasping a sword in one hand and a shield in the other.

"How are you able to conjure those if you're not a Spirit, treacherous villain?!" Marshal seethed.

He then lunged. Fiery sparks flew all round them as their swords clashed with a deafening furore. Al had never imagined he would ever wield a sword, let alone prove to be a skilful swordsman – he was becoming more and more confident with every stab and blow he blocked. Marshal was soon shrieking with sheer frustration and fought with more and more fervour. Suddenly, his efforts bore fruit. Al's sword was sliced into two and fell spinning to the ground.

But he was not prepared to give up. Another sword appeared in his hand. Marshal almost immediately destroyed this one too. And no less than a dozen more after that. Desperately trying to think what to do next, Al hid behind his shield – but Marshal hacked at it and hacked at it until it shattered. Both Al's mind and body were now utterly exhausted. He could not fight any longer, however much he wanted to.

He dropped to his knees, resigned to his fate. The only hope he had remaining was that if Marshal *did* somehow have the power to kill him, he would remain in Luxfons as a Spirit. He would then, at least, not lose the chance of rescuing his family.

"I sincerely wish the fire cleanses you of your evil!" spat Marshal as he raised the sword high above Al's head.

It remained where it was, though.

Marshal had become distracted by a loud metallic jangling emanating from the place he had left unguarded far behind him for some time now. Al gasped as he looked towards the Orangery. The tiny figure of Silvester was punching and kicking and clawing at the bolts, chains and padlocks on the wooden door. Marshal let out a scream of fury and flew like a hurricane after the little Spirit-boy, who scurried away behind the dark structure.

The very next moment, something heavy and golden fell out of the sky and, like Silvester, disappeared behind the Orangery. It was Alfred's carriage. Marshal let out yet another scream, even more horrific than the last, as he continued to tear through the air. The carriage rose into view again and whizzed past him towards Al. Clearly suspecting that this was a new ploy to lure him away again, Marshal did not give chase and landed squarely in front of the still-locked wooden door.

"Come," Alfred said urgently, stepping out of the carriage as soon as Robin placed it in front of Al. His lined face was drooped with sheer worry.

Al, feeling enormously relieved, smiled apologetically at his grandfather, but he continued to look as worried as ever.

"Come," he repeated, stepping aside to allow his grandson to get into the carriage.

Before Al could do so, however, the ground shook, and his eyes darted towards the Orangery again. Marshal had not moved, but he was no longer holding his sword – it was embedded in the sludge. He pulled it out with great difficulty, and the ground shook even more violently, forcing Al and Alfred to cling onto the carriage door to stop themselves from losing their balance. And then a thick stone wall came crashing out of the sludge from the place the sword had struck it. It grew taller and taller and wider and wider, hiding Marshal and the Orangery from view and encircling itself round them. Huge towers with battlements then erupted out of the top, making it look no less mighty than the wall of a fortress.

"Come," Alfred said for a third time. He did not seem surprised by what he had just witnessed.

Al climbed into the carriage followed immediately by his grandfather, who swiftly closed the door behind them as they sat down side by side. Silvester was slumped on the opposite seat, but he was not alone: Frederick was sitting next to him. The young blacksmith, too, looked very worried. Before anyone could say a word, Robin carried them off into the air.

"What you did was not at all wise, Al," Alfred sighed, looking at the floor instead of his grandson. "I don't exaggerate in the slightest when I say your actions have now made it more difficult than ever to rescue our family."

He turned his head slowly to look at his grandson. The look of disappointment etched on his grandfather's face left Al in no doubt about the seriousness of what he said. And Al broke down. He placed his head in his arms and wept uncontrollably.

"I can't give you false hope, my dear boy," said Alfred. "We might still be able to get them out of that terrible place ... but I simply don't know how anymore. A sound plan had been approved by Her Nobleness Mistress Magistery to breach the Orangery, but that will no longer work because of what Marshal has erected around it, not to mention his now heightened sense of paranoia."

"We *will* think of something else, though," said Frederick, leaning over to pat Al's trembling shoulder.

Al looked up, his face awash with tears. "I … I know I sh-should've waited. But I just couldn't any longer …"

"You should never be hasty when it comes to such important matters," Alfred said firmly. "I suppose your decision to face Marshal was influenced by what you found out about yourself in Sundomum … Am I right?"

Al nodded.

"You must remember, Al, that your powers have not been fully unlocked – only a fraction of them have come forth. The beings of this world will always have an advantage over you. Never assume you can contend with them on your own.

"Marshal was created by Raja Nawab, who certainly made sure his Spirit-creature had the ability to prevent the evil ones imprisoned in the Orangery from ever being freed. His sword will entomb any Spirit attempting to free them in flames, and the pain will undoubtedly force them to Depart Luxfons. Now, you would have suffered the same fate if his sword had so much as grazed you – the only difference being that, as you're not a Spirit of Luxfons, you wouldn't have had the luxury of Departing."

Al shuddered, and then caught Silvester's eye.

"Thank you so much for what you did," he said to the tired-looking Spirit-boy. "Silvester distracted Marshal just in time," he told Alfred and Frederick. "He saved me."

"Would've expected nothing less from him," said Frederick, ruffling his son's hair.

"I'm *so* sorry for asking him to come with me."

Frederick shook his head, smiling kindly. "I'm just grateful we got to you both in time. Thanks to Kiang. We knew almost instantly where you were after we saw the state he was in when he flew back to Vulcanest. Only Marshal can have such an effect on another Spirit-creature."

A loud chirping sound from above made Alfred chuckle, and his face brightened, even though it was only for a moment. "Robin wants you all to know that Marshal doesn't scare him in the slightest."

9

The Merciful Hawkanine

After what had seemed like an eternity of discussions involving countless arguments and disagreements, Alfred, Mistress Magistery and the Spirit-nobles and Future Spirit-nobles had formed a brand-new plan to rescue the Babas. Although Al, still having little knowledge of the ways of Luxfons, had not had much of an input, he felt satisfied with everything that had finally been decided. He thought it was a very robust plan, and his beacon of hope was burning brightly.

It had been established who would be going, how they would get there, how the newly erected wall would be breached, how Marshal would be distracted and subdued if necessary, how Metanos would be captured and how they would arm themselves against Spiritsnuff, should the Hawkanines attack.

As for who would be going, it had been unanimously deemed wise from the very beginning, in light of the enormity of the task, that all Spirits involved in formulating the plan – as well as Al – were needed to implement it. But then, as their final discussions had ebbed away, Mistress Magistery stated that this was not actually wise after all and declared that one of the five

Spirit-nobles would have to remain behind. If she and the other Spirits were all struck by Marshal's sword, then Luxfons would not, at least, become automatically leaderless – the Spirit-noble to remain behind would inherit Mistress Magistery's powers and succeed her as Spirit-noblest. In order for them to do so, Mistress Magistery would elevate their rank to that of Chief Spirit-noble before she and the others set off for the Orangery.

Ivar had immediately volunteered himself before lamenting, "My only regret is that Metanos will not now face the wrath, which, now I come to think of it, I had mercifully subdued in Ancient Gates Wood!"

◆ ◆ ◆

Al, Alfred and Robin returned to Sundomum after spending some time resting and recuperating at Mistress Magistery's insistence. They would embark on their task with the others after the Ennoblement – the ceremony in which Ivar would be made a Chief Spirit-noble. Once the three of them took their usual places next to Mistress Magistery in the hall, Alfred rang the silver bell to summon the Spirit-nobles and Future Spirit-nobles.

"I'm surprised Ivar isn't here by now," Alfred said after a while as he looked round the semi-circular bench, which now only had two spaces remaining – those of Ivar and Frederick. "In fact, I was quite sure he'd be the first one to arrive. It's not like him to turn up late to his own Ennoblement."

But there was no sign of him. Frederick eventually walked through the open golden doors, but he was accompanied only by Morfox and seemed as surprised as those he was joining to find his Spirit-noble absent. The Spirits on the bench started to murmur worriedly.

"We were waiting for Lord Havelock in the clearing, but then thought he must already be up here when he didn't show up," Frederick told them as he sat down after bowing to Mistress Magistery and stating his name and title. "Has he sent a message explaining why he's been delayed?"

"No," said Mistress Magistery.

"Perhaps the old boy didn't hear the Noble Bell," suggested Admiral Keel.

"With all due respect, Admiral," piped up Hexa, "if you were able to hear it, I'm sure Lord Havelock would've heard it too."

"Well, I cannot argue with that," said Admiral Keel. He doffed his bicorn hat to Hexa. "You are very rationally minded, Miss ... um ... Please forgive me, but remind me of your name ..."

"Oh, never mind!" said Hexa, half-smiling. "I hope nothing untoward has happened to him."

"Oh no!" squealed Cloelia. "He might be in grave danger!"

"Think we should all head to Bloomturrim, in case he needs our help," said Polemus, his permanent frown intensifying somewhat.

"All of us?" squeaked Kerr, taken aback. "What if we're being lured to some sort of trap? What if Metanos is behind this?"

"Wouldn't be very logical for all of us to go," said Hamelin, conjuring a raspberry and giving it to Fickle, who was a white mouse and sitting on her master's shoulder.

"I very much doubt Ivar has been delayed because

of something out of the ordinary," said Lady Tyto. "We cannot always be punctual. He's most probably on his way as we fret needlessly." She looked round at the other Spirits on the bench for support …

None came, however. Their attention had been captured by Alfred and Mistress Magistery, who were on their feet and looking towards the golden doors. A split second later, Al, too, was on his feet. Those on the bench turned to look over their shoulders in unison.

A swarm of little red-and-white roses had flown into the hall, their petals fluttering together harmoniously. It rose higher and passed over the bench before splitting into three distinct columns. Each fell in a flurry at the feet of Al, Alfred and Mistress Magistery. The three piles of roses then arranged themselves into the shapes of three arrows and then – what were unmistakably three flowery models of Bloomturrim.

"It seems some of us may have to travel to Lord Havelock's abode after all," said Mistress Magistery.

"How can we be sure this message is actually from Lord Havelock, Your Nobleness?" Kerr's mousy little eyes were narrowed with suspicion.

"Because the doors of Sundomum would've slammed shut before any of these roses had come anywhere near them if they were part of an evil ploy," replied Mistress Magistery. "I have now granted the Oculus Plume the ability to detect the products of bad intentions too."

"The wisdom of Your Nobleness knows no bounds!" exclaimed Virginia, clapping her hands together. "That settles it – this message is undoubtedly from Lord Havelock," she added firmly, glancing at Kerr.

Mistress Magistery turned to Al and Alfred. "Shall we proceed to Bloomturrim?"

"Yes, please," Al said at once. He had a feeling that something rather significant had warranted Ivar to invite him and the two most senior Spirits in Luxfons to Bloomturrim. *Hopefully, it's not anything bad.*

Alfred nodded, looking a little anxious, and Robin flew onto his shoulder.

"We aim to return as soon as possible," Mistress Magistery told the Spirit-nobles and Future Spirit-nobles.

She turned into a sphere of white light, which grew to engulf Alfred and Robin and then Al.

The thrilling journey was over in mere moments, and they found Ivar standing under the archway of his transparent tower. He seemed relieved to see them.

"Please forgive me, Your Nobleness, for not presenting myself at Sundomum but circumstances were such ..." he said, bowing deeply. "Do come in."

As Al, the two Spirits and Robin followed him inside, Ivar pointed his cane at the lone chaise longue on which Al had lain in the very centre of the bright space. A slender, bare-footed figure in pyjamas, with dark brown hair tied up in a ponytail, was sitting on it. They had their face in their hands and looked up as the new arrivals approached them –

"*Karen!*"

Al felt faint. He sprinted across the glassy floor towards his pale-faced and puffy-eyed sister, who jumped up, and they embraced tightly. The moments that followed were full of laughter and tears. By the time they parted, they had been joined by Alfred. Mistress Magistery and Ivar remained a few feet behind him.

"Oh gosh!" Karen said with awe as she looked at Alfred. She sounded weak, however, and her voice was a little hoarse. "It's you, Grandad. It's *you*! So it's true. I really am in a world of Spirits."

Alfred nodded and smiled warmly.

"But we're not dead?" She had turned to Al. "We're not, are we?!"

"Definitely not," he assured her. "You wouldn't look like you if you were!"

Karen sighed with relief.

"Oh, Grandad ..." She started to sob and then embraced him too. "You have to get Mum, Dad and Granny out of that place. *Please*. I don't even know whether they're still alive ..."

"I can assure you that they are, my dear," Alfred told her, patting her gently on the back, "and we will rescue them."

"How did *you* get out of there?" Al blurted out; he was finding it impossible to contain his curiosity any longer. "What happened?"

"Now, take your time, Karen," said Alfred as she slid out of his arms and sat back down on the chaise longue. "If you are able to tell us everything you remember, we're bound to be in a better position to carry out the task before us. None of us will interrupt you."

Karen nodded and wiped away the tears trickling down her cheeks with the sleeve of her pyjamas. Al sat next to her, and Mistress Magistery and Ivar moved closer to stand next to Alfred. Three transparent chairs, glittering almost as much as the crystals on Mistress Magistery's magnificent gown, appeared out of thin air, and the three Spirits sat down too. After being introduced to the Spirit-noblest of Luxfons, who was observing her unblinkingly, Karen proceeded to enlighten the four attentive listeners:

"I woke up on Christmas morning to find a massive hawk in my bedroom. Before I could make a sound, something gold came out of its wings, and I blacked out. Next thing I remember is coming round on the floor of this horrible place full of thorns and weeds and gargoyles and this disgusting smell. And there was a m-man in a red metal robe thing standing over me. I was just so, *so* scared – I didn't know what was going on. I tried to scream and get up and run away but ... just felt so weak. The man started talking to me. He told me I'd been brought to a world of Spirits, and I should feel privileged to be amongst his kind and honoured, too, because I was a vital part of his plan, which would lead to his ... um ... revolution.

"He then closed his eyes – his face was screwed up with concentration. After a while, he became really agitated, and ... Don't know whether he was still talking to me or himself or someone else, but he said whatever he was doing wasn't working and he couldn't *find* something ... but was sure he'd be able to if he looked deeper.

"And then he left. I heard something creak and saw that he'd left this big wooden door open. I knew I had to try and get out. It was really hard, but I managed to get up, and that's when I saw them – Mum, Dad and Granny. They were lying on the floor amongst the rotting stuff and ... they were ... they were completely s-still, and their eyes were closed."

Karen stifled a sob before continuing:

"I tried to get them up but couldn't. Just felt so helpless. I tried looking for you, Al, but couldn't find you. It looked like I was their only hope. I was determined to get out and get help, even though I couldn't stop shaking. And I just went for it ... and managed to sneak out.

"A shiny sandstorm was raging outside. I just stood where I was, too scared to move. But then it began to die down, and I realised that the particles flying all round me were being absorbed by something enormous near my feet. It was a creature of some sort, which looked like a jumble of metal and red scales, and it had a big sword lying next to it. And I was just able to make out the man too: he was looking at this poor creature from a distance and, thankfully, didn't see me. The creature then thrashed its tail, and the sandstorm became more intense again. Just before it did, I saw what was causing it – what looked like four of those massive hawks in the air. The particles were coming out of their wings ... and I thought that must be the same substance that had made me pass out on Christmas morning.

"The sandstorm began to die down again, and I crept round the building to hide. When I looked back round the corner, I saw the man locking the wooden door as if by magic, and one of the hawks came down to him, and he flew away on it. When the air became clearer, I ... I lost all hope of escaping. I saw that the building was surrounded by a castle wall and realised there was no way out.

"And then I heard a horrible screeching sound, and one of the other hawks landed in front of me. Though I thought it was probably futile and I'd be sprayed with the shiny sand thing at any moment, I pleaded with it to help me get out of that place. It stared at me for a while, like it was thinking about what to do with me ... and then grabbed me by my shoulders with its claws and flew me straight here."

The four listeners remained silent, but were all looking at each other – Al, Alfred and Ivar were stunned. And so was Mistress Magistery: the barrier that kept her emotions from escaping had been breached once more. But before her face transformed back into the blank canvas it usually was, a flicker of unmistakable relief passed over it.

"This means one of Metanos's Hawkanines isn't that loyal to him after all!" Al said excitedly.

"It certainly does, young one!" boomed Ivar. "I could scarcely believe my eyes when the monster of a Spirit-creature stormed into my abode with this young lady dangling from its talons. When she informed me who she was, I was overcome with happiness at the thought of Metanos being betrayed. Good news, indeed!"

Alfred did not share Al and Ivar's enthusiasm. "It's gratifying to learn that at least one Hawkanine has retained some of its light, but I'm very concerned about the facets of Metanos's plan about which we remain ignorant." He turned to Mistress Magistery. "It's clear, Your Nobleness, that he didn't have members of my family abducted solely to compel me to ask you to lift the suppression of powers. There was another reason for doing so."

Mistress Magistery's emerald-like eyes darted towards Karen again. "May I enquire whether you felt at all as though you were losing control over your own thoughts when the individual you mentioned was standing over you with his eyes closed?"

"Um ... don't think so," replied Karen, frowning.

"So his intention wasn't to Possess," Mistress Magistery said more to herself. "The only other activity which demands the level of concentration described is—"

"Delving into another's mind," finished Alfred, looking extremely uneasy.

Mistress Magistery nodded and said, "Whatever Metanos requires is in the mind of this young lady, and perhaps also in the minds of the other members of your family, Alfred."

"What could it be?" Al asked heatedly. "What do we have buried in our minds that will help him get the Power to Kill?!"

Before any of the Spirits could respond with any kind of conjecture, Karen burst into tears again.

"I just d-don't know what's g-going on," she spluttered. "I'm just so ... so *confused*!"

Al thought it was about time Karen was enlightened too – she, after all, had been gracious enough to enlighten them. He did not want to overwhelm her with how surrealistic their situation was, though, and hesitated. He looked at his grandfather.

"Go on, my dear boy," said Alfred, smiling approvingly.

It took Al quite a while to get through the *whats*, *whys*, *whos*, *whens*, *wheres* and *hows* – with a little help from the Spirits – before Karen's confusion had fully evaporated. *Her* capacity to accept what she was told was highly complemented too. And although she still sounded quite weak, she became markedly less sombre, especially after being reassured about the robustness of the plan to rescue Edward, Helen and Margaret. Her mischief, which Al knew so well, soon returned.

"Really struggling with the idea of you having these great powers and fighting a knight and dragon rolled into one, little brother!" she said, grinning.

"Watch this ..." said Al.

Instead of pyjamas, Karen was now in her favourite spotty jumper and jeans; she was no longer bare-footed, but wearing hiking boots, and a big bowl of marshmallows – a delicacy she always claimed she could not live without – appeared between her and Al on the chaise longue. Karen looked extremely impressed and ruffled Al's hair affectionately whilst helping herself to a handful of marshmallows.

"Looks like you haven't had these in a long time!" Al joked.

"I haven't," whined Karen, observing the spongy nuggets longingly. She suddenly looked up. "How long have we been in this world?"

"Don't know," said Al, surprised that he had not yet wondered the same.

"Today is your twelfth day in Luxfons," Alfred told them. "We're beyond the realm of time here, so we only have an essence of it through those in the Domain of the Living our minds are Connected to. Right, I think—oh, that looks magnificent, Ivar."

An array of brightly coloured flowers were zooming round outside the glass tower like they were trying to imitate a fireworks display.

"Thank you, old chap," said Ivar, sounding a little sad. "I've animated the flowers in my pond to occasionally provide me with such amusement. It makes up somewhat for the lack of Communicative Flowers from my mentees – I do miss advising them on how best to use their powers."

"Do cheer up, Ivar," said Alfred. "You are about to be elevated in rank after all. You'll be the only Spirit in Luxfons with two titles: Spirit-noble *and* Chief Spirit-noble."

Ivar beamed and declared, "I'm determined to prove worthy of such an honour by carrying out my new duties as fervently as my current ones."

"We ought to go back to Sundomum for the Ennoblement," said Mistress Magistery, rising to her feet. "I'm sure the others are eagerly awaiting our return, and we have much to tell them."

"Indeed, Your Nobleness!" exclaimed Ivar, also rising.

Alfred and Karen did the same, but Al remained where he was. Something had just occurred to him, which alarmed him a great deal.

"Now that we know Metanos has definitely left the Orangery for whatever reason, will we have to wait until he's back inside before we try and breach it?" Although Al had recently discovered how wise it was to be patient, the idea of his mother, father and grandmother being in that abysmal place of decay any longer than necessary was still difficult to accept.

"No," said Mistress Magistery. "Our plan will be implemented as discussed. The greatest priority at present is to free the innocent, not to capture Metanos. It'll be fortunate, indeed, if he has returned to the Orangery by the time we get there; I believe we would then have a good opportunity to capture him. Nonetheless, we cannot know whether he has returned until we're there – I'm not prepared to risk the mutilation of any more Spirit-creatures like Io by requesting that they spy on him for me."

Al nodded and rose to his feet, his heart feeling lighter than it was a few moments ago.

Robin, who had been hovering above them, came down and chirped in his master's ear.

"It would seem so," replied Alfred.

"What a little beauty!" Karen squealed with delight, stroking the fiery-red feathers on Robin's chest with her finger. "What did he say?"

"Well ..." said Alfred, "he's just pointed out that the Hawkanine's decision to bring you to Bloomturrim must have been influenced by his own decision to bring Al here on Christmas morning."

Al and Karen laughed as Alfred turned to Mistress Magistery. But she had already morphed into an expanding sphere of white light.

"Brace yourself for the best rollercoaster ride ever!" Al told his sister just before they were engulfed by it.

When the subsequent thrill came to an end, they found themselves facing many pairs of keen eyes under the dome of Sundomum. And every one of these became fixed on the unfamiliar young individual who had appeared in front of them: a rather nervous-looking Karen.

Ivar immediately took his place on the bench. And as Alfred resumed his seat on his mahogany throne with Robin, another turquoise armchair appeared next to Al's, and the Baba siblings sat down too. Mistress Magistery, however, remained standing. Before long, she commanded the full attention of all those in the hall. Al felt a great deal of empathy for his sister as her ordeal was relayed in fine detail and she was bombarded with shocked glances. He was not at all surprised – and somewhat amused – when Karen avoided the glare of the spotlight she was in by looking at her feet.

The newly enlightened Spirits had much to say once Mistress Magistery finished speaking and was sitting on her throne. They were all intrigued by the idea of a Hawkanine proving to be so merciful and having the courage to betray Metanos. Karen's saviour was commended across the bench.

But then Hamelin indignantly changed his mind after his nose twitched and Fickle transformed from the white mouse into the black rat. ("It *must* have had a sinister agenda for doing what it did!") Another twitch of the nose soon afterwards turned her back into the white mouse, and Hamelin immediately changed his mind again – less indignantly on this occasion. ("No, it's clear that the valiant Spirit-creature was moved by this young lady's plight.")

They were all troubled by the mystery of what Metanos had been searching for in Karen's mind. A great many theories later, Al suspected that everyone in the hall was just as perplexed as before regarding this matter – he certainly was.

"The Ennoblement will now commence," Mistress Magistery said finally, nodding at Ivar and rising to her feet again.

Ivar's face ignited with pride, and he rose from the bench so quickly that his powdered wig nearly fell off his head. He approached Mistress Magistery and, using his cane for support, knelt in front of her on the ermine-patterned floor.

"Do you, Lord Havelock, believe you're fit for the tasks you're about to be entrusted with?" she asked him.

"I do, Your Nobleness," he replied. The sincerity in his voice was unmistakable.

"Taurbrum – kindly present me with the Sceptre."

"Oh gosh," gasped Karen.

The enormous black bull had remerged out of thin air, right beside Mistress Magistery this time. He bowed his head in front of her, allowing her to procure its crown-like horns in the form of the Sceptre before vanishing again. Mistress Magistery tapped the top of Ivar's wig once with the end of the Sceptre – a spurt of golden light streamed out of the ornate rod and took on the shape of a many-arched crown. It hovered above Ivar's head for a few moments before fading into nothingness.

"As a Chief Spirit-noble, you now have the power, Lord

Havelock, to peer into the minds of all those in the Domain of the Living who aren't fortunate enough to have loved ones in Luxfons," declared Mistress Magistery. "I wish you luck in helping Alfred and me in alleviating their many hardships. It won't be an easy task to accomplish, nor will the others that will support me in upholding the Laws of Luxfons. But this will make the accomplishment of these tasks all the more gratifying."

Ivar then rose but seemed too overwhelmed with emotion to say anything. Mistress Magistery stood aside and gestured towards the empty mahogany throne next to her own, which Al assumed must have once been occupied by Metanos. Ivar marched over to it and sat down as all those on the bench bowed. The new Chief Spirit-noble could not have looked statelier, sitting there on his throne in his sumptuous outfit and grasping his silver-topped cane like a sovereign's sceptre.

"You may now bring into existence the Spirit-creature who'll be flying your carriage," Mistress Magistery told him. "It'll be your vehicle during your tenure as Chief Spirit-noble and awaits you next to Alfred's beneath us." She pointed the Sceptre at the great golden doors.

"My gratitude to Your Nobleness knows no bounds," Ivar said finally, beaming tearily.

He raised his arm in a manner reminiscent of someone looking at their watch, and a fat magpie materialised on his hand. It bobbed up his arm and came to rest on his shoulder.

"Wow, another little beauty!" exclaimed Karen, craning her neck to get a better look at the Spirit-creature.

Robin chirped loudly – he sounded annoyed, prompting all three of the Babas to start chuckling. He clearly did not appreciate this reaction to his expression of woe and chirped louder, sounding even more annoyed than before. But the Babas had already stopped chuckling.

Mistress Magistery had just announced that it was now time to take the first step on their journey to the Orangery. Al felt like he had put on an armour of determination.

"Karen," Alfred said earnestly, "I'm going to ask Robin to take you in the carriage to my abode. You'll be comfortable there as it's almost identical to—"

"I'm coming along with all of you!" Karen interrupted loudly, bringing herself squarely back under the glaring spotlight. "You might have one less Hawkanine to deal with then!"

10

Hermit's Endeavour

Having left Sundomum together as a beam of light, Al, Karen, the eleven Spirits and the three Spirit-creatures were now squeezed together in the mouth of a small cave. This was where a Spirit called Hermit the Apothecary lived. He was in possession of the Dormshield Concoction: a defence against Spiritsnuff. According to Mistress Magistery, he had spent centuries trying to create it – his sole aim all that time – and had only succeeded fairly recently.

The cave was in the foot of a range of rocky hills, which overlooked a vast meadow of wildflowers. Inside, it was lit by golden light emanating from a stoppered glass bottle on a marble pedestal. A plethora of non-luminous bottles, on the other hand, of all shapes and sizes and colours were dotted around a large mortar and pestle made of brass. Hermit was nowhere to be seen, but Mistress Magistery was sure he had not ventured very far, and Robin and Morfox were sent by their masters to look for him.

Al and Karen, meanwhile, resumed their argument – which had flared up in Sundomum.

"I still think it's a really bad idea for you to come along,"

Al told his sister firmly.

"Oh, not this again!" Karen huffed. "It'll be OK. I'll be really careful."

"But you don't stand a chance if you get in Marshal's way," persisted Al. "If his sword touches you—"

"I know – you've told me a hundred times! Do you think I'd go back to that place if I thought I wouldn't make a difference? That Hawkanine seemed quite taken with me – pretty sure it wouldn't attack any of us with me being there. Might even switch sides. And the more help we have against Marshal and Metanos and so on, the better."

"You're just assuming everything!" Al retorted heatedly. "The fact is you're in real danger if you go back!"

"So are you!" Karen said equally as heatedly. "Your powers don't make you invincible!"

"That's quite enough," said Alfred. "Al – I, too, would have less cause to worry if Karen stayed behind, but I can't make her change her mind. And nor can you. Her reasons for wanting to play an active part in this task are not meritless." He then turned to Karen. "This doesn't mean your brother's fear isn't justified. Out of all of us, you *are* in the most danger."

Karen gulped and nodded.

"Just don't want to lose you again," Al said to her in a much calmer manner.

"I know, little brother," Karen sighed. "But I want to do my bit for Mum, Dad and Granny. I have to."

Although he still felt uneasy about her decision, Al could not help but admire Karen's unfaltering zeal – the kind he was now familiar with. "I'll do everything I can to protect you. I promise."

Karen smiled at him warmly.

"I'm very proud of you both," Alfred told them,

beaming.

"We'll all support you in this noble task, Al," said Frederick. "You're not alone."

"Hear, hear!" cried the rest of the Spirit-nobles and Future Spirit-nobles in unison, their voices echoing off the bare walls of the cave.

Just then, a Spirit accompanied by Robin and Morfox entered the cave. He had long, stringy grey hair and an even longer beard, which hung like a drape above his sandalled feet; he was wearing a ragged purple toga with a large number of pockets and carrying a bulging brown sack over his shoulder.

"Greetings, Hermit," said Mistress Magistery.

"Greetings! Greetings! Greetings to you all!" Hermit said enthusiastically. He grinned broadly, displaying a far from full set of teeth. "Never have I had so many visitors. Never! Welcome! Welcome! Welcome!"

The throng of visitors parted with great difficulty to let him deeper into his rocky abode. Hermit smiled and nodded at every single one of them as he shuffled past before throwing his sack onto the ground next to the mortar and pestle. He then spun round to face them, almost toppling over onto the numerous glass bottles at his feet.

"How may I be of service, Your Nobleness?" he asked Mistress Magistery with a bow.

"We're in need of the Dormshield Concoction."

"Aha!" yelled Hermit. "Queen Lamiobra – or Queen Sisyphus as I like to call her – has returned armed with her Spiritsnuff! I knew she would. I told him … I told Raja Nawab she was far too cunning to remain imprisoned. I told him the Spirits of Luxfons would need to be protected from her golden venom. I told him!"

A fair few of the listeners exchanged bemused looks.

"She hasn't returned, Hermit," said Mistress Magistery. "She's entombed in stone and cannot easily be freed – such an act would lead to the destruction of the Orangery itself. Her Spiritsnuff, however, is now being utilised by another."

It was Hermit's turn to look bemused. "Oh ... well ... well ... I ... I cannot give you the Dormshield Concoction in that case."

"We'd be *very* grateful if you'd reconsider," implored Alfred. "We don't ask for it lightly. You'll be doing a great service by providing us with it."

"But ... but I made it to show Queen Sisyphus that she's not as powerful as she thinks ... that I'm strong enough to defend those she attacks."

Hermit removed a clear vial of ebony-coloured liquid from a pocket in his toga and held it up, looking at it with awe.

"This is all I have," he said. "Just this. If I give it away, I'll be left with nothing."

"Couldn't you just make some more?" asked Al.

Hermit started to laugh. Al was taken aback, and so were those around him. Although he was bouncing on the spot and howling with laughter, Hermit's face was still plastered with agitation. And then he stopped quite abruptly.

"I'm unable to remember the steps I took and the ingredients I used to make what this tiny, tiny container holds," he lamented, continuing to hold the vial aloft. "That is what happens when something takes so, *so* long to make. The experiment which lasted centuries finally gave me what I wanted, but it cannot be replicated. Tragic, isn't it? Quite tragic – and funny at the same time.

In short, this is all I'll ever have."

"It's your prerogative to choose the circumstances in which you'll dispense your creation," Mistress Magistery told Hermit. "Your reasons for creating the Dormshield Concoction are noble, but I can assure you that our reasons for requesting it are equally as noble."

Hermit replaced the vial in his pocket and, stepping gingerly over the glass bottles, backed away until he stood directly against the wall. He turned to face the luminous glass bottle on the marble pedestal and began to mutter to himself in a consultative manner. After a short while, he fell silent.

"Well?" said Mistress Magistery.

"You may have it!" Hermit replied instantaneously, as though he had suspected he would have changed his mind if he had faltered even for a moment. He smiled as a look of peace irradiated his face, replacing the agitation.

Al felt incredibly relieved. He could not help but express his sincere gratitude with a hearty "Thank you!" after Hermit shuffled over to them and handed his highly prized creation to Mistress Magistery.

"You're welcome, Orpheus," said Hermit. "Very welcome, indeed!"

Al chuckled sheepishly but did not reveal his actual name; he was quite sure Hermit would be unaffected by it.

"May I enquire how much is needed for it to be fully effective?" piped up Mistress Magistery, holding the vial up to her eyes.

"The magic number is twelve! Twelve drops. Only twelve drops reside within me. You can have more, but you'd just be wasting it."

"How can you be sure it works, Hermit?" asked Alfred.

"What a tremendously appropriate question!" enthused Hermit, breaking into applause. "After all, important matters should not be accepted without any scrutiny. I do admire your great wisdom, Apollo." He bowed theatrically to Alfred.

"Hope I'm given an exotic new name too," Karen whispered to Al with a mischievous smile.

Hermit shuffled back to the marble pedestal and picked up the luminous glass bottle. He removed its stopper and tiny specks of golden light shot out of it before it was quickly stoppered again, losing none of its dazzling luminosity. The specks of light now floating in the air collectively formed an arrow pointing at Hermit ... and then fell to the floor.

"Spiritsnuff fails yet again," Hermit said with child-like pride as he shook the bottle vigorously. "I'm still conscious. I can see you. I can communicate with you. And this is why I can say with unshakeable confidence that the Dormshield Concoction works!"

"I see that Raja Nawab was kind enough to grant you what you desired before he Departed," said Mistress Magistery, nodding at the bottle of Spiritsnuff in Hermit's hand.

"Only after he had finally calmed down about the tunnel business," Hermit sighed. "I still think digging it all the way to the Orangery to capture Queen Sisyphus's Spiritsnuff-creating power shouldn't have warranted his wrath – it really shouldn't have! How was I supposed to know I had unwittingly created a Marshal-bypassing passage for a Spirit wanting to release her? How was I supposed to know I'd wasted my efforts because her powers had not even been detached from her?"

"They were detached," Mistress Magistery corrected

him. "That's now become evident."

"Oh, maybe I misremember what he said," Hermit conceded. "It *was* hundreds of years ago."

He grimaced at the bottle as he replaced it on the pedestal and then started talking to it: "I spent very nearly all that time trying to find a way to combat you. It was a maddening endeavour – in fact, I'm sure I *must* have come close to actual madness on more than one occasion. Raja Nawab himself doubted I would succeed, even though he was gracious enough to create you at my insistence. But in spite of all the trouble you've given me, the Dormshield Concoction wouldn't exist without you, and I wouldn't have been able to help our visitors." Hermit patted the bottle's stopper like he was patting the head of a small child, his grimace transforming into a wide grin.

"Forgive me, Hermit, but we need your assistance in another matter too ..." said Mistress Magistery.

Hermit looked up eagerly. "What other concoction of mine is required, Your Nobleness?"

"None presently. However, I'd be grateful if you could kindly point out the entrance to your secret tunnel."

"Of course, of course, of course!" cried Hermit. "*But* it's my duty to warn you all that it's highly unlikely that you'll be able to venture very far inside without being apprehended. And even if you did manage to reach the end, it's now impossible to break into the Orangery from underground."

"Understood," said Mistress Magistery, and the others nodded.

The use of Hermit's tunnel was an integral part of their plan to breach the wall around the Orangery without alerting Marshal. According to Mistress Magistery, the nature of the wall was such that its foundation was going to be embedded deep underground and be no less remarkable than the structure it was supporting. The tunnel would provide access to that foundation, and the task was to break it down to reach the other side. Mistress Magistery herself would be travelling through the tunnel to carry it out along with Al, Alfred, Robin, Karen, Frederick, Morfox, Hamelin and Fickle.

The other Spirit-nobles and Future Spirit-nobles would remain aboveground as barely visible Spirit-creatures. They would position themselves near the Orangery, awaiting Alfred's signal to distract Marshal when the time was right.

"Follow me, follow me!" said Hermit as he quickly shuffled past his visitors out of the cave.

"We'll join you shortly, Hermit," Mistress Magistery called after him.

"Take as long as you like," he replied without looking back. "The longer you take, the longer I'll have to admire this glorious view. It's remained unchanged for centuries, but I never tire of beholding it!"

He proceeded to sit cross-legged just beyond the mouth of the cave like he was about to meditate and began to hum loudly.

Mistress Magistery unstopped the vial and gave it to Alfred. "Kindly ingest twelve drops as Hermit said," she told him. "Administer the same amount to Robin before passing it on. I, like your grandson, don't require the Dormshield Concoction."

Al blushed as Karen beamed at him with pride. Before long, Alfred handed the vial to her.

"You've missed out, little brother," she said with a smile after having her dose of the ebony-coloured liquid. "It tastes delicious!"

"Really?" asked Al, though a part of him suspected his sister was being sarcastic.

"Yes ... a bit like liquorice. I'm pleasantly surprised!"

"Karen's right," Alfred chuckled. "It *was* quite nice. My commiserations, Al!" He winked at his grandson as Robin chirped happily on his shoulder.

The vial was nearly empty when it finally got round to the last of those in the group who needed to arm themselves against Spiritsnuff: Cloelia. She looked anxious as she poured the contents into her bony mouth.

"Don't think that was quite twelve drops, Your Nobleness!" she squealed as the empty vial disappeared into thin air.

"You may stay behind if you wish, Miss Iceni," said Mistress Magistery.

"No," Cloelia sighed. "Have to do my duty. I'd be ashamed to be a Spirit of Luxfons otherwise, let alone a Future Spirit-noble."

"Obviously chose my successor well," Hexa said proudly. "Do we have the permission of Your Nobleness to go forth and take up our positions?"

"You do."

Hexa turned into a tiny bluebottle fly. And a moment later, Kerr, Admiral Keel, Polemus, Lady Tyto, Virginia and Cloelia had done the same. All seven of them whizzed out of the cave. Those they left behind joined Hermit, who stopped humming and stood up.

"Oh," he said, looking a little disappointed, "I must have imagined I had more visitors than I actually did again. I had a funny feeling it was too good to be true. Oh well, never mind. This way ..."

Al, Karen, the four Spirits and the three Spirit-creatures followed Hermit as he began to shuffle through the meadow. Al could not remember enjoying a pleasanter walk as he looked round at his surroundings and did not blame Hermit for praising them so highly. Each flower that brushed against his trousers looked like it had been individually painted by a meticulous artist using the brightest colours available, such was its exquisiteness; even the blades of grass had a certain elegance, with their rich, waxy sheen and rigid uprightness, which remained unaffected by those walking through them.

And Al soon discovered that this seemingly endless stretch of beauty was a haven for many Spirit-creatures: a melodious mixture of birdsong and buzzing filled his ears as birds and insects of all kinds caught his eye. It was almost as though they were popping out of their little abodes to greet them. A couple of blue tits and goldfinches even circled round their heads for a while, amusing Robin a great deal. But Al was more familiar with the Spirit-creature who subsequently came up to them.

"Io!" Mistress Magistery cried happily.

It was the first time Al had seen her smile.

Although Io's wings were still the colour of rust and each still had a grey patch in the centre, they no longer twitched as she fluttered alongside her mistress.

"You're looking very well, indeed, Io," said Alfred.

Io moved her antennae back and forth and side to side.

"I'm glad to hear it," said Alfred. "And you're very welcome."

"The Meadow has done her a lot of good," Mistress Magistery told Alfred, looking relieved. "And, of course, that concoction from Hermit cannot be praised enough."

Hermit turned round and broke into applause before leading on again.

"I'd give anything to have her as a pet ..." Karen said to Al, looking at Io longingly.

"Not surprised," Al laughed. "Bet you thought the same thing when you first saw Robin and Morfox *and* Fickle!"

Karen unglued her eyes from Io to look at the three Spirit-creatures Al had mentioned in turn, her expression of longingness not diminishing in the slightest.

"I still do!" she declared.

"Don't think Morfox would need much persuasion to swap me – his master – for another mistress instead," Frederick told Karen. "I'm sure he prefers female company – tends to communicate a lot more with my good wife, Alcea, than he does with me!"

"I'm sure m-my little Spirit-creature would never leave me," Hamelin said shyly; Fickle, whose head was poking out of the breast pocket of his patchwork overcoat, was in the form of the harvest mouse.

"You should resume your rest now, Io," said Mistress Magistery. There was a touch of sadness in her voice, and her smile began to wane.

Io fluttered off and vanished amongst the sea of wildflowers, and her mistress's face soon became as expressionless as it normally was.

By the time Hermit came to a halt again, they had all walked so much that the rocky hills behind them looked like a dark, jagged line tucked under the blue sky. At first, Al wondered why Hermit had brought them to this particular spot: as pretty as it was, it did not seem to differ in any noticeable way from the rest of the Meadow. But then he became aware of a horrible smell wafting towards him – that of rotting vegetation.

Hermit pointed out a group of flowers that, on closer inspection, were woven together to form a kind of canopy. "Here it is, here it is!" he cried. "Here's what you seek! My task is done. It's done! Oh, by the way, you can be as noisy as you like down there without any fear of being heard by Marshal ... but use as little light as possible – for all our sakes. Farewell!"

He spun round and shuffled past them back in the direction of his cave.

Alfred and Mistress Magistery pulled the canopy of flowers apart with their hands. It had been obscuring a mossy, oblong stone, which was the size of a small table. The stone drifted away, as though it was nothing more than a feather caught in a breeze, to reveal a gaping hole in the ground. Mistress Magistery peered inside it.

"The tunnel has been built quite near the surface," she told them, "so it's only a short way down. Shall we descend?"

"No," Hamelin said indignantly – Fickle had just turned into the black rat. "Let me first get the taste of that disgusting concoction we were forced to drink out of my mouth." He spat forcefully over his shoulder a few times. "Didn't even see the point of having it! How can you be sure the Hawkanines are actually going to attack us?" He turned to Alfred. "They didn't attack your grandson and Frederick's boy when *they* were at the Orangery. It's preposterous to be so pessimistic!"

"It's best to assume that the worst scenario imaginable will unfold when it comes to such matters," Alfred said calmly. "The Hawkanines didn't attack Al and Silvester simply because they didn't want to reveal themselves to Marshal. Should the need to subdue Marshal arise, which is likely, and we succeed in doing so, they're then bound to intervene to stop us getting to my family."

Hamelin gave an angry huff in response but did not argue. He joined the others as they encircled the very edge of the hole.

"Don't forget to glide," said Mistress Magistery. "A nasty fall awaits you otherwise."

In a flash of blue-and-yellow, she plunged into the hole and was swallowed by the darkness. The remaining Spirits (along with their respective Spirit-creatures) followed her in quick succession. As Al prepared to jump, he caught Karen's eye. She looked rather nervous.

"Don't worry," he assured her, "I'll help you."

"Thanks, little brother."

Al took the plunge. The thrill that would have accompanied such an action was non-existent. He had imagined himself to be as light as air and floated down into the earthy-smelling darkness until his feet landed on something solid.

"I'm ready," Karen called from above.

"Go for it!" said Al.

He closed his eyes to concentrate on the mental image of his sister descending as gracefully as he had just done. It worked. Karen came to rest beside him and hugged him gratefully.

"It looks like my grandchildren have made it down safely, Your Nobleness," Alfred said with pride.

"Right," said Mistress Magistery, "Mister Hancock – we require Morfox to light the way. He cannot be too luminous, however. Hermit's warning must be heeded."

Frederick instructed his Spirit-creature as per Mistress Magistery's wish. A swarm of fireflies rose into the air as it had done inside the Fallen Tree. But its orangey glow was not nearly as bright on this occasion; it hovered near their heads as a sphere, barely lighting up their immediate vicinity.

Although the tunnel was extremely wide, it was just high enough for the tallest of the party (Alfred) to walk through it without having to crouch. It *had* been skilfully constructed, though, using a mixture of chunky, glass-like flint and long, thin bricks. Al could not help but admire Hermit for creating such a marvel underground and wondered what had motivated him to find a defence against Spiritsnuff in the first place ...

"Did Hermit have a bad experience with Spiritsnuff?" he asked his grandfather as they made their way vigilantly through the tunnel.

"Yes, I'm afraid he did," said Alfred. "I'm only vaguely aware of what happened, not obviously having witnessed the event in question—"

"I, on the other hand, did," Mistress Magistery said abruptly.

Al, whose curiosity was now surging, was eager for her to elaborate. He was not disappointed.

"A long time ago, Hermit and I were both Chief Spirit-nobles under Raja Nawab: the first Spirit-noblest of Luxfons. Raja Nawab's status was shared by his beloved consort: Queen Lamiobra, who was almost as powerful as he was. He built the Orangery in her honour. At the time, it was a wondrous place full of the most beautiful plants imaginable. Raja Nawab's wish was to reside in it in peace with Queen Lamiobra when they both felt their tasks were becoming too burdensome. Unlike other Spirits who came to feel the same, he didn't want to Depart Luxfons because he feared he'd never see his consort again. Even if they Departed together, he wasn't to know whether they'd remain together. In short, Raja

Nawab was adamant that his bond with Queen Lamiobra should last forever.

"But his love for her was not reciprocated. She was full of darkness. After recruiting a number of followers who possessed as much darkness as her, Queen Lamiobra cornered Raja Nawab in Sundomum in the presence of Hermit and me. For reasons she didn't share, she wanted the key to the vessel that contains the Power to Kill – a wish which, lovestruck as he was, Raja Nawab didn't grant. She exploded with rage and struck him with all her dark powers – including Spiritsnuff. Hermit and I came to his aid, but he didn't require it and single-handedly defeated Queen Lamiobra and her cronies. He wasn't affected by Spiritsnuff, and nor was I. Hermit wasn't so fortunate, however, which is something he's always been ashamed of."

"What did Raja Nawab do to Queen Lamiobra and her followers?" asked Al, feeling intrigued.

"They were entombed in stone in the Orangery, and a fully armoured Marshal was then created to guard it. Raja Nawab was heartbroken and turned the place he once adored into a grotesque prison. He Departed Luxfons soon after, and I succeeded him as Spirit-noblest. Before he left, however, he decreed that all Newly Departed Spirits should undergo the Noble Possession to stop history from repeating itself. Alas, what he feared has come to pass again."

Al heard a sniffing sound beside him and turned to see Karen teary-eyed.

"Not like you to start crying after hearing a sad story!"

"I know, I know," Karen conceded, wiping her eyes with the sleeve of her jumper. "Can't help having a heart, though!"

They were approaching a sharp bend in the tunnel when something suddenly alerted them to its presence by growling loudly.

11

The Sceptre and the Horns

The four Spirits looked at each other in alarm and hurried towards the bend, the sphere of fireflies floating after them. Al was about to follow, but his grandfather came to a halt and spun round.

"Stay back," he said sharply. "Look after your sister. Robin will keep you both company."

The little bird flew off his master's shoulder and landed on Karen's instead as Alfred disappeared round the bend after the other Spirits. Al acted at once: a dome of impenetrable steel erected itself round Karen and Robin before either of them could protest.

Robin chirped angrily.

"Is this *really* necessary?!" Karen sounded even angrier.

"Yes, it is," said Al. "It's for your own good!"

"Whatever that thing is, it can't exactly kill me!"

"Maybe not," retorted Al, "but it can probably cause you serious harm."

Karen sighed defeatedly and fell silent.

The growling sound echoing through the tunnel, on the other hand, was getting louder and louder, and it was making Al feel extremely uneasy. It was suddenly accompanied by the sound of what he thought was rapid digging. And then a babble of confused voices. And then – by a cacophony of horrified yells. Without thinking, Al sprinted round the bend and froze.

A badger, three times the size of the kind he was familiar with, was using its shovel-sized claws to fill up a deep pit with rubble and dirt at a colossal speed. Lying inside it side by side, quickly disappearing from view and struggling to get out, were the four Spirits. Barely a moment later, they had been completely buried by the gigantic Spirit-creature, who proceeded to sit on the newly created mound as a mother hen would on her eggs. It had not yet noticed Al; its jet-black eyes were fixed on the fireflies hovering near the ceiling. When it did finally spot him, standing mere feet away, its growl turned into a horrendous snarl, but it remained where it was.

Suddenly, Alfred's voice filled the tunnel –

"You're our only hope now, Al. We can only emerge from this grave if the Spirit-creature that created it is dislodged from above us. Do not look at it in the eyes!"

"How do I get it to move?!" cried Al.

He received no response. Al was becoming more and more panicky and finding it almost impossible to gather his thoughts as the badger continued to snarl loudly.

"Is everything OK?!"

"Karen!"

As quick as lightning, Al sprinted back to the steel dome.

"Karen – I need your help! What are badgers scared of?"

"Um ... humans, I suppose."

"Well, this one doesn't seem to be!"

"That thing we heard is a badger?" Karen sounded fascinated.

"Yes, it looks like one. It's massive, though, and it's

buried Grandad and the others in a pit it dug and is now sitting on top of it. They can't get out. It's really, really angry and won't budge."

"Oh no. Sounds like it has the personality of a honey badger. And nothing really scares them that much. They even eat poisonous snakes and stuff! The only animal that probably has a chance of winning against it is something like a leopard … perhaps. But it needs to be a big one."

Al sprinted back to the badger. Keeping his eyes averted from its fierce glare, he visualised a gigantic and ferocious-looking leopard. But the one that subsequently appeared out of thin air beside him had neither of those attributes.

"Focus!" he commanded himself.

Al stared at his creation with narrowed eyes, concentrating as hard as he could on the image burning into his mind … The leopard began to grow and become more muscular; it opened its mouth, now studded with needle-like whiskers, to reveal long fangs and let a heart-stopping hiss to escape … And then it became smoky and shapeless and evaporated into nothingness. Al stomped his foot and cried out in frustration. *I need to use my powers in a different way.*

He closed his eyes. When he opened them again, they were bright yellow, and he was no longer a fourteen-year-old boy, but a vastly overgrown leopard. He was still very much conscious of who he was and in control of his thoughts and actions, but he no longer felt an iota of fear. He had an instinctive urge to do battle. And he let that urge overcome him. With a tremendous roar, tantamount to that of an aggrieved lion's, Al pounced on the badger. His sharp claws dug into its black-and-white face, and it yelped and fell backwards, hitting the tunnel wall in a puff of thick dust and dirt. He had done it.

As Al morphed into himself again, the Spirits sprang out of the mound, unscathed and completely speckless. Their re-emergence seemed to reignite the badger's wrath: it jumped back up, and its snarl returned with increased ferocity.

"Not again," said Mistress Magistery.

The badger began to shrink until it was no bigger than a skunk before scuttling off past them round the bend and out of sight.

"I don't possess the power to keep it like that permanently," Mistress Magistery told them. "Although not as powerful as Marshal, this Spirit-creature, like him, was created by Raja Nawab, which means it cannot be vanquished so easily. It had managed, temporarily, to disarm all four of us." Her eyes came to rest on Al. "You've earned my sincere gratitude for what you did, young man."

"No problem," said Al, reddening a little. "Karen helped too."

"Did she, indeed?" piped up Alfred. "Splendid, splendid."

Frederick came over to shake Al's hand, thanking him with the kindest of smiles. Even Hamelin nodded at him appreciatively, which surprised Al a great deal: Fickle, who had just left the safety of the chest pocket of her master's overcoat and was now lounging on his shoulder, was still in the form of the black rat.

"We shall move on with swiftness," said Mistress Magistery.

"Where are Karen and Robin?" Alfred asked Al.

In a matter of moments, the steel dome had been

demolished and those it had been protecting had been reunited with their fellow travellers. Together, they continued on their long course through the tunnel unhindered until they finally reached their destination – the foundation of Marshal's wall. The tunnel's newly constructed dead end was, indeed, no less remarkable than the huge, fortified structure aboveground that it was supporting. It was made of a mixture of crushed stone and tall rods of what looked like –

"Pure diamond," observed Mistress Magistery, placing her hand on one of the rods glittering in the light from the fireflies. "Taurbrum – kindly present me with the Sceptre."

The horns of the enormous bull almost touched the flint-and-brick ceiling of the tunnel as he appeared in their midst. Once he had been made hornless by Mistress Magistery, he habitually disappeared again.

"I require your kind assistance," Mistress Magistery said to Alfred, offering one end of the Sceptre to him whilst tightly grasping the other.

His grip on it, too, was vice-like. The two elderly Spirits closed their eyes, and the rod began to vibrate violently, as though it had sprung into life and was determined to escape from their clutches. Soon, Alfred and Mistress Magistery's arms were shaking with it, and then they began to tremble horrifically from head to toe. Robin careered off his master's shoulder in alarm to land on Karen's again. She did not seem to notice, being utterly transfixed by what she was witnessing, as were Al, Frederick and Hamelin. There was a great clang, and the Sceptre finally managed to free itself. It whooshed through the air in the direction of the stunned spectators – namely Al – who caught it.

"I'll take that." Mistress Magistery had rushed over to Al at once.

"Of course," Al said awkwardly.

As he placed the Sceptre in her outstretched hand, he realised with a jolt that it was no longer a sceptre, but a sledgehammer.

"I don't think you'd ever be able to make something like *that* in your little forge, Frederick!" Hamelin scoffed.

"You're right," Frederick chuckled. "I really wouldn't. That thing is sure to do some serious damage."

Mistress Magistery turned to face the foundation. Holding the sledgehammer aloft, she flew towards it in a flash of yellow crystals and struck it at its very heart. The sound of the blow was tantamount to that of a mountain crashing down. But the foundation remained stubbornly as it was – entirely and solidly intact.

"Why won't it break?" Al asked anxiously. "Grandad ..."

"Perhaps it just needs to be weakened somewhat," said Alfred, frowning at the foundation.

"I agree, Chief Sir," said Frederick.

"As do I," declared Mistress Magistery, placing the sledgehammer at her feet and taking a step back. "All those who possess the ability to do so, follow my lead."

She raised both hands in unison with the palms facing each other like she was lifting something large and heavy and invisible in the air. An iron cannonball encrusted with chunky diamonds appeared between them, and she flung it forcefully at the foundation. The resultant sound was no less deafening than that of the sledgehammer-assault. The cannonball bounced off the structure and vanished. Mistress Magistery barely let a moment pass before launching an even bigger diamond-encrusted cannonball at the foundation. And then another. And then another. The other Spirits quickly joined in, bombarding their obstacle with iron and diamond.

"You should help, too, Al!" Karen yelled over the almost unbearable cacophony.

Al was a little hesitant to do so. He doubted he would be able to contribute much to the efforts of four Spirits with limitless access to their powers. But his grandfather, like his sister, did not seem to agree –

"Come on, my dear boy!" Alfred commanded over his shoulder as he conjured a monumental canon ball made mostly of diamond in his old hands. "Now's certainly not the time to be shy!"

Al did not require any further encouragement. Although his cannonballs were much smaller than the countless ones the Spirits were conjuring (and also more iron than diamond), Al's fervour to help weaken the obstacle before him could not have burnt more fiercely. And the smiling faces of his mother, father and grandmother flashing across his mind kept it burning. He fired cannonball after cannonball from his hands like bullets. He was panting heavily and felt exhausted by the time Mistress Magistery finally asked them all to stop.

She took up the golden sledgehammer and struck the foundation once more. Al's heart leapt joyously. An enormous crack had appeared across the entire structure, splitting every single one of the rods of diamond into two. Mistress Magistery struck it again with a loud grunt, and the foundation was reduced to nothing more than a pile of stone and diamond fragments strewn across the tunnel floor. The sledgehammer changed back instantly into an ornate sceptre.

Al and Karen cheered in unison.

The *true* end of the tunnel was now revealed and was

only a couple of dozen or so feet away from where they were gathered. It was partially concealed by heavy iron chains, which were wriggling like tentacles trying to feel their surroundings.

"Remain well away from those," Mistress Magistery said at once, pointing at the chains.

She walked effortlessly through the pile of stone and diamond until she was beyond the point where the foundation had stood.

"Quickly!" she cried all of a sudden, whizzing round.

The others froze before becoming aware of what had warranted this unexpected interjection. Looking down, they saw that the stone fragments were rapidly turning into diamonds, which were aggregating with the old ones to form an even stronger foundation. Al's heart leapt with horror this time.

Hamelin was the first to join Mistress Magistery, skipping over the self-constructing structure with an angry sniff.

"Karen – you should go next!" said Frederick.

"*Quickly!*" Alfred echoed Mistress Magistery.

Without slipping or tripping even once, Karen sprinted across the mobile diamonds and skipped graciously over the growing obstacle with Robin still perched on her shoulder.

"Go on, Frederick!" ordered Alfred.

Nearly a quarter of the foundation had already been built as Frederick reached the other side, followed closely by the swarm of fireflies.

"Right – after you, my dear boy!"

Al had not taken more than a couple of hurried steps before a familiar snarling sound made him stop in his tracks and turn round. The badger – regrown to its full size and looking almost demonic with rage – was hurtling towards him.

Al fell backwards in shock, landing painfully on the diamond-strewn floor. And then ... the badger was on top of him. He squirmed and struggled to free himself, but it was futile against the enormity of the monstrous Spirit-creature, whose black eyes were piercing his blue ones. If he was not finding it difficult to breathe, Al would have let out a terrible scream: the badger had opened its mouth and was about to sink its shard-like teeth into his face. A bolt of lightning struck it on the head just in time, and it was the badger's turn to fall backwards.

"Thank you, Grandad," Al panted as Alfred helped him to his feet.

"I'm not quite finished with this Spirit-creature ..."

Alfred eyed the badger sternly as it tried to get back up. It was soon the size of a mouse and shot off in the direction it had come from.

Al, having been somewhat preoccupied with the unwelcome return of the badger, had not taken much notice of the cries and shouts from Karen and the Spirits and the very high-pitched ticking from Robin. And neither, it seemed, had Alfred. They exchanged looks of horror as they faced a fully formed diamond dead end. The new structure was giving off its own luminosity, lighting up their immediate vicinity as the fireflies had done.

"Can this one be broken down too?" Al asked desperately. "We can try, can't we?"

Alfred surveyed the foundation and shook his head.

"Those on the other side will have to carry on with the task without us," he said, looking dejected.

"But they need your help," argued Al. "They need *our*

help. If they fail, we could lose our family forever!"

"I know," Alfred sighed. "I know."

He leant back against the tunnel wall, closed his eyes and began to massage his wrinkly forehead, deep in thought.

"I have an idea that might just work," he announced after a short while, his blue eyes glinting.

Al had been observing him with anticipation and now smiled with sheer relief. Before he could ask him to elaborate, Mistress Magistery's voice filled the tunnel –

"Alfred – as you're unable to proceed and are still in possession of the Noble Bell, kindly await—"

"Forgive me, Your Nobleness," Alfred interrupted loudly, "but my grandson and I may still be able to proceed as planned. I believe I know how our obstacle can be torn down ..."

"How?"

"Taurbrum. He can bring it down easily. He has immense strength, far more than any of us. If the Spectre were replaced on his head and he charged at this foundation, it would shatter instantly."

His words were met with a prolonged silence.

"It would," Mistress Magistery said finally, causing Al and Alfred to beam at each other. "But because of his circumstances, I cannot assign him with a task. It's up to Taurbrum whether he wants to help us in the way you've described."

"I'm sure he will," Alfred said quietly to Al. "Just this once."

"Feels unreal that we're nearly there," said Al. "You'll soon be reunited with Granny and Dad. And you'll meet Mum. Wonder how each of them will react when they see you!"

Alfred chuckled and said, "With pleasure, I hope! I thought I'd never have the chance to meet you all in my true form like … I hadn't died, and in that sense, it feels unreal to me too. The idea naturally fills me with happiness – however painful our parting once more is bound to be. At least I'll get to say goodbye properly this time. Something I hadn't been able to do."

"Stand well back," warned Mistress Magistery's voice.

No sooner had Al and Alfred complied than the tunnel began to vibrate. The thunderous crash that followed made them back away even further. An avalanche of tiny diamonds clattered to the floor: the second foundation, too, had been obliterated.

Neither hesitated this time. As the great, golden-horned bull, having successfully accomplished his task, was swallowed up by nothingness, they raced across the carpet of diamonds. It was a joyous reunion, even though the separation had lasted only a short while. Karen tearfully embraced them both, whilst Robin, chirping melodiously, flew onto Alfred's shoulder and dug his little feet into the tweed as though he was determined to stay with his master forever. It seemed that Taurbrum had damaged the diamonds quite extensively with his horns: they remained where they were, motionless.

"Not so active this time, are they?" said Hamelin, pointing at them and roaring with laughter. (Fickle was now in the form of the red squirrel.)

"Mister Buck …" said Mistress Magistery.

"Yes, Your Nobleness?" Hamelin stopped laughing, though he still looked very much amused.

"Kindly get us out of this place as discussed."

"Of course!" said Hamelin. "Fickle, my love, you're going to have to change again. It's one of those funny occasions when *I* get to decide which of your identities you'll adopt."

He grinned as he scooped the squirrel off his shoulder and raised her high above his top hat until her whiskery face was almost touching the tunnel ceiling. And then Hamelin's nose twitched. The squirrel had gone; a small, russet-coloured beaver was being held aloft by him instead. Although not fully grown, the beaver was far plumper and hairier than her predecessor, and the bright orange teeth protruding from her jaws were long and sharp. Fickle's mouth was twitching like she was desperate to start gnawing on the flint and bricks above her.

"Go!" said Hamelin, raising his arms a fraction higher.

Fickle lunged at the ceiling. Using her chisel-like teeth, she began hacking at the ancient masonry and breaking it down into chunks. Not a single, minute piece of it fell to the floor; she was ingesting the lot with a loud crunching sound. The hole she had created was getting bigger and bigger, and *she* was also getting bigger and bigger.

Soon, Hamelin was struggling to hold up a now adult-sized beaver, but he did not complain. Even when his top hat was knocked off by Fickle's flat, scaly tail, he laughed dismissively and encouraged her to continue chomping with greater vigour still. When she had chopped her way through the flint and bricks, she leapt out of her master's hands and disappeared into the hole. The crunching sound was replaced by the sounds of digging and sloshing for a while. Finally, light began to stream into the tunnel and with it came the smell of rotting vegetation.

Hamelin twitched his nose, picked up his hat and raised it upside down. Fickle fell into it as a snowy-white mouse, having created a hole that even Polemus would have fitted through quite comfortably if he were with them.

"It's time to signal to the others to distract him," Mistress Magistery said quietly.

Alfred produced the tiny silver bell from his jacket and muttered, "Marshal should be used to hearing this noise by now, like all others who inhabit Luxfons – I am positive he will ignore it." He rang the bell.

As the resultant peal died down, a grating, icy voice far above them cried out, "You're all *doomed*!"

12

The Culmination of the Plan

"Shall we go up?" whispered Al.

Alfred and Mistress Magistery shook their heads and moved closer to the hole in the tunnel ceiling.

For a few moments, nothing could be heard. But then the sound of great wings flapping fiercely ripped through the silence. As soon as the sound died away, Mistress Magistery spun round like a ballerina and rocketed out of the hole. Hamelin, placing his top hat on his head with Fickle still inside, followed her in the same manner. And so did Frederick, with the fireflies closely behind him (turning back into Morfox's true form as they swarmed out).

"Definitely sure you want to go up there?" Al asked Karen. "You could stay here in a steel dome or something – safe and sound and—"

"No way!"

"Come, you two," said Alfred. "Let's get our family back."

He and Robin, too, vacated the tunnel as swiftly as the others. Al took his sister's hand into his own, and the two siblings floated up into the bright light after their grandfather.

The ring of stench-filled space between the Orangery and the colossal wall was not much wider than an alley. Those who had sprung out of the ground in the very middle of it were huddled together like a group of statues. Al's heart began to pound as he, once again, faced the grotesque building and its securely locked wooden door. The idea of leaving it behind without his family again seemed far-fetched – *of course they're going to be freed this time. How could it be otherwise?* The very moment this heartening thought crossed his mind, Al found he could just make out the voices of Kerr, Admiral Keel, Polemus, Lady Tyto, Virginia, Hexa and Cloelia speaking in unison beyond the wall. And it seemed that the others could too because they all remained in a state of stillness and silence, listening closely.

"—so our intention is not to attack your esteemed self, nor is it to gain access to the prisoners that you have so nobly guarded for centuries. We're here for one purpose and one purpose only: to commit ourselves, our powers and these swords we carry to you. We wish to spend our remaining time in this world helping you to keep the evil ones enclosed by that wall where they are. We implore you to permit us to share your burden."

"It's not a burden," said Marshal. He did not sound angry anymore, but his voice was as cold as ever. "Carrying out the task I was entrusted with by my noble master, Raja Nawab, is an honour and a privilege! It's your good fortune that I find you to be sincere, but I find the implication that I alone am not sufficient for this task quite offensive."

"No offence is intended," replied the unified voices. "Your capabilities make you extraordinarily adept – that cannot be disputed. However, each of us, too, have many qualities, which you might judge to be valuable and can make use of."

"Go on ..." urged Marshal.

The Spirit-nobles and Future Spirit-nobles now ceased to speak with a single voice made up of seven: each of them began to list their own various skills and accomplishments at the same time.

"One – at – a – time!" Marshal's threatening voice cut across the babble of self-praise. "You can go first."

Marshal had selected Virginia because she alone could now be heard by those rooted to the sludgy ground inside the wall. Al's eyes had barely strayed from the door of the Orangery, and he was beginning to wonder when they were going to move closer to it. He was about to catch his grandfather's eye when Mistress Magistery saved him the trouble of doing so.

"We shall proceed," she whispered.

The door was so close that they could have sprinted across to it in a matter of seconds. But they took their time, edging forward together – one careful, soundless step at a time. After what seemed like an eternity, Al was now once again within touching distance of the obstacle which stood *literally* between him and his loved ones.

The Spirits were going to concentrate on removing each bolt, chain and padlock individually, and Al was going to help them. Mistress Magistery pointed out their first target: the biggest padlock of the lot; it looked as though it weighed a ton and was keeping a cucumber-sized bolt firmly embedded into the stone. Al and the Spirits pierced it with their gaze, and the heavy chunk of iron buckled without making a sound and fell. Before it could hit the sludge and alert Marshal however, it vanished. And so, in this fashion, the wooden door steadily became less and less secure, and the presence of the intruders remained undetected by the Guard of the Orangery.

"Can't do this anymore! I'm t-too scared."

The look of terror on Hamelin's face could not have been a clearer indication of his earnestness. Fickle, who was still under his top hat, was undoubtedly a harvest mouse once more. He took a step back and nearly tripped over his long overcoat.

"Careful!" hissed Mistress Magistery.

"Come now, Hamelin," whispered Alfred. "We're nowhere near unlocking the door yet and need your assistance. Can't you try and change Fickle into something else?"

Hamelin tapped his nose in frustration and shook his head. "Don't think I can," he bleated. "Shouldn't have brought m-my Fickle to this place. She needs to be at home."

Hamelin took another step back. This time, he fell into the sludge with an almighty splash. The others froze in horror. Al hoped as hard as he could that – somehow – the sound had not reached Marshal's ears. No such miracle came to pass, though.

"Silence!" cried Marshal.

The ramblings of Admiral Keel (who was having difficulty remembering his many attributes) came to an abrupt close. Those on the other side of the wall were struck with sheer panic as they heard the air being thrashed by Marshal's great wings.

Just before he leapt to his feet again, Hamelin's nose twitched and the fear on his face gave way to a vicious scowl. Al found the lateness of this – normally trivial – transformation almost unbearable.

He and Karen were rapidly forced against the door behind the Spirits and the Spirit-creatures, who were ready to fight. Alfred, Mistress Magistery, Frederick and Hamelin were now all armed with swords and shields. Robin, meanwhile, had grown to the size of an eagle, and Morfox had turned into a perfect clone of the monstrous, red-breasted bird.

But *they* were not anywhere near as monstrous as the knight-and-dragon hybrid who rose high above them from behind one of the many towers, screaming and brandishing his golden, copper-tipped sword. With his helmeted head pointing at his cornered prey like an arrow, Marshal began to descend.

He had not managed to get very far when he was stopped in his tracks by what Al first thought were seven angels. They were not – though they may as well have been. The Spirits who had sworn their undying allegiance to him mere moments ago were now barring Marshal's way. Each of them had a pair of pure white wings and, like the four Spirits on the ground, were armed with swords and shields. The realisation that he had been tricked by them made Marshal scream in a way that Al had never heard him scream before. It was a truly terrible sound. And then – metal clashed violently against metal.

"They need our help, Your Nobleness!" cried Frederick.

A pair of majestic white wings sprouted out of Mistress Magistery's back. Soon, the other three Spirits were sporting wings which were no less majestic than those of their leader.

"You alone must carry on unlocking the door, my dear boy" said Alfred, turning to Al. "You can be as crude and noisy as you like now, which should make it a little easier. In the meantime, we'll do our best to hold him back. But *please* don't go in without me – you can't face Metanos by yourself if he's in there." He turned to Karen. "Stick close to your brother."

He then spread his wings and flew directly into the midst of the raging battle with the other Spirits and the two gigantic robins.

"It's in your hands now, little brother." Karen had tears in her eyes. "Wish I could do more to help you or those up there."

"Just focus on staying safe!" said Al, giving his sister's arm a little squeeze.

He swiftly directed his attention to a chunky chain snaked around no less than a dozen padlocks. His grandfather was right in that it did not require much concentration to make the chain rip itself off and fling itself into the sludge, but he still needed to focus; there was a long way to go. Trying his utmost to ignore the din of clangs and yells and screams high above (and the gasps and squeals from Karen), Al continued unfalteringly to strip the ancient door of its iron. It was nearly bare when Karen let out a terrified scream, making him look up.

Marshal had managed to slip through the ring of Spirits surrounding him and was hurtling towards the Orangery. The two eagle-sized robins fiercely flapped their wings, and two huge tornadoes erupted out of them. They struck Marshal squarely in the back. The screaming Spirit-creature crashed onto the battlements of a nearby tower. But he rose and swooped down once more, his sword pointing directly at Al and Karen.

"WE NEED TO RUN!" yelled Al, pulling on his sister's hand. "NOW!"

"THERE'S NOWHERE TO RUN TO!" cried Karen. "*We're trapped!*"

Splash! A golden, horseshoe-shaped necklace had fallen at their feet, which turned into a golden, winged horse.

"I'm here to fly you away on the orders of my mistress, Cloelia Iceni!" the horse told them in a frantic voice. "Get on – quick!"

THUD! Marshal was on the roof of the Orangery. It was too late. He was holding his sword like a javelin and was about to launch it at the young siblings, who fell into each other's arms, trembling from head to toe. And then – no less than a miracle occurred.

What looked like a shimmering sandstorm descended upon Marshal, engulfing him entirely. The Spiritsnuff seeped into his silver armour and scaly skin, and he swayed and fell off the Orangery into the sludge, attacking the air feebly with his sword.

The Spirits landed mere feet away from him. Polemus hurried up to Marshal and struck his sword with his own. The great copper-tipped weapon flew out of the gauntleted hands and fell into the sludge like its master. The Spirits, now wingless, surrounded Marshal once more and held their swords aloft. An enormous wiry net streamed like a fountain out of the shiny tips and wrapped itself around the Spirit-creature, entrapping him where he lay. Marshal had been defeated.

"Where did the Spiritsnuff come from?" asked Kerr, turning his head in every direction imaginable.

"Look!" said Lady Tyto, pointing at the sky.

Al could just make out a tiny black speck surrounded by the vast blueness, but it was getting bigger and bigger. And then one of Metanos's Hawkanines came into view. It soared down to land beside a gleeful Karen, its bright yellow eyes fixed on Marshal.

"The ... Spiritsnuff ..." said Alfred, gazing at the Hawkanine. "Was that your doing?"

Without taking its eyes off the Spirit-creature stirring weakly beneath the net, the Hawkanine nodded.

"I'm most grateful to you," said Alfred. "Most grateful – for saving my grandchildren."

The two robins, who were now robin-sized again and hovering near their respective masters, chirped with delight.

"See!" enthused Karen, turning to Al. "I was ri—"

"Let me out of here at once!"

Marshal was himself again. He struggled in vain to free himself from the net clinging to him like it was part of his very self.

"You'll be let out when the Orangery has been vacated of those who shouldn't be in there," said Mistress Magistery.

"Who do you think you are?!" shrieked Marshal.

"I am the Spirit-noblest of Luxfons – your master's successor."

"You're nothing more than a traitor! I – cannot – allow – you – to – open – that – door! Never!"

But Al had. The very last padlock and bolt dived together into the sludge at his bidding, and the ancient door creaked loudly. It was now ajar. Although the joy that Al felt at this moment made his eyes moist, he braced himself for Marshal's volcanic wrath, expecting to be cursed and threatened. But he need not have.

"I should have taken the Orangery elsewhere ... far, far away," lamented the entrapped Spirit-creature. "What a fool I've been. I have failed you, Master. Forgive me."

As Al somehow found himself pitying his foe – he who had been so determined to engulf him in eternal flames

– Marshal became smoky and shapeless and faded into nothingness. He had Departed. The Spirits placed their swords and shields on top of the empty net and bowed before it, too, vanished.

"Morfox," Frederick said to the robin nearest to him, "it's time to fetch the chain, my friend."

"Go with him, Robin," said Alfred. "Quickly!"

The two little birds sped off over the towers and out of sight.

Alfred and Mistress Magistery left the circle and joined Al. They were about to step into the Orangery when the sound of soul-piercing screeching froze them to the spot. All of a sudden, they were repelled by a grey-and-copper blur. The other Hawkanines had crashed in front of the door, barricading it. Al cried out in pain as drops of blood fell onto his cardigan; he had received a deep scratch from one of them just below his eye. Alfred and Mistress Magistery were clutching their arms – they, too, had been injured. The Hawkanine beside Karen clicked its beak at the other three, but they ignored it and spread their wings, which began to flap ...

"Farrier!" snapped Cloelia. "Come here this instant!"

As the winged horse headed towards his mistress, gale upon gale of Spiritsnuff choked the ring of space with a thick, golden haze. When the air became clear again, the sludgy ground was carpeted with ever-brightening particles of Spiritsnuff. The Hawkanines lowered their wings and looked round with bulging eyes – none of their intended targets had lost consciousness ... yet.

"Oh, Cloelia!" cried Hexa.

She managed to catch her future successor, whose eyes were closed and whose limbs were limp, in her arms just in time. Cloelia's Spirit-creature, who had not quite reached his mistress's side, was not so fortunate. Farrier's legs crumpled, and he toppled onto the ground in a heap of gold. The tip of one of his wings was almost touching the partially camouflaged sword of Marshal. And then his wings twitched. The golden tip brushed against the copper one, and Farrier became a ball of flames. The sound of anguished neighing made Al and Karen cry out in horror. Farrier's ordeal did not last long, though – he Departed, and the flames disappeared with him.

"You evil monsters!" Karen screamed tearily.

But the three Hawkanines ignored *her* too and spread their wings again, ready for another attack. The Hawkanine standing beside Karen now thrust itself into the air and launched itself at the other three. A torturous cacophony of screeching ensued as tufts of torn feathers swirled all round.

Al wiped the blood off his cheek with his hand (along with the wound itself) and looked at his grandfather, who was no longer clutching his arm. As their almost identical eyes met, they understood each other. Alfred nodded.

"Stay close to the others!" Al ordered Karen.

And in the following moments, whilst Mistress Magistery rallied the other Spirits to help her stop the battling Hawkanines, Al and Alfred slipped past the slashing beaks and talons into the Orangery.

The door creaked closed behind them, muting the noise beyond. The Orangery was lit by a gloomy, reddish light without a discernible source. Its numerous stone pillars were carved with hideous grotesques, and the vegetation housed in its broken pots and urns was in a state of rot and smelled just as bad as the sludge they had left behind.

Al looked round desperately for any sign of movement,

his heart about to explode ... And then he heard the tinkle of chainmail. The sound had come from behind a cracked marble urn, which was directly opposite them on the other side of the building. It was monumental in size, being nearly as tall as the pillars, and was decorated with cobra heads. Without so much as a split-second's hesitation, Al and Alfred raced towards it.

"GET AWAY FROM THEM, METANOS!" roared Alfred.

Al let out something that was between a cry and a laugh. There they were – his mother, father and grandmother. Their limp, pyjama-clad figures were levitating side by side, and although he could not remember feeling happier than he did right now, Al wept at the sight of them looking so pale and lifeless.

Metanos, who had been leaning over them with his eyes closed and his taut face screwed up with concentration, had been flung back before he had even had the chance to look up. He had hit the murky stone wall behind him with a metallic thud and seemed unable to move.

Alfred turned to Edward, Helen and Margaret, and a protective bubble sprang into existence round them. And the next moment, that bubble was being navigating round the pillars, pots and urns towards the heavy wooden door by Al, who remained rooted by his grandfather's side. The door creaked open, and the bubble floated out of the Orangery. *It's done. They're free.* The screeching could no longer be heard outside. Instead, it was the sound of cheering that flooded into the Orangery, lightening Al's heart even more.

With a loud grunt and rattle of chainmail, Metanos straightened up. He was seething with rage. But so was Alfred, whose blue eyes were piercing *his* bloodshot ones.

And then Al felt uneasy: the anger contorting Metanos's face vanished, and he looked – fleetingly – as proud and satisfied as ever.

However, it was with an expression of mournfulness that he said, "I have no choice but to concede defeat. My plan is in tatters, and the glorious revolution I'd envisaged will not now take place. It would be foolish to believe otherwise."

"It was always foolish to believe your twisted vision would become a reality!" spat Alfred. "Tell me, why were you delving into the minds of my loved ones? How was such an audacious act going to help you get the power you wanted?!"

"It doesn't matter anymore," Metanos sighed. "What a shame that you and your grandson failed to do as I'd asked. What a shame."

"We got them back on our own terms," Al said proudly. "The only shame I feel is that I wanted my grandad to do what you wanted. So glad he didn't!"

"I'm getting the impression, Non-Spirit, that you think yourself to be highly noble," Metanos sneered. "You may have some feeble powers at your disposal, but you can never be ranked amongst us. And you'd never have been able to get your family back without the help of my kind. Talking of which ..." Metanos turned to Alfred. "Where's the *noblest* of my kind? Why has Mistress Magistery not joined you as yet in this little confrontation? I wish to congratulate her on—"

"I'm here, Metanos."

Mistress Magistery was striding towards them, the crystals on her gown shimmering eerily in the reddish glow. She had her hands behind her back and seemed unable to look at Metanos as she joined Al and Alfred.

Before any of them could utter another word, there was a blinding flash of white light and a great clatter of metal. Mistress Magistery had bound Metanos with a thick iron chain, which she was grasping like a leash.

"What's the meaning of this?!" he yelled. "I can't release myself!"

"I know," said Mistress Magistery, still not looking at him. "The fact that this chain has subdued even your powers is a testament to Mister Hancock's skills. You'll be taken to Sundomum, where your fate and that of your Spirit-creatures who still remain loyal to you will be decided."

She turned round and strode back out of the Orangery, effortlessly dragging a protesting Metanos behind her. Al and Alfred beamed at each other before following Mistress Magistery and her prisoner into the bright light.

Karen and the other Spirits were gathered against the wall opposite the door, with the bubble encasing Edward, Helen and Margaret floating above them. They were all observing Metanos with disgust as he continued to demand that he be released in an increasingly frantic manner; Hexa, who still supported an unconscious Cloelia, had the most disdain on her face. Each of the four Hawkanines, meanwhile, were suspended – silent and unmoving – high up in the air in cages made of countless rays of white light. The two robins were whizzing round them and began to chirp happily at the sight of the chain they had brought from Vulcanest being put to its intended use.

Al sprinted over to Karen, and they hugged each other, both shedding tears of unadulterated joy.

But as soon as they parted, Al knew that there was something wrong. Metanos's protestations had come to an abrupt end, and he was staring at Marshal's sword, which still lay where it had fallen, almost buried in Spiritsnuff. And then he let out a gleeful cackle. It was so loud that the whizzing and chirping robins above him flew down onto the shoulders of their respective masters in alarm.

Looking back at the Orangery, Metanos cried, "Your Highness now has nothing to fear – Marshal has Departed!"

13

The Double Possession

The recipient of Metanos's news did not reveal themself but acted at once. Al, Karen and the Spirits gasped in unison – no less than a dozen gold cobra heads with rubies for eyes shot out of the Orangery as though they had been fired from a canon one after the other. They surrounded Metanos, baring their long fangs, and proceeded to devour the chain entrapping him and his powers.

Mistress Magistery staggered towards Alfred and Robin as the ends of the great chain were ripped out of her hand and disappeared inside the chomping mouths. She had never looked more shocked, or more shaken, or more fearful. Al was sure the barrier keeping her emotions buried deep inside her had shattered irreparably this time.

Once Metanos was free, the cobra heads spun on the spot with a loud hiss to face the statue-like spectators. They snapped their powerful jaws, warning them not to come any closer.

"Did you really imagine, Alfred, that I'd concede defeat so easily?" Metanos's taut face was ablaze with pride and satisfaction once more, and his bloodshot eyes were bulging with excitement. "Did you really imagine that the glorious revolution would not come to pass? I'm surprised my little pretence in there was able to fool you so easily."

Alfred opened his mouth to respond, but no words came out. He was as dumbstruck as Mistress Magistery, whose wide eyes kept darting from the cobra heads orbiting Metanos to the open door of the Orangery.

"You see, Alfred," continued Metanos, "you were too late. Had your little rescue mission culminated a fraction of a second earlier, I wouldn't now have what I required – from the minds of those you rescued. Like I said, it's a shame that you didn't carry out the task I'd set because now I have no choice but to conduct a little experiment. Its outcome may very well be detrimental, but it's worth the risk."

"What do you m-mean?" Alfred had found his voice, and it was brimming with fear.

"I'm assuming you've been under the impression that the Connection between your mind and the minds of your family ceased to exist when they were brought to Luxfons. Am I right?"

Alfred gulped and gave a small nod.

"Well, you were wrong," said Metanos. "Quite, quite wrong! It remained intact. It did become weaker, however. Considerably so. Although it wasn't an easy task, I managed to find that Connection in the minds of the members of your family remaining in my custody and manged to extract it from not just one of them, but all three. And now, Alfred, your mind is Connected to *my* mind. Oh, what a powerful Connection it is."

Al's thoughts were entangled in a torturous state of confusion, but his uneasiness had increased with every word Metanos uttered. *Whatever's about to happen next surely can't be worse than being torn apart from my family ...*

The gold cobra heads amalgamated and twelve became one. At the same time, Metanos turned into a beam of red light. It hit Alfred squarely in the forehead and disappeared inside him.

Al felt numb. He was surrounded by cries of horror, but all he could do was stare in silence ... not understanding what was going on ... not understanding how to help his grandfather.

Alfred remained as he was for a moment and glanced at his grandchildren. And then he, *too*, turned into a beam of light, making Robin career violently towards a tearful Karen. She caught him in her hands as this beam of light, changing from red to white and then back again, now hit Mistress Magistery squarely in the forehead and disappeared inside *her*.

The eruption of exclamations all round was tantamount to an explosion. Mistress Magistery's head began to shake like it was about to fall off. It then jerked upwards, and the vast blueness above them was immediately swallowed up by a flash of white light. As soon as the sky re-emerged, her head stopped shaking and jerked down again. A beam of red light then shot out of her forehead. It morphed into Metanos. Just Metanos. There was no sign of Alfred.

Mistress Magistery and Metanos could barely stand upright, and it seemed like they did not even have enough strength left to speak. Lady Tyto and Virginia broke away from the others and gingerly hurried past Metanos and the hissing cobra head to support their leader.

"Where's my grandad?" Al asked desperately, looking round.

None of the Spirits (who were able to) responded or met his gaze.

"Frederick – please ... Tell me."

The blacksmith looked sombre as he raised his head. But before he could utter a single word, someone else took the opportunity of enlightening Al instead:

"Your grandfather has *obviously* Departed, Non-Spirit. You'll never see him again."

The voice had come from the Orangery. It was shrill and full of arrogance – and pure hatred. And the one it belonged to was soon amongst them. A tall female Spirit had stepped out of the Orangery. She had a handsome, alluring face and short, sleek black hair. And she looked regal to the highest degree: she was wearing a scarlet, scale-patterned sari made of silk, was adorned with a great many gem-encrusted necklaces, bangles and rings and was crowned with a chunky gold circlet.

The cobra head attached itself to this circlet as if by a powerful magnetic force, and Metanos hobbled over to join her. The other Spirits looked afraid – none more so than Mistress Magistery.

"What did you say?" Al asked the new arrival abruptly.

She looked at him with unequivocal disgust and said, "You heard, Non-Spirit. He's gone. And if you are going to have the audacity to address me in future, it'll be in your interest to remember to be more respectful."

The sickening feeling of dread that had begun to rise inside Al was now frothing and bubbling as he turned his face towards Frederick. The blacksmith nodded, fat tears running down his face into his moustache.

Al may as well have been back in his garden – standing there in the cold in his pyjamas and watching his family being taken away by the Hawkanines. *But there's no chance*

– however tiny – of being reunited this time. How could fate be so cruel?

A scream from Karen roused him – but only partially. Al looked down to see Robin becoming smoky and shapeless in her hands, and then his grandfather's loyal little companion, too, was gone.

But the Spirit whose shrill voice was drilling into Al's ears clearly did not care. He wished with all his might that everything would come to a standstill ... that silence would fall. But she carried on speaking. And he was forced to listen, though the pain made it difficult to make sense of what she was saying.

"How times have changed in a mere millennium or so. It's astonishing that those finding themselves in my presence – that of Queen Lamiobra herself – haven't deemed it proper to bow even once. Quite astonishing! Perhaps you believe yourselves to be more superior now because most of you have made yourselves immune to my Spiritsnuff ..." Her narrow, hate-filled eyes came to rest on Mistress Magistery. "How weak you've become, Mistress Magistery. Not much of a leader anymore, are you? Certainly not worthy of the rank of Spirit-noblest of Luxfons."

Apart from Hexa and Cloelia, the Spirits next to Al and Karen rushed over to Mistress Magistery, Lady Tyto and Virginia and stood in a protective line between them and Queen Lamiobra and Metanos.

"If you possessed any real wisdom," Queen Lamiobra said to the five Spirits now facing her with even more disdain in her voice, "you'd abandon your so-called leader and join my consort, Metanos, and me. We are *truly* the noblest Spirits in Luxfons because we *truly* value our powers. They're not meant to be used sparingly for the sole purpose of benefitting Non-Spirits. They're meant to be unleashed in their entirety, giving rise to the most extraordinary spectacles imaginable! And that's what'll happen – no foolish so-called leader or ridiculous Unsighted Gate will be able to hinder the glorious revolution!

"Those Spirits who continue to carry out their tasks in a feeble manner, whether by choice or not, will be obliterated, and so will their loved ones. In the end, we'll have an army so powerful that no force of any kind *anywhere* will be able to stand in its way. After all, who knows how many undiscovered realms are out there that require true leadership?

"But I know that you're not as wise as my consort and me … as well as others. I know you'll remain loyal to that weak creature you seek to protect. Raja Nawab would be proud of you, I'm sure – much more than you should be of him because he was easily tricked into believing that he'd actually managed to entomb *me* in stone!" The shrill cackle that followed her words sounded more horrific than Metanos's ever could.

"If you're entertaining the idea of harming Her Nobleness Mistress Magistery," piped up Lady Tyto, "be sure that we'll succeed where Raja Nawab failed. Her Nobleness may have been weakened, but you and Metanos are still outnumbered."

"My noble consort has just restored the powers of every single Spirit!" Queen Lamiobra seethed. "Are none of you aware of what that means? And yet you're supposedly the noblest Spirits in Luxfons. Astonishing! You're about to discover that it is not us who are outnumbered, and also pay the price for having the audacity to threaten *me*!"

She spun towards Metanos and lunged at his leather

quiver, snatching up the Noble Trumpet poking out of it. She was about to bring the archaic-looking instrument to her bright red lips when she yelped in fear. Something had risen out of the Spiritsnuff in front of her of its own accord …

It was Marshal's sword. The gigantic weapon hovered in mid-air for a moment, its copper tip pointing directly at Queen Lamiobra, before hurtling towards Al.

It was not because he was half-frozen with grief that he did not move out of its way: there was no doubt in his mind what would happen if the sword so much as touched him. But something inside him – some unfathomable force – told him to remain where he was. And that same force made him raise his hands just in time to grasp the ornate hilt of what had looked like a golden missile heading towards him and stop it in its tracks. Al was now wielding Marshal's sword. He had not been engulfed by flames.

"NO!" yelled Queen Lamiobra. "HOW?!"

"We – must – go, Your Highness," Metanos said weakly, his bloodshot eyes bulging with fear this time.

In a flash, Queen Lamiobra and Metanos turned into reddish mist. It enveloped the cages of light in the air. Every single bright ray was extinguished in unison, and all four of the freed Hawkanines, too, turned into reddish mist. The resultant veil was heavy and almost completely opaque, but it rapidly vacated the ring of space, drifting upwards and over the towers into the unending vastness beyond.

"I wish to take the Babas to A-Alfred's abode." Mistress Magistery had found her voice, but it sounded strained. "The rest of you should go to Sundomum. Once inside, make the doors as secure as you can and then await my arrival."

She stood upright in her usual stately manner, and Lady Tyto and Virginia relinquished her arms. The five Spirits standing in front of her dispersed as she strode towards Al.

She looked down at the boy full of sorrow and confusion, who was still holding Marshal's sword.

With a voice which was now markedly less strained and very gentle, she said, "I'll explain everything I can, Al – to you and Karen. It's the very least I can do."

Her green eyes swept the length of the sword, and it began to shrink until it was the size of a dagger.

"This belongs to you now, Al. Please place it in your pocket and keep it there."

As Al robotically did as he was told, Mistress Magistery turned into a sphere of white light. It grew outwards and upwards, submerging every Baba in blinding brightness.

Al and Karen sat down opposite each other in the green velvet armchairs by the fire in the Spirit-twin of their sitting room. An identical armchair appeared beside them, and Mistress Magistery sat down too. Edward, Helen and Margaret were no longer in a protective bubble. They were still unconscious, however, and had been placed side by side on settees near the window. Mistress Magistery thought it was best to awaken them from their deep trance only after she had fulfilled her promise of enlightening Al and Karen.

"Where to begin?" she sighed, looking at the silent siblings in turn. Her eyes came to rest on Al. "There's no doubt in my mind, Al, that you'll succeed me as the Spirit-noblest of Luxfons."

Her words were like a hammer blow, which shattered Al's own trance-like state.

"But … but …" he spluttered.

"I'm well aware that you're not a Spirit. But you will be one day. And you'll return to Luxfons and go on to take your rightful place on the Great Throne in Sundomum. Does such an idea sound strange to you?"

"No – it doesn't." Al was astonished. He found this extraordinary insight into his future no more surprising than being told that he would die one day. As strange as it was, it seemed just as inevitable. Just as natural. "Why *me*, though? What made the sword come to me? And what made me grab it? Why did it not burn me? *Why do I have the powers I do?*"

"I wish I had knowledge on such matters, so I could share it with you," said Mistress Magistery. "The fact is that there are many influential unknowns present all around us, which we cannot even begin to understand but must accept, nonetheless. Raja Nawab simply told me that I'd have clear signs of who my successor would be. He was right, Al. You – whose powers have not even been fully unlocked – are now the only one in Luxfons who can wield Marshal's sword. I will receive no clearer sign than this."

Mistress Magistery fidgeted in her seat, struggling to maintain her stately uprightness.

"And now …" she said, "now the time has come for my confession – a secret only I'm aware of. Ultimately, I'm the one who's responsible for the premature Departure of your grandfather from this world. It's because of me that you'll never see him again. And I must beg your forgiveness."

Both Al and Karen had tears in their eyes as they looked at Mistress Magistery questioningly. Her eyes, too, were glinting in the firelight like the crystals on her gown.

"Metanos shouldn't be in Luxfons," she said, shaking her head. "He wouldn't be here had I not intervened in the ways I did. He had no loved ones in the Domain of the Living, but I ... I grew to love him as a mother loves her child."

Al and Karen's intense gaze did not stray from her face even for a split second as she continued:

"Well over a century ago, during my task of helping those in the Domain of the Living who had no Spirits watching over them in Luxfons, I was very moved by the plight of a young beggar woman and her new-born. The mind of this woman was polluted with utter misery, and I set out in the guise of a passer-by to bring a little light into her life and that of her poor child. My intention was to provide her with the means of getting off the grimy streets she had been compelled to beg on without much success. And so I immersed myself in a crowd that would eventually walk past the dilapidated wall in the shadow of which she was sitting on a pile of filthy rags – with her half-naked boy clinging to her red shawl and wailing non-stop.

"When the time came for me to leave the crowd and approach them, I found that the woman had stopped begging. She was looking at her distressed son in a way that filled me with horror. Her face looked almost demonic with rage – the kind of rage that makes one take leave of their senses. She got up, unaware that she was being watched, and placed the crying child on the rags. She then picked up one of the large stone fragments that had fallen off the wall behind her and held it aloft above her own flesh and blood, who she was about to strike and silence forever. But I didn't let her. I found myself being consumed by the same kind of rage she had been consumed by ... and ... and before I could stop myself, I caused her life to end. Her dead body fell against the wall, still clutching the stone, as the now motherless child continued to cry. That child – who I had saved – was Metanos." Mistress Magistery lowered her head and wiped away the tears leaking from her eyes.

"You don't need to feel bad for saving his life," Al said quietly after a few moments of silence.

"Al's right," Karen said gently.

Mistress Magistery looked up and said, "I could've saved him without resorting to murder. I committed an act that is alien to my principles. It makes me no less heinous than Queen Lamiobra and Metanos. I wouldn't have been able to take *any* life if the darkest power in existence remained where Raja Nawab had left it and where it is now: locked away in its vessel. But I foolishly thought it would be prudent to carry it with me ... and then ended up doing what I wanted to prevent others from doing. Nothing will ever alleviate the shame I feel. That's my punishment. And yet, I carried on making unquestionably shameful decisions. Both of you have every right to know what they were.

"By the time Metanos died, he was rich and powerful – I'd done everything over the years to make him as content as possible. He had no family and was friendless, but, unknown to him, he had me – a surrogate mother, who loved him dearly. I was there the moment his Spirit left his body, and I soon realised that its destination was not Luxfons as I'd hoped. I just couldn't bear the idea of never seeing him again – *just couldn't.*

"Without his knowledge, I took him with me through my own Unsighted Gate by force, against the wishes of my Spirits-liminal. I left him wondering Ancient Gates Wood to make it look as though he'd been admitted naturally. Lord Havelock brought him to Sundomum, and during his Noble Possession, I—" Mistress Magistery seemed unable to carry on, bowing her head again.

"Frederick told me that Metanos hoodwinked you and the Chief Spirit-nobles," said Al. He had an uneasy feeling he was about to be corrected.

Mistress Magistery raised her head slowly and lamented, "That was the only conclusion those who undeservedly think highly of me could come to."

"So you did see the terrible darkness inside him?" Al asked dejectedly.

"There was light there too. But the darkness was more profound. It was I who hoodwinked my Chief Spirit-nobles by shielding Metanos's true nature from their eyes. I wasn't prepared to allow him to Depart Luxfons. I thought I'd be able to nourish whatever little light there was inside him ...

"How wrong and foolish I was! His betrayal broke me. I stripped myself of warmth and friendliness and became aloof from all those in my presence to stop myself from becoming close to any other individual ever again – in case history should repeat itself. But I had no idea how treacherous his betrayal was until now. I had no idea he'd allied himself with the evillest Spirit to have ever set foot in this world. No other being in my affections could ever come close to emulating such a betrayal!"

Al could not help but feel sorry for Mistress Magistery; he looked at Karen and could tell that she felt the same.

Although he conceded that Mistress Magistery's actions could never be fully justified and had directly resulted in evil flourishing in Luxfons ... evil that had cost him his grandfather, he could not bring himself to blame the self-loathing Spirit for his loss. She who was being so open and heartfelt.

"What did Metanos do to make G-Grandad Depart?" he asked her. "What exactly happened back there?"

"What you witnessed was a so-called 'Double Possession.' Now, even peering into the mind of a Spirit of Luxfons is extremely difficult and could harm both the observer and the one whose mind is being observed. Our powers naturally repel any external force seeking to undermine us in such a way. As you can, therefore, imagine, *Possessing* a Spirit of Luxfons is almost impossible. But if such an act is carried out, it's only a matter of time before the Spirits in question are destroyed due to the resultant clash of powers—"

"So how come the Noble Possession thing is safe?" interrupted Karen, looking perplexed.

"Because a Spirit's powers are only unlocked after they've been Accepted as a Spirit of Luxfons," said Al. "So there is no repulsion or clash."

"That's correct," continued Mistress Magistery as a hint of pride flickered on her mournful face. "Considering how powerful Alfred was, Metanos wouldn't even have come close to Possessing him in a conventional manner. He needed to bypass the repulsion and also avoid the ensuing clash; he did this by hijacking the Connection between your grandfather's mind and the minds of your parents and grandmother. By procuring it, he became at one with that Connection and a part of Alfred himself. He was able to then Possess him without much difficulty.

By using the combined strength of his own powers and those of Alfred, he Possessed me. I couldn't stop him, and he forced me to restore the powers of all Spirits.

"Knowing that all three of us were quite possibly about to be obliterated ... and perhaps hoping that by doing so, he might just stop Metanos from succeeding, Alfred ... Alfred Departed, giving me the chance to expel Metanos. Your esteemed grandfather valued my tenure in Luxfons above his own, but I don't. I most certainly don't!"

"If all the Spirits have their powers back," Al said with dread in his voice, "does that mean that Lamiobra and Metanos now have followers which are really powerful again?"

"Yes – and it's an army," Mistress Magistery corrected him. "Considering how much Metanos believes in his cause, he will have been busy amassing nothing short of an army. Sooner or later, it *will* be coming to Sundomum for the Power to Kill. And I cannot suppress its powers because Metanos will have ensured that his soldiers have the ability to repel me, just like he and Queen Lamiobra can."

"Was she about to call them using that trumpet thing just before the sword came to Al?" Karen asked with as much dread in her voice as her brother.

"I believe so," said Mistress Magistery. "She would've commanded them to destroy us, and there would've been another battle. Although Queen Lamiobra is exceptionally powerful, she's full of cowardice and will avoid putting herself in danger at all costs. That's why she only revealed herself when Marshal had Departed ... when she knew his sword no longer posed a threat. But now she's discovered otherwise – as we all have. You'll be at the forefront of her mind, Al—"

"I'm not hiding!" Al interjected fiercely. "I won't hesitate to use the sword on her or Metanos or their soldiers or anyone else who helps them with their disgusting plan!"

"You want to stay in Luxfons and help us?!"

"Yes, I do," Al said without any hesitation whatsoever. He had made up his mind and did not have the slightest doubt it was the right decision.

He looked at his sister, who smiled at him encouragingly.

"Al – you need to think about this properly," said Mistress Magistery. "You and your family deserve to spend the rest of your lives together in peace: you've all been through quite enough. I never imagined that you'd even contemplate the idea of being separated from them again."

"It will be hard to leave them," Al sighed, "but as long as I know they're safe and happy, I'll be happy.

"You have a better chance of winning with that sword, and only I can touch it without being harmed. So, of course, I'm going to help. Lamiobra and Metanos are probably already planning on how to get rid of me, and I know they won't rest until they've captured me or ... or killed me if they get that Power. I won't really be at peace anyway knowing that. And plus: I want to carry on where my grandad left off – trying to stop their plan from succeeding!"

"He would've been so proud of you," said Mistress Magistery, her voice full of emotion. "I'm going to feel his loss enormously. The fact is that Queen Lamiobra is right: I am becoming weaker. I can feel it. It was such a relief to be able to rely on Alfred's wisdom. Such a blessed relief."

"Wish they'd had the chance to meet him," said Al,

glancing at his mother, father and grandmother. "He was looking forward to it. Told me he didn't get the chance to say goodbye to Dad and Granny before he died, and now ... he'll never get that chance." Tears started to stream freely from Al's eyes again. "I understand why he would never have revealed himself if we *hadn't* ended up in Luxfons ... but because he'd been forced to reveal himself, do you think he would've decided to become a part of our lives until he Departed Luxfons naturally? Meant to ask him. I really would've liked that, regardless of what form he took."

"Me too ..." lamented Karen.

"He ... he told me that he wanted to," said Mistress Magistery. "It would've been crueller not to be a part of your lives after you'd found out that he existed as a Spirit in Luxfons."

All three of them broke down and wept in unison.

14

Darkness and Light

After returning from Sundomum, Mistress Magistery had brought all five Babas to the site of Alfred's Unsighted Gated: the leafless oak tree he had pointed out to Al on the Ragnarsson. It stood in the middle of a luscious field and was as gnarled and ancient-looking as its twin in the Babas' garden – but they were not quite identical. This one was taller, and its trunk was girthier; even the ivy garlanded around its exposed roots had bigger and greener leaves. It was as though this tree, having been separated at birth from its twin, had had a more indulgent upbringing.

"So … we'll be flown into those branches up there and we'll be back where we belong?" Edward asked Mistress Magistery, sounding nervous.

His thin face was still stained with tears, as was Helen and Margaret's. After having their consciousnesses restored by Mistress Magistery, the three of them had naturally demanded an explanation. They had paid the price for their enlightenment by being overwhelmed by an exhausting array of emotions. Al had provided them with food, drink and appropriate clothes, but the wonder at his powers had not been sufficient to avert their thoughts from Alfred's Departure.

"That's correct, Mister Baba," replied Mistress Magistery. "I'll now summon the Spirit who will take you to the Domain of the Living. No other in Luxfons knows your homeland better – he will have very little trouble finding a safe abode for you and your family. Alfred's Spirits-liminal have already agreed to let you all through at my request."

She conjured a small silver bell (not dissimilar to the one Alfred used to have).

Just before ringing it, she brought it close to her lips and muttered, "Lord Havelock."

"Is it really necessary for us to abandon our home and relocate?" Edward demanded all of a sudden after the peal had died down.

The others stared at him.

"Yes, it is!" Al and Karen cried in unison.

"You two don't understand," said Edward. "Not easy to uproot yourself—"

"You've already been uprooted!" Karen went bright red. "And now we're all in danger of being captured again! Those two Spirits are pure evil: our lives don't mean anything to them! They'll make us suffer to make Al give up the sword. We have to go into hiding!"

"Can't bear to lose any of you again," Al sighed. "You have no idea what it was like."

"I do have an inkling of what it's like to lose someone I love ..." said Edward, his voice shaking.

Al immediately regretted his poor choice of words and apologised.

"I concede that it'll be difficult to adjust, Edward," said Margaret, "but let's be sensible now. Your children are absolutely right. Alfred and I brought you up to be selfless, and that's exactly what you'll be!"

Edward opened his mouth to respond, but Helen stopped him by gently squeezing his arm.

"Putting our lives on hold for a while longer *is* a big sacrifice, darling," she said lovingly, "but it has to be made."

Edward sighed and nodded.

"Ah, here's Lord Havelock," said Mistress Magistery, looking up.

A brightly coloured speck zoomed across the blue sky before coming to a halt above them. As it began to descend, an enormous wheelless carriage came into view; it was a much grander version of Alfred's, decorated all over with enamelled flowers and surmounted by a much larger arched crown. The fat magpie carrying it acknowledged them with a loud chattering sound before placing it on the ground with a soft thud.

"Greetings!" boomed Ivar, bursting out of the carriage.

As hearty as his salutation was, his face looked even droopier than usual. Al did not need to wonder why this was the case: he knew that Ivar was affected by the loss of Alfred and that, though the two elderly Spirits had not always agreed with one another, they had cared for each other greatly. Ivar bowed deeply to Mistress Magistery, supporting himself as ever with his cane, and then to Edward, Helen and Margaret after being introduced to them.

"The sooner you go, the better," Al urged his family.

"Don't fret, young one," Ivar said kindly. "They will almost immediately be safe and secure in seclusion, where even the Hawkanines won't be able to find them. It's an honour to help dear Alfred's family – the family of our Future Spirit-noblest."

Al, feeling a little embarrassed, thanked him earnestly.

"And you're absolutely sure that you want to stay, my little darling?" Helen looked concerned as she gave Al a peck on the cheek.

It was not the first time she had asked him that question since being made aware of his decision.

"I'll be fine, Mum – honestly."

"*I* know that you definitely will be, son," declared Edward, shaking an emotional Al's hand. "I'm very proud of the person you've become. Very proud."

Once Karen and Margaret, too, had bade Al affectionate farewells, Ivar exclaimed "Follow me!" and made his way back to the carriage with his five charges.

"Whoever knew you were born to save worlds, younger brother?!" yelled Karen, waving, as she climbed into the carriage after Edward and Helen.

Margaret struggled a little to get onto the step and through the door, prompting Ivar to hand over his own cane to her for support. He then conjured an even more elaborate replacement, made entirely of silver, and followed her inside. As soon as he closed the ornate door behind him, the magpie flew the carriage through Alfred's Unsighted Gate and vanished.

Over the course of what Al now thought had been many, many days, he and Mistress Magistery had travelled the length and breadth of Luxfons, visiting as many Spirits as they could. Their purpose for doing so was twofold: request vows to help defend the Laws of Luxfons if called upon to do so *and* attempt to discover those who had been tempted by Queen Lamiobra and Metanos to become soldiers in their army.

The Spirit-nobles and Future Spirit-nobles were also employing themselves fully in the same task. Mistress Magistery had temporarily granted each of them one of her own exclusive powers: the ability to suppress and reinstate the powers of other Spirits. If the powers of a particular Spirit could not be suppressed, their guilt would be confirmed.

Even though she had not yet received any reports confirming it to be true, Mistress Magistery was sure that Queen Lamiobra and Metanos were being just as industrious by trying to amass an even greater army than the one they already headed. And she was absolutely certain that Queen Lamiobra was desperately finding a way of – somehow – arming herself against Marshal's sword.

"Another one!" cried Al.

Even though they had naturally come across many empty abodes when the Unsighted Gates were open (all Spirits of Luxfons now able to resume the task of helping their loved ones, having had their powers reinstated), this was the dozenth consecutive time they had come across an empty abode since the Gates had closed. They were outside a red-brick mansion beside a deer park. After growing tired of repeatedly announcing their presence with the large lion-shaped door knockers, Al and Mistress Magistery walked back down the stone steps of the stately building.

Mistress Magistery looked very uneasy. "There's something wrong."

"What do you think's going on?"

"I believe that this abode and many of the others we've

found to be empty belong to soldiers of Queen Lamiobra and Metanos. It looks like they were aware that our visit would lead to the discovery of their true allegiance, and that's why they've fled."

"How do you think they found out? All the Spirits we have seen so far have proven to be loyal, and they were told not to reveal what we're doing. And surely if the others had come across bad Spirits and they'd somehow escaped to tell Lamiobra and Metanos, you'd have been told."

Mistress Magistery was lost in thought.

After a few moments, she sighed deeply and said, "There are a number of possible answers to this mystery, and some of them are more concerning than others. I can only hope that we come up with a satisfactory explanation when I summon the Spirit-nobles and Future Spirit-nobles back to Sundomum. In the meantime, we need to persist with our task with even more fervour than before."

She turned into the rapidly expanding sphere of white light and the two of them beamed away.

They arrived in the middle of a large hillside village comprising many simple stone houses amidst a rich variety of plants. Out of the many pleasant villages Al had now visited in Luxfons, this one lightened his heart the most. It was teeming with friendly-looking Spirits of all ages who were determined to fill the air with a fusion of cheery conversation and hearty laughter. Al was wearing a peacock-feather sash over his cardigan at Mistress Magistery's behest as a symbol of his future position, and both of them were greeted with waves and cheers as they made their way up the pretty path of a tiny house. Mistress Magistery knocked gently on its green door, and it was opened by a young female Spirit in a flowery shalwar-kameez with a long, colourful scarf draped over her shoulder.

"Oh, what an honour!" The round, ruddy face of the Spirit glowed with happiness as she bowed and welcomed them inside.

They were led into a cosy sitting room adorned with vases of fresh flowers. A little Spirit-girl, who could not have been more than two years old, was sitting cross-legged on a rug in the middle stroking a black-and-white kitten with wings. A handsome, smartly dressed male Spirit was sitting in an armchair next to her, reading what looked like a letter he had just written. He jumped up in delightful surprise as he looked up at his guests and bowed.

"I don't know whether you remember us from our Noble Possessions, Your Nobleness ... but this is my husband, Jay Khan, and that's our daughter, Jasmine. And I'm Alisha. Please do take a seat."

Al and Mistress Magistery sat opposite Alisha and Jay on small settees. Jasmine and her winged kitten remained where they were and continued to enjoy each other's company in their own blissful little bubble.

"Of course, I remember you," Mistress Magistery said with a kind smile. "You were brought to Sundomum by Mister Buck along with another young family. I remember being extremely pleased at how much light resided inside all of you."

"My good lady here deserves the credit for nurturing the light in both our daughter and me, Your Nobleness," said Jay.

Alisha went bright red and placed her hand, which was beautifully decorated with henna, on top of Jay's.

"Right," Mistress Magistery sighed, "on to the matter that has brought us here ... Forgive me ..." There was a flash of white light – Alisha and Jay's powers had successfully been suppressed and then reinstated. "As you might already be aware, Metanos is still at large and he's not alone: he's formed an alliance with Queen Lamiobra, who is no longer imprisoned in the Orangery. It's unquestionable that they already have a large number of soldiers, whose identities I don't know – and who now have powers I can no longer suppress. My belief is that they're attempting to expand their army as we speak—"

"Forgive me for interrupting," interjected Jay, "but Your Nobleness is absolutely right. Queen Lamiobra and Metanos were both here in this village and left mere moments ago."

Al and Mistress Magistery exchanged looks of shock.

"What did they want?!" demanded Al.

"Precisely what Her Nobleness has just stated her belief is, young Sir," said Jay. "They announced their arrival in the village square with voices that penetrated our abodes and invited us all to gather before them. When we'd all done so, they told us about their so-called revolution in great detail and how we could benefit from it by becoming a part of their great army. We were all—"

"Absolutely disgusted," finished Alisha. "And none of us were afraid to make our sentiments known to them. They gloated that they'd soon have the Power to Kill, and the loved ones of those who defied them would not be spared."

"But when we told them this cowardly threat made us even more determined to defy them," continued Jay, "they were quite taken aback and left very abruptly."

"I'm not surprised!" said Mistress Magistery, looking

emotional. "They realised that ordinary Spirits are willing to defend the Laws of Luxfons – to fight for what's right, even though none of us were meant to fight for anything at all in Luxfons. We were just meant to project a little light across the divide. That's all. But now we must fight. We must!"

"Indeed!" cried Alisha. "And we vow to stand up for our noble ways – whatever and *whoever* we have to face!"

"We certainly do," said Jay. "Alisha and I thought it would be prudent to inform Mister Buck at once about what we'd witnessed so he could inform Your Nobleness in turn" – he held up the letter in his hand – "but there's no need now."

"You're both very brave." Al could not help but express his admiration. It was the first time since embarking on their task that he and Mistress Magistery had come across Spirits who were actively defying Queen Lamiobra and Metanos – without any fear of the consequences.

After bidding farewell to the Khans, Al and Mistress Magistery went on to visit every single house in the village and found themselves being overwhelmed by a torrent of passionate declarations of loyalty. And the Spirits they subsequently visited in other villages were just as loyal, just as determined to defend the Laws of Luxfons. Al had never seen Mistress Magistery's old, pearly face so full of delight before.

"I'm much less fearful about the future than I was," she told Al just before they departed a pretty seaside village.

They now came upon a solitary abode on a desolate moor: a rusty old cabin not much bigger than a garden shed. Al was convinced that it had long been abandoned. He could not think why a Spirit with endless choices would choose such an abode in the first place. But much to his surprise, the lopsided corrugated door flung open before they had taken more than a couple of steps towards it. The Spirit-youth who emerged out of the cabin froze at the sight of them. He was big and warty, had unkempt blonde hair and was wearing a long, maroon-coloured leather coat with huge collars.

"Greetings," said Mistress Magistery. "The Future Spirit-noblest and I wish to see you. You're Mister Poley-Babington if I remember correctly? Agrius Poley-Babington?"

"I am, yes!" he replied as quick as lightning in a nasally voice. "But I can't stop. Really sorry. Must go. Have to um – see my Spirit-noble, Lady Tyto, about new ways I'd like to use my powers in the Domain of the Living. Sorry again!"

"I'm afraid all the Spirit-nobles are occupied with more pressing matters and aren't able to carry out their conventional tasks," Mistress Magistery told him. "Were you not informed?"

"No," shot back Agrius, his warty face screwed up in an almost cartoonish manner with confusion. "I wonder why I wasn't told ... Never mind! There's another Spirit who can help me, though! He uses his powers in a similar way – but um – but he told me he's Departing soon. Quite, quite soon! It's really important to get his opinion before he goes. Please excuse me, Your Nobleness."

A sound like a thunderclap filled the air. Agrius yowled and jumped back.

"There's no need to be alarmed." Mistress Magistery's voice was devoid of any warmth, and she was piercing Agrius with an icy stare. "I've just discovered that I'm unable to deprive you of your powers. You cannot, therefore, deny the fact that you're a soldier of Queen Lamiobra and Metanos."

"P-please don't make me Depart," spluttered Agrius. "My family need me to help them! It was a tough decision – joining their army. It's tearing me apart even now. But I did it for my family! Only for them! I was promised I'd be able to help them with all their troubles constantly! They need me."

"And helping Queen Lamiobra and Metanos to murder millions – to obliterate countless families – is justifiable to that end, is it?" asked Mistress Magistery, making Agrius whimper. "You do know that if the use of your powers in helping your loved ones doesn't result in the kind of carnage Queen Lamiobra and Metanos desire, you *and* your loved ones will be obliterated by them?"

"I'm sorry!" wailed Agrius. "*Please*. I can't Depart!"

The Spirit-youth swished his leather coat and spun in the air towards them. Al whipped the copper-tipped dagger out of his pocket, and it was a sword again. Agrius fell to the floor at their feet with a thud, cowering.

"No!" he cried. "Please! No! I regret my decision! I repent!"

But Al had already replaced the great weapon in his pocket as a dagger. The idea of forcing such a pitiful individual to Depart Luxfons by engulfing him in flames seemed wicked – even though that same individual had launched himself at them like a missile in order to attack and escape.

"Rise," said Mistress Magistery as she and Al stepped away from him. "You will certainly not be harmed or forced to Depart Luxfons by any of us. Where have you been summoned? And how did Queen Lamiobra and Metanos gain knowledge of our activities?"

Agrius lumbered up to his feet, gulped and said, "Please don't make me betray them."

"You have nothing to fear," Mistress Magistery assured him. "You will be under our protection."

"Th-they'll kill my family when they get the power to do so."

"*If* they get the power to do so," Mistress Magistery corrected him.

"You can help us stop them from getting that power in the first place by telling us what you know!" piped up Al.

"I can't!" retorted Agrius. "They'll destroy me. They'll find a way – I know it! I'll be rendered useless and have no choice but to Depart. But I'm repentant. Truly, I am. I just want to focus on helping my family – as before. That's all."

Mistress Magistery sighed deeply. The frostiness on her face thawed a little, and she spent a few moments lost in thought.

"You cannot be pardoned so easily, Mister Poley-Babington," she said finally. "As I'm unwilling to take the risk of peering into your mind, and you cannot now undergo the Noble Possession again, I cannot determine whether you truly are repentant. My decision, therefore, is as follows: you'll be confined to your abode until our ways are no longer threatened by dark forces. You'll then be brought to Sundomum, where the Spirit-nobles and Future Spirit-nobles and I will determine whether you're fit to resume your task."

Agrius shuddered as he said, "What if Queen Lamiobra and Metanos triumph?"

"You should sincerely hope that they don't," Mistress Magistery replied crisply. "It is only I who can set you free."

Looking crestfallen, Agrius turned and trudged back into his cabin, closing the door behind him. Mistress Magistery raised her forefinger, and a thick chain made of white light erupted out of the tip. It wrapped itself round the rusty cabin with a great clang. The entire structure was then swallowed up by the moor, leaving not a trace of it behind.

"The right decision?"

"Yes ... I think so," said Al, taken aback.

"I believe you made the right decision too." Mistress Magistery nodded towards his pocket before smiling at him.

"Hope I don't hesitate to use it when I know I have to," Al sighed.

"You possess a great deal of wisdom, Al," Mistress Magistery said with earnestness, placing her hand on his shoulder. "It will steer you in the right direction – don't fret."

As Al, feeling comforted by her words, expressed his appreciation, he noticed that Mistress Magistery suddenly had that air (now rather familiar to him) of being alerted by something.

"Unsighted Gates?"

"Indeed. They're open again."

A short while later, the sky had turned into a packed thoroughfare, its blueness drowned in a sea of colour. It was buzzing with Spirits making their way to the Domain of the Living, many of whom were atop all manner of extraordinary Spirit-creatures. Al and Mistress Magistery remained rooted to the spot, admiring the glorious scene until it subsided. But then they were distracted by another phenomenon. One occurring on the moor itself.

Dozens of white, smoky figures were floating towards them in a congregation. Al and Mistress Magistery had occasionally come across a lone Newly Departed Spirit during their travels, but never so many all at once.

"I think the Noble Possessions have been neglected long enough," Mistress Magistery told Al as the silent congregation turned round in an aimless fashion and began making its way in the opposite direction. "It's cruel to keep these Spirits in the dark and deny – at least some of them – their true forms. We'll adjourn our task for a little while, I think."

Al nodded before being whisked away on a thrilling rollercoaster once more.

"Oh, so you can't go straight through anymore?" he asked Mistress Magistery a few moments later.

They were standing in the clearing beneath Sundomum, surrounded by the jagged rocks.

"It's not much of a sacrifice. Quite a trivial one in fact, considering what's at stake. Queen Lamiobra is probably more than capable of impersonating me and fooling Sundomum itself. This place can never be fully secure as long as she's at large."

The pair of them having been deemed fit to enter Sundomum by the Oculus Plume, the jagged rocks rose and constructed the mighty stairs leading up to the palace. They began to climb them side by side. Al soon noticed that the great golden doors of Sundomum were gone. They had been replaced by a portcullis that looked semi-molten: it was glowing a bright orange, and Al began to sweat profusely as he got closer and closer. When they reached the top, the portcullis cooled into gleaming gold and whooshed up into the ochre-coloured stone at once – like it felt ashamed to bar the Spirit-noblest of Luxfons from her place of residence even for a split second.

Instead of striding into the hall, though, Mistress Magistery remained where she was. Al looked at her questioningly but did not receive a response – she seemed transfixed by the silver spire mounted on the great dome high, high above them.

"I could certainly do with a little more peace of mind," she muttered before raising a forefinger and pointing it at the spire.

A small peacock shot out of her fingertip with a high-pitched hoot. As he flew towards the spire, the Spirit-creature grew larger and larger, his majestic blue-and-green tail fluttering behind him like a regal mantle. When he finally reached his destination, he was the size of a Hawkanine and began to circle the gleaming monument on the dome, his lustrous blue head turning in all directions in rapid succession.

"He has my eyes," Mistress Magistery told a fascinated Al with a hint of pride in her voice, "which means I can see exactly what he's seeing at any given moment if I choose to. And his call will be able to reach me wherever I am – in Luxfons or even the Domain of the Living itself."

"Has he been positioned there *only* because it gives him the best view of Sundomum and its surroundings?"

"Very admirable, Al," said Mistress Magistery, smiling. "You, of course, imply that that's not the only reason, and you're correct." She leaned towards him and in a barely audible whisper, said, "I'm about to share something with you that not even your grandfather was privy to ... After Metanos tried to take it from me, I embedded the key to the vessel that contains the Power to Kill deep in that spire up there."

Al was struck by a crescendo of hope. "So even if they manage to get their hands on the vessel, they wouldn't be able to open it without the key?!"

"That only *may* be the case." Mistress Magistery

straightened up. “It would be a grave mistake to underestimate the combined might of Queen Lamiobra and Metanos *and* their army.”

15

A Friend's Loyalty

As the handsome peacock continued to orbit the silver spire without the slightest falter, Al and Mistress Magistery stepped into the hall. The gold portcullis came crashing down behind them before glowing bright orange again. Al's sorrow resurfaced at once at the sight of Alfred's empty throne – it seemed unnatural to be walking towards the trio of thrones without his grandfather and Robin by his side. Trying his best to suppress his tears from flowing, Al conjured his customary turquoise-coloured armchair, which, on this occasion, appeared so close to his grandfather's throne that the turquoise arm was touching the mahogany one.

Once they had taken their seats, Mistress Magistery brought the silver bell that had appeared in her hand close to her lips and said, "Spirit-nobles and Future Spirit-nobles, kindly return to Sundomum and bring Newly Departed Spirits with you." She then rang it as the enormous semi-circular bench materialised before them.

Ivar, Frederick and Morfox were the first to return, leading a huge group of Newly Departed Spirits into the hall. Before taking his place on the bench, Frederick, looking emotional, went up to Al.

"Sorry for your loss," he said, patting Al on the arm. "I think you're very brave to stay in Luxfons and help us. You've probably been told this already, but Chief Alfred would've been very proud of you."

All Al could do was nod and smile in response, not daring to say anything, lest he should break down.

Soon, the hall was brimming with phantom-like figures as the other Spirit-nobles and Future Spirit-nobles arrived with their invitees. They stood in silence in dozens of rows behind the now fully occupied bench.

"Before the Noble Possessions commence," began Mistress Magistery, looking grave, "we must address an issue which gave me cause for concern during my travels with Al and which should've given you all cause for concern too."

"The fact that Queen Lamiobra and Metanos knew about our task and had warned all their soldiers?" piped up Kerr.

"Indeed, Mister Weston," Mistress Magistery sighed. "We won't be able to fully accomplish our task as a result. Could any of you kindly shed some light on the matter?"

Her words were met with silence and blank faces all around.

"You didn't come across any suspicious characters who might've been observing your visits and could've then betrayed us to Queen Lamiobra and Metanos before you'd had the chance to visit *them*?"

The Spirit-nobles and Future Spirit-nobles shook their heads.

"Even though I find it hard to believe that any such Spirit would've been able to evade our notice," Hamelin said thoughtfully as he stroked Fickle (who was in the form of the white mouse), "it's still possible that one of their soldiers *was* cunning enough to do so."

Mistress Magistery nodded and said, "If this happens to be the reason behind the mystery, I'd certainly be disappointed in some of your abilities, but it would be the least concerning in the long run."

"Perhaps we're all being spied on by those dastardly hawk creatures," murmured Admiral Keel, turning his ancient head all round like he expected to spot one lurking in the hall. "I forget their names, but I do wish I had their spyglass-like eyes."

"Not all of them are bad," said Al, frowning. He could not help but defend the Hawkanine who had come to his sister's aid – not once, but twice.

"You're a very just young man." Admiral Keel doffed his bicorn hat to Al. "An essential quality for a Future Spirit-noblest, in my humble opinion."

"I, for one, don't believe any of the Hawkanines are spying on us," declared Lady Tyto. "Forgive my vulgar boast, Your Nobleness, but I'd have spotted them in spite of the great heights they can reach. My sight, after all, is only fractionally inferior to theirs."

"Really surprised we haven't touched upon another – far more disturbing – yet perfectly plausible reason behind the exposure of our task," complained Hexa. "We might have been betrayed by a Spirit who had already vowed to defend the Laws of Luxfons."

"Believe me, Miss Parr," asserted Mistress Magistery, leaning forward on the Great Throne, "that particular reason was the first to cross my mind, and the one that filled me with the most horror. If a Spirit has, indeed, joined the ranks of Queen Lamiobra and Metanos's army after assuring us of their goodness and loyalty, then they're full of as much darkness as their new masters, meaning that the calamity upon us has worsened a great deal."

"Oh, I hope beyond hope that's not the case!" cried Cloelia. "Don't think I could cope with any more downturns!" Her skeletal hand shot up to her equally as skeletal neck, which was now devoid of her horseshoe-shaped necklace.

"It's just a thought, Cloelia," Hexa assured her future successor.

"NO PUNISHMENT WOULD BE TOO HARSH FOR SUCH A SPIRIT!" thundered Polemus.

"Regardless of whether or not the existence of such a Spirit happens to be little more than a figment of our imagination," said Mistress Magistery, "we can be certain that a vast number of Spirits now stand against us under the protection of their master and mistress – hidden and unpunished. But Al and I were, at least, able to prevent one of them from escaping ..." She turned her head towards Lady Tyto. "A certain Agrius Poley-Babington."

Lady Tyto gulped. "I confess his recent change in apparel and demeanour did arouse my suspicions," she said.

"And yet you didn't act upon them ...?" Mistress Magistery's eyes widened with astonishment.

"I felt it was wrong to jump to conclusions without any proof," muttered Lady Tyto, averting her owl-like eyes from the unblinking green ones.

A long, intense silence followed her words before Mistress Magistery responded. "It's *unwise* to suppose that a wise principal may be applied in all situations. In these dark times, we cannot afford to be lenient."

"Of course, Your Nobleness," said Lady Tyto, nodding. "Of course."

"I'm glad to say that Al and I visited countless Spirits whose deep loyalty to our ways could not be questioned, however. And I hope you've all had a similarly heartening experience so far ..."

There was a general murmur of agreement all round.

"Some of my courageous mentees even sent me Communicative Flowers confirming what Your Nobleness had wisely assumed: that Queen Lamiobra and Metanos are, indeed, busily trying to amass more soldiers," boomed Ivar. "Having such courage in abundance in our arsenal surely means that we'll be victorious. I'm certain of it!"

"I'm glad you're optimistic, Lord Havelock," said Mistress Magistery, "but we must still continue with our task with no less fervour."

"Do we have Your Nobleness's permission to resume the task of helping our loved ones in the Domain of the Living at the same time?" asked Kerr. "Surely, I'm not the only one keen to do so, am I?" He leaned forwards and jerked his head from left to right a few times in rapid succession, the tassel on his mortarboard bouncing hither and thither.

Virginia was the first to assure him that he was not, followed by some of the others on the bench.

"Very well," said Mistress Magistery. "But in order to make up for the slower progress as a result, you should visit the remaining Spirits as individuals rather than in pairs. Future Spirit-nobles, you may go."

Without uttering a single word, Kerr and Virginia jumped off the bench, bowed to Mistress Magistery and were out of the hall before Frederick, Polemus and Cloelia had even finished saying their farewells. As the three Future Spirit-nobles and Morfox started to make their way through the vast crowd of silent Newly Departed Spirits, Ivar's booming voice made them stop and turn round.

"I've just had a remarkable idea!" he announced, a self-satisfied smile lighting up his large face. "Alongside carrying out our conventional tasks in the Domain of the Living, we can all share the privilege of being responsible for another task. One no less noble – that of guarding dear Alfred's family in their new abode!"

Al felt as though an invisible, icy claw had suddenly tightened round his throat. "They're not too exposed, are they?!"

"Not at all, young one," said Ivar. "I've ensured that they're remarkably well-hidden in a glorious spot on my own estate. They're also in possession of trumpets that will alert Her Nobleness at once if sounded and lead her directly to them. However, the resourcefulness of our enemies can never ever be underestimated, and it would be devastating if you were, once again, subjected to the pain you and dear Alfred went through – that of losing them. Hence, this extra measure!"

Al felt a great surge of affection for Ivar.

"It's settled," declared Mistress Magistery. "Your idea is truly commendable, Lord Havelock, and I'm sure Alfred would've been quite touched by it. I propose that this task commence immediately. As long as there's a need to carry it out, all Spirit-nobles and Future Spirit-nobles will no longer have restrictions imposed upon their freedom to visit the Domain of the Living."

She closed her eyes and murmured inaudibly under her breath for a little while.

"The Spirits-liminal are now aware of this particular Law," she said before turning to Ivar. "I suggest you show the Spirit-nobles and remaining Future Spirit-nobles where Al's family is residing right away."

Ivar bounced off his throne and gave Mistress Magistery one of his deep bows.

"Gather round, my noble fellows!" he commanded, tapping his cane with gusto on the ermine-patterned floor.

As Frederick and Morfox led Polemus and Cloelia back towards the bench, those sitting on it stood up. They all formed a compact semi-circle round Ivar.

"It really is a great idea, Chief Sir," Frederick told Ivar. "Morfox and I would be happy to be the first ones to carry out this task."

The handsome fox nodded and growled in approval.

"And you both shall," said Ivar. "We can then continue ... alphabetically. It's as good an order as any!"

He raised one of his fingers in the air and a glorious garland of red-and-white roses shot out of the end; it wreathed loosely round the whole group, including Ivar himself, who caught the two ends and fashioned them into a bow-shaped knot.

"Would you like to pay your family a little visit, young one?" he asked Al, smiling.

Al hesitated. He was missing them a great deal but knew how difficult it would be to leave them again if he was back in their midst. It also seemed more fitting to reunite with his loved ones in triumph – when the evil he was determined to help defeat no longer posed a grave threat to either world.

"I'm okay for the moment," replied Al. "Thanks, though."

Ivar looked a little surprised as he gave him a polite nod and turned back to those he had just festooned with roses.

"This will be a short but *far* from unpleasant journey," he told them before beseeching his Spirits-liminal to bring his Unsighted Gated to him as he had done on the Ragnarsson.

The entire garlanded group disappeared, as did the bench, leaving Al and Mistress Magistery facing a silent sea of smoky whiteness.

"Right," Mistress Magistery said with a friendly smile, "I'm afraid the Noble Possessions, which every Newly Departed Spirit in Luxfons must undergo, can only commence in the presence of Lord Havelock. Whilst we await his return, kindly introduce yourselves."

Not a single one of them mustered up the courage to speak, however.

"There's no need for coyness," persisted Mistress Magistery, her smile retaining its friendliness.

"*I* am not coy!"

One of the Newly Departed Spirits had bobbed forward from their position at the very centre of the frontmost row; they were extremely tall and looked particularly ghoulish.

"And what's your name?" Mistress Magistery's smile waned a little.

"Philip Armada."

"Welcome to Sundomum. I understand that you may be feeling a little impatient—"

"Yes, I am!" snapped Philip, prompting Al and Mistress Magistery to exchange looks of surprise. "You don't know how long I've been waiting to leave behind this ... this useless existence! I followed that buffoon who was sitting beside you for what seemed like days and days, listening to his lies about how soon our ordeal would be over.

He rambled on and on about the so-called privileges of being a true part of this world – which I found quite insensitive."

"Mister Armada," Mistress Magistery said sternly, "it's not in your best interest to criticise your potential mentor so harshly—"

"Even the scruffy blacksmith seemed less insufferable," interrupted Philip. "He was a little too sycophantic, though. I'm sure those who were with me would agree that the most tolerable of the trio was the fox!

"Anyway, to be *frank*, I want to be the first to undergo whatever it is we need to undergo when *His Lordship* returns."

Philip, though he had now fallen silent, remained firmly where he was.

"Kindly continue," Mistress Magistery said to the other Newly Departed Spirits, looking a little flustered.

None of them managed to introduce themselves in a noteworthier fashion than Philip Armada, however.

Shortly after the last of them (a rather nervous Jane Earnshaw) had done so, Ivar reappeared along with Hamelin, Admiral Keel, Lady Tyto and Hexa. As the other Spirit-nobles took their place on the bench (which had also reappeared in their midst), Ivar remained standing and was swiftly joined by Mistress Magistery.

The Nobles Possessions lasted for hours and hours, but Al felt no sense of relief when they came to an end. He had found trying to guess what form a Newly Departed Spirit would take once they had been Accepted rather fun, and his unspoken predictions were quite accurate more often than not. Almost every one of the Newly Departed Spirits present in the hall had become a Spirit of Luxfons. Philip Armada, though, was amongst a handful who had not and had to Depart. The Spirit-nobles who had been sitting on the bench – and, like Al, played no part in the Noble Possessions – joined their new mentees and began leading them out of the hall.

Soon, a mere thirteen newly Accepted Spirits remained. They were waiting in silence for Ivar – their mentor – who was slouched on his throne, his cane in danger of clattering to the floor.

"Lord Havelock," Mistress Magistery prompted him, "it's time to help your new mentees find abodes."

"Of course, Your Nobleness. Forgive me, forgive me."

Ivar almost lost his balance as he struggled to his feet. He then hobbled towards the knot of Spirits waiting patiently.

"Then again," said Mistress Magistery, "you may wish to return to Bloomturrim first for a little while to recover your strength ... Carrying out one Noble Possession can be strenuous enough, let alone dozens and dozens."

Ivar turned round slowly with a look of resoluteness on his face and said, "I'm confident that I'm able to fulfil the duty I owe to my new mentees immediately, but I wish to return to Bloomturrim for a short rest once it's been fulfilled – with Your Nobleness's permission ..."

Mistress Magistery gave him a firm nod, and he bowed in return.

"Come," he said to his mentees, "we must not keep our feathery chauffeur waiting any longer."

As soon as the portcullis had crashed down behind them, Mistress Magistery rose to her feet.

"Let's resume our noble task, Al – we have many more Spirits to see."

◆ ◆ ◆

Al and Mistress Magistery were standing on a wooden bridge in a gloriously autumnal part of Luxfons. They had visited a dozen more abodes and just left what looked like the Spirit-twin of a small, octagonal tollhouse, which was inhabited by a fiercely loyal elderly Spirit-couple. Before continuing with their journey, they were spending a few short moments admiring the array of colourful leaves floating down the River; the sheer beauty of the reds, yellows and bright browns in a bed of undisturbed blueness made Al feel like he had stepped into a painting. But he had not forgotten how untranquil the River could be too. And then he realised that he never discovered the reason behind its episode of mania …

"When we were going to Ancient Gates Wood on Lord Havelock's longship, the River suddenly became out of control—"

"Why wasn't I made aware of this?"

"I thought Grandad might have mentioned it – he wasn't there when it happened, but he definitely knew about it."

"I'm afraid he didn't, but I'm not at all surprised: he was concerned with more pressing matters at the time."

"So was I …" Al said with a shudder. "Was what the River did significant somehow?"

"It may very well be," muttered Mistress Magistery, her eyes glued to the enigmatic body of water flowing beneath them as though she was searching its depths for clues.

Just then, a gigantic red-and-white rose fell from the sky and came to a halt in front of them. Al and Mistress Magistery stared at it with wide eyes as its white petals turned red. And then the rose burst into a shower of blood-like droplets.

"Something's happened to Lord Havelock!" cried Mistress Magistery. "We must go to Bloomturrim at once!"

She, herself, burst into white light and they were away.

When their feet hit the ground again, they found themselves on a mound that was now not only covered in roses, but shards and shards of glittering glass too. Al and Mistress Magistery both jumped back and squirmed. The bottom portion of Ivar's face – completely detached from the rest and his neck – had risen into view out of the glassy rubble in a cushion of white vapour and come to a standstill mere inches from *their* faces. His mouth fell wide open and froze. A laboured and mournful voice flowed out of it – unmistakably his.

"They've destroyed my abode. My possessions. My Spirit-creature. And me. I'm in terrible pain. It's excruciating, and I long to Depart. But before I do, I must reveal that they want something of mine ... When they didn't acquire it from me, their rage was extraordinary. As extraordinary as the army they've amassed."

"What are they after?" Mistress Magistery gasped.

"My old cane. But I don't know the reason. It's in the Domain of the Living – I gave it to Old Missus Baba."

The terror Al was feeling rocketed. "Do Lamiobra and Metanos know this?" he choked.

"No," said Ivar. "I refused to reveal its whereabouts. I'd never betray dear Alfred's family. I told them to do their worst."

"I'm so, *so* sorry." It was all Al could say.

"Your grandfather wasn't only my friend, but a Spirit I truly looked up to. Luxfons needs him more than ever right now. Much more than it needs me. I admit I was petrified of the evil that flourishes in these dark times and knew deep down that my abilities were better suited to happier times – however much I tried to pretend otherwise due to the shame I felt."

"Your unwavering loyalty to your friend and his family and to our Laws has elevated you above all the Spirits of Luxfons in my eyes, Lord Havelock," Mistress Magistery said tearily.

As Al nodded with all his might, the half-face began to fade, and a moment later, it was gone.

16

A Relic from the Distant Past

Al and Mistress Magistery left the site of Bloomturrim's destruction behind and headed directly to Vulcanest.

They had agreed that it would be best to tell Frederick about Ivar's Departure first, before resummoning the Spirit-nobles and Future Spirit-nobles to Sundomum as a whole. As the Unsighted Gates had just closed, Mistress Magistery thought Frederick and Morfox would be back at Vulcanest for a little recuperation after their visit to the Domain of the Living. Al knew that Frederick would be devastated on hearing the news and would appreciate some time in the company of his loved ones to come to terms with the loss of his friend and mentor.

The beam of white light morphed into the figures of Al and Mistress Magistery at the foot of the hillock. They had only taken a couple of steps towards Vulcanest when a sudden cry of "Your Nobleness!" stopped them in their tracks and made them turn round. Alcea, carrying Morfox in her arms and looking somewhat flustered, was descending the hillock towards them. As she placed Morfox on the ground next to her, Al noticed that her curly hair was now adorned with many more gold stars, though her dress looked as shabby as ever.

"We've come to see Mister Hancock," Mistress Magistery told her, the solemnity in her voice remaining unmasked.

The smile on Alcea's moon-shaped face faded, and she said, "He's with Silvester – I'll take you to him."

She and Morfox led them to the red door of Vulcanest in silence, and it flung open of its own accord when they reached it.

"After you." Alcea stepped aside and nodded curtly at her guests.

Morfox leapt out of their way to wait beside Alcea, and Al and Mistress Magistery crossed the threshold into the sitting room of Vulcanest, closely followed by the handsome Spirit-creature and his mistress.

"Your Nobleness! Al! What a pleasant surprise!"

Frederick, who had been sitting with Silvester on the settee and mending one of his tin toys by candlelight, got to his feet immediately, his face aglow with warmth. He bowed to Mistress Magistery and shook Al's hand before offering them the two chairs opposite the settee. As he sat back down next to a now shy-looking Silvester, Alcea slid onto the settee beside him.

"I'm afraid we don't bring glad tidings, Mister Hancock ..."

Al found it heart-breaking to witness his friend's increasing despair as Mistress Magistery enlightened him about Ivar's fate; the young blacksmith's kind face was studded with tears by the time she finished, and he placed his head into his arms and sobbed. Alcea and Silvester moved closer to him and put their arms round him, whilst Morfox rubbed his head affectionately against his master's legs.

"Does this mean my husband is now a Spirit-noble?"

Alcea asked Mistress Magistery with wide eyes.

"It does."

"That doesn't really matter right now," Frederick sighed, looking up and drying his hairy face with the back of his hand. "The question we should be asking is: why do Queen Lamiobra and Metanos want Chief Ivar's old cane?"

"I wish I had an answer," lamented Mistress Magistery, "but I don't."

"I think I do, though." Al sat up. The realisation had struck him like a lightning bolt; *that has to be it.* "The cane has protective powers. I'm sure of it. When Robin rescued me from the Hawkanines, he took me straight to Bloomturrim because he sensed I'd be safe there, and he was right: the Hawkanines couldn't follow us inside. And the Hawkanine that rescued Karen also took her to Bloomturrim – it must have sensed that the building was somehow protected too!"

"That's it!" cried Frederick. "It all makes sense! Metanos tried really hard to harm Chief Ivar in Ancient Gates Wood, but he wasn't able to. He must have worked out that Chief Ivar had something which protected him and probably wanted to make sure he was right!"

Mistress Magistery seemed to have frozen in her chair. The shock on her pearly face soon dissipated into what was unmistakably guilt, however.

"What a fool I've been." The self-loathing in her voice was such that Al found it almost heart-wrenching to hear. "I could very well have saved Lord Havelock from annihilation if I hadn't been so, *so* foolish. When I found out that the decision Robin had made on Christmas Day turned out to be the right one to protect Al, I ... I quite wrongly assumed that Metaons still harboured some respect for his former Spirit-noble at the time, and that's why the Hawkanines didn't dare infiltrate Bloomturrim. And I didn't even question why the Hawkanine that rescued Karen took her there of all places! Oh, how utterly foolish of me."

"No Spirit is perfect, Your Nobleness," said Frederick. "No Spirit is immune from making mistakes. Just like those in the Domain of the Living."

"The Spirit-noblest, however, cannot always use that excuse to disregard their mistakes and be at peace. I'm responsible for the welfare of Non-Spirits and the Spirits of Luxfons alike – a truly unenviable task."

She glanced at Al as she finished speaking. He avoided her gaze and stared at the floor, fiddling with his peacock-feather sash and feeling daunted by the inevitable tribulations he would have to face when he was in the same position as the Spirit sitting beside him. But his thoughts were soon displaced by a more pressing matter.

"So, what needs to be done about the cane?" he asked Mistress Magistery, looking up. "It must be a powerful object if Lamiobra and Metanos had to bring their army in order to retrieve it from Lord Havelock."

Mistress Magistery remained silent for a few moments, the others observing her closely.

"That decision is entirely in your hands, Al," she said finally. "The choice you make will have a direct impact on the welfare of your loved ones.

"On the one hand, the cane can remain where it is, providing them with a powerful layer of protection but at the same time, giving Queen Lamiobra and Metanos another reason to find them if they discover where it is. On the other hand, the cane can be hidden elsewhere, which means your loved ones will lose that extra layer of protection, *but* the risk of them being hunted reduces dramatically. Remember, if you decide that it should stay with them and our secrets become known to Queen Lamiobra and Metanos, the combined might of their powers and the powers of their soldiers may overcome the protection the cane affords."

Al gulped and was about to tell Mistress Magistery that he needed time to think before he could make such a momentous decision, but there was no need …

"There's no rush," she told him. "You can inform us all about the decision you've made back in Sundomum after Mister Hancock's Ennoblement."

"*What?* Your Nobleness wants me to replace Chief Ivar as a Chief Spirit-noble?"

"I could really do with a Spirit like you by my side, Mister Hancock."

"But I've just acceded Chief Ivar as a Spirit-noble," argued Frederick. "Surely, the other Spirit-nobles are more qualified than I am."

"But Her Nobleness has chosen you, dearest," Alcea told her husband, squeezing his arm. "She – has – chosen – you. This isn't the time to be modest."

"You'll be amazing, Frederick!" enthused Al.

Frederick smiled appreciatively at Al before informing Mistress Magistery – not without an air of hesitancy – that he would accept the role of her deputy.

"I'm glad," said Mistress Magistery, smiling.

She rose to her feet and gestured that Al and the Hancocks should do the same.

"I've parted with tradition somewhat, Mister Hancock, by conjuring the vehicle of your tenure before your Ennoblement. It's outside. I thought a certain Spirit-creature of yours, who will no doubt be flying it, might like to get acquainted with it as soon as possible."

They all followed Mistress Magistery out of the house to look at what Al assumed was going to be a grand wheelless carriage, quite like the ones his grandfather and Ivar had been given, but he was wrong. Standing near the open doors of the forge was a bronze chariot; its long pole, which was not yet attached to any Spirit-creature, was painted brightly with peacock feathers, as were each of the spokes on its wheels.

Frederick seemed too overcome with emotion at the sight of the chariot to say anything apart from a teary "Your Nobleness – thank you."

Alcea, on the other hand, remained completely silent.

The sound of creaking metal filled the air, and they all looked up.

"Kiang!" cried Al.

The bronze donkey was circling down towards them, his huge wings looking no less graceful than that of a bird, and he landed in front of the chariot with great skill.

"It certainly seems like you've embraced your new role, Kiang," Mistress Magistery chuckled, going over to him to pat his shiny head. "It won't be too long before your master summons you to Sundomum. The skies are yours to roam as much as you like in the meantime!"

A moment later, Kiang was fully harnessed and hitched to the chariot. He rocketed towards the unending blueness with a deafening clatter, and Silvester burst into gleeful applause.

◆ ◆ ◆

"Well," said Mistress Magistery, turning to Al, "have you come to a decision regarding Lord Havelock's cane?"

Frederick had just been Ennobled and was now sitting on Ivar's former throne with Morfox beside him, and Al, once more, found himself being scrutinised by many pairs of keen eyes. But he did not avert his gaze this time.

"I have," he declared. "The cane should stay where it is – with my family."

He had thought long and hard and felt sure it was the right decision. He could not imagine how Queen Lamiobra and Metanos would ever discover that the cane was with his family, nor where they themselves were. And the idea of his loved ones having a powerful, albeit mysterious, object that was further cocooning them from any evil intentions was one he found very comforting.

Mistress Magistery nodded and smiled at Al before turning to the eight Spirit-nobles and Future Spirit-nobles on the bench before her.

"Now, you're not excused from the task of guarding Al's family because I cannot say with any certainty that the level of protection the cane affords is impenetrable. When the Unsighted Gates open, it will be your turn to carry out this noble task, Miss Iceni. Kindly take Mister Weston and Miss Walsingham with you to show them the location."

Cloelia nodded vigorously, looking as anxious as ever.

"You must make Al's family aware about the importance of what they now have," Mistress Magistery continued with earnestness. "And this is what you must do if—"

Whoosh!

Mistress Magistery gasped. And so did Al. And so did Frederick.

The portcullis had been sucked up by the thick stone and a Hawkanine had flown into the hall. The enormous

Spirit-creature was finding it difficult to stay airborne, however, and staggered to the floor near the base of a pillar as the portcullis crashed down behind it.

Al, the Spirits and Morfox hurried across the vast space to where the Hawkanine lay in a flailing heap. Its plume was heavily scorched and had even burnt away completely in places, and its once bright, yellow eyes were now dull and blackened and had receded into their sockets. It opened its sabre-like beak and started to speak in a deep, clear voice that exhibited no trace of antagonism whatsoever:

"I'm Clemerc, Lord of the Hawkanines, and I've come here to ask for help."

"Are you the same Hawkanine who took my sister to Bloomturrim and then saved us both from Marshal's sword?!" cried Al.

"The very same," said Clemerc. "I paid a heavy price for those actions, but I wouldn't hesitate to repeat them. My former master's growing darkness wasn't able to extinguish the light inside me, but the same, alas, can't be said about my remaining brothers."

"What happened to you, Clemerc?" Mistress Magistery asked gently, crouching to observe his injuries.

"Immediately after the events at the Orangery, I was stripped of my powers and imprisoned on Epis Islet," Clemerc replied with a terrible flinch. "And I wasn't the only one. Queen Lamiobra created chains with minds and wills of their own. They not only keep those she's deemed to be traitors bound on that rock, but also inflict the worst kind of pain I've ever experienced on their prisoners. They're *searingly* hot. Rather like the gate you have here to deter evil."

"These Spirit-creature-like chains were first created

by Raja Nawab," said Mistress Magistery, looking very uneasy, "but his never harmed their prisoners. I'll be back in a moment or two with something that will, to some extent, alleviate your injuries, Clemerc."

Mistress Magistery sprinted back to her throne, and when she rejoined the throng around Clemerc, she was carrying a bright blue vial. Al recognised it immediately as the one that contained the concoction with healing properties. She unstopped it, and its watery contents spurted out all over the distressed Hawkanine before the vial and stopper vanished. The effect was almost instantaneous: Clemerc's plume was whole again, though a little thin and blackened here and there, and his eyes regained their colour, but they were not quite as bright as they once were and still stuck deep in their sockets. He thanked Mistress Magistery, however, and managed to lift himself up onto his clawed feet without much difficulty.

"How did you escape from the chains on the islet thing?" probed Al

"With the aid of the latest prisoner," replied Clemerc. "She happened to be powerful enough to resist the chains for a few moments and was also noble enough to free me. This led to her being doubly bound from head to toe – she had no choice but to end her suffering and Depart." His partially healed eyes filled with tears. "And then another prisoner – already bound – gave me a voice and told me to seek out Your Nobleness; he suffered the same fate. I implore you to help the others on the Islet and bring their suffering to an end. I fear that their desire to continue with their task in the Domain of the Living and to make amends for their wrongdoings will not sustain their resilience to such torture for long!"

"Of course, I'll help them, Clemerc," declared Mistress

Magistery. "Will you join me, Al? Your sword will be an invaluable tool in this particular task."

Al nodded without hesitation, subconsciously slipping his hand into his pocket and closing it round the cold handle of the miniaturised weapon.

"Would it be wise for any of us to join Your Nobleness too?" enquired Kerr.

"I don't believe so, no," Mistress Magistery said firmly.

"But Your Nobleness ..." protested Polemus, the permanent frown etched on his large, sweaty face becoming more intense, "you may need further assis—"

"These chains were made to have an extremely powerful affinity for the Spirits of Luxfons," said Mistress Magistery. "Their affinity for Spirit-creatures, on the other hand, is not as powerful; this is why Clemerc was able to be freed. The remaining prisoners on Epis Islet cannot be freed by *any* of our powers. The only chance of hope they now have is Marshal's sword. In these calamitous times, I cannot allow the Spirit-nobles and Future Spirit-nobles to go anywhere near the Islet and risk being bound and tortured until they're forced to Depart!"

A tense silence followed her words until it was finally broken by Frederick.

"Your Nobleness," he said with trepidation in his voice, "as your Chief Spirit-noble, I must humbly discourage *you* to go to Epis Islet as well. Because of what you've just told us."

The other Spirits murmured their agreement.

Mistress Magistery seemed taken aback for a moment before sighing and saying, "Al may require guidance ..."

"I'll be fine on my own," said Al. And he meant it. There was not an infinitesimal amount of fear or self-doubt festering inside him.

The Spirits surrounding him were full of high praise. (Admiral Keel doffed his bicorn hat twice and Hamelin and Kerr doffed their respective hats too.)

"I'll gladly take you to that place," Clemerc told Al, bowing his copper-coloured head. "But before I do, I have another duty to fulfil. I must break the vow of silence I made to my former master and reveal that he and Queen Lamiobra do not only desire the Power to Kill, but also—"

"Lord Havelock's cane," finished Mistress Magistery.

Clemerc expressed surprise that they were already aware of this.

"We've figured out that it will provide its possessor some protection from harm," Mistress Magistery told him. "But that's all we know. We don't know why it has such powers or where Lord Havelock got it from – whether he created it or—"

"He didn't create it in its entirety," interrupted Clemerc.

It was as though the Hawkanine was suddenly in the midst of numerous stone statues, the frozen eyes of which were on him and him alone as he continued:

"The cane's rose-shaped finial was created long, long before Lord Havelock was even born. It's actually a very small silver trinket box, and it contains a lock of Raja Nawab's hair, which he gave to Queen Lamiobra as a token of his love. It had been lost for many centuries, and when the alliance between my former master and Queen Lamiobra was formed, the task to find it was given to us Hawkanines – our eyesight made us the perfect candidates. Queen Lamiobra gave us the power to create Spiritsnuff as a reward for accepting the task.

"She refused all opportunities to escape from the Orangery when Marshal was momentarily under the influence of Spiritsnuff until she had the lock of hair again – the ultimate protection from his sword. Although we scoured Luxfons and tried our utmost to find it, our efforts were to no avail. And then by chance, we discovered that Bloomturrim had the sort of protection the lock of hair would afford. When it was confirmed by my former master in Ancient Gates Wood – in my very presence – that the lock of hair was, indeed, in Lord Havelock's possession, Queen Lamiobra declared that as soon as her army was vast enough, it would have a second purpose: help her retrieve what was once hers from Lord Havelock.

"He must be protected along with his cane: I fear that he'll be attacked at any moment ..."

Mistress Magistery stayed stone-like for a few moments, her mouth slightly open, before rousing and muttering, "It's too late to protect Lord Havelock, but they don't have the cane." She then smiled widely, looked round at the others and cheerily said, "And they never will, unless it's handed over to them, which is a ludicrous idea! Queen Lamiobra is wrong. The protection provided by the lock of hair could never be breached, even if all the Spirits in Luxfons tried to breach it in unison. It's part of Raja Nawab himself." She turned to Al. "Did you by any chance come into direct contact with Lord Havelock's cane on the Ragnarsson before the River ceased to be serene?"

Al thought long and hard and then he remembered. "I did. Just before the River went all crazy, I picked his cane up because it had fallen down. Why is that important?"

"That proves beyond any doubt whatsoever that Raja Nawab's lock of hair is contained within the cane!" Mistress Magistery's smile progressed swiftly into a jovial laugh – the delight on her pearly face made it look even more lustrous. "The River mistook you for Raja Nawab when you handled the cane, Al; the fusion of the extraordinary powers you possess and a part of Raja Nawab temporarily awoke the River from a deep sleep. It behaved as it used to behave centuries ago whenever it sensed that Raja Nawab was near, in reverent tribute to him. Raja Nawab – the first Spirit of Luxfons – was not born in the Domain of the Living, but emerged from the River itself. As strange as it may seem, their relationship was like that of a mother and her child.

"The fact that we have a part of Raja Nawab is more comforting than I can convey!"

"Does this mean we'll surely be victorious?" enthused Kerr.

"We can never speak of the future with certainty, Mister Weston," said Lady Tyto.

"We can make an exception on this occasion, Lady Tyto," argued Hexa. "Just consider this: *all* their attacks on Sundomum will fail miserably if we bring the cane here in time from the Domain the Living. We are all sure to survive these dark times, and believe me when I say, I know a thing or two about surviving!"

"If the cane is brought here, Miss Parr," Lady Tyto replied cuttingly, "Al's family will no longer be as protected."

"There's actually a simple solution to this quandary," remarked Hamelin as he conjured a blackberry for Fickle (who was in the form of the white mouse and perched on his shoulder). "Al's family can be secretly relocated to Sundomum too ..."

"That's what I was going to suggest, Mister Buck," Mistress Magistery told him, nodding. "What do you think, Al?"

"Seems like the only concrete way to stop Lamiobra and Metanos from getting the Power to Kill *and* keep my family safe," Al sighed. "Happy for them to be brought here if they don't mind – I'm sure they'll understand, considering what's at stake here."

"Thank you, Al," said Mistress Magistery. "Miss Iceni, Mister Weston and Miss Walsingham will be seeing them when the Unsighted Gates reopen and can propose the idea of relocation then.

"Right, Mister Hancock ... Frederick – I suggest you find your future successor amongst your new mentees as soon as possible. Do you already have a Spirit in mind?"

"Well ..." began Frederick, but he was interrupted almost at once –

"Mistress!" growled Morfox.

Frederick smiled apologetically at Mistress Magistery, but she seemed humoured by the abruptness with which Morfox had spoken.

"I'm sure Missus Hancock will be delighted with the news and make a fine Future Spirit-noble," she said before turning to the other Spirits. "I would still like you all to resume your task with no less fervour than before. Lady Tyto is correct in that we cannot take anything for granted when it comes to the future, and the more allies we have vowing to come to our aid if called upon, the better." She turned to Al. "You must take this to Epis Islet."

She conjured a small silver bugle attached to a green cord. She put this round Al's neck, and the bugle came to rest on his chest, against his peacock-feather sash.

"Sound this if you need my help," she told him. "I'll await your return here after I've paid Hermit a visit."

Al nodded and thanked her as Clemerc crouched in

front of him, allowing him to climb onto his back. The Hawkanine's feathers were incredibly tough, as though they not only resembled copper in colour, but had been infused with it too. As Al's ears rang with farewells and yet more praise, Clemerc rose into the air and glided towards the portcullis, which, in an instant, had turned from bright orange to gleaming gold and shot up to let them pass.

17

Epis Islet

It felt to Al that they had now been flying for at least a day, but Clemerc still seemed determined to carry on. They had passed over snowy terrains and summery meadows; forests, fields and many a mountain, mire and moor; and countless abodes – from inconspicuous huts to mighty castles. A hungry and exhausted Al requested that they stop and rest for a short while, and Clemerc, to his enormous relief, agreed.

He circled down from the sky to land on a hillside sheltered by richly blossoming trees and shrubs. Al climbed off Clemerc's back and settled on the grass against a mossy tree trunk, visualising a hamper full of delicious delicacies appearing next to him, which it did. As he feasted on turkey sandwiches and jam tarts, savouring every bite, Clemerc kept fidgeting and looking up at the sky.

Al was about to tell Clemerc, with a degree of reluctance, that he was willing to continue with their journey without further delay, but he then resolved that it was more important – for both him and Clemerc – to recuperate as much as possible for the task ahead. He decided, therefore, to try and distract the Spirit-creature from the worries born out of his nobleness for the duration of their respite.

"So, Clemerc ..." he began a little awkwardly before taking a sip of some tea, "which of the Hawkanines were you exactly in our garden on Christmas Day?" It was the only question he could think of, but it had the desired effect.

Clemerc embarrassedly said, "I was the one who failed to subdue your Spirit with my Spiritsnuff and was then attacked by Chief Alfred's Spirits-liminal."

"Oh," was the only response Clemerc got in return, which was uttered with no less embarrassment than his own.

It was followed by an uncomfortable silence for a short while before Al asked him another question – one that he genuinely wanted to know the answer to:

"What do the Spirits-liminal actually look like?"

"They're indescribable," Clemerc said at once. "I can't give you an idea of what they look like because they're nothing like any other beings I've seen in Luxfons or the Domain of the Living."

"How would Lamiobra and Metanos deal with them *if* they succeeded in keeping the Unsighted Gates open permanently? They're bound to object, aren't they? It's their job to object."

"My former master would create many more Hawkanines – one for each Unsighted Gate. They would keep the Spirits-liminal inactive indefinitely with their Spiritsnuff."

"The nasty piece of work has thought of everything!" Al said through gritted teeth.

"He wasn't always so villainous," Clemerc said a little sadly. "But his greatest vice has always been excessive pride – even when he was in the Domain of the Living."

"How would you—?"

"Like my brothers, the Connection I had with my former master was very similar to the one between a Spirit of Luxfons and their loved ones in the Domain of the Living – perhaps even more profound because it worked both ways and allowed us to communicate telepathically. I was able to look into his thoughts *and* his memories. His pride, ultimately, led him to the dark path that he's taken."

Al listened closely as Clemerc continued:

"For many years, he carried out his tasks nobly as a Chief Spirit-noble and managed to ignore his pride, which was constantly making him feel that his powers weren't being utilised to their full potential. Everything changed when, out of curiosity, he persuaded Marshal to let him into the Orangery and discovered that Queen Lamiobra was not, in actual fact, entombed in stone at all. She ensured that he could no longer ignore his pride, and then it grew, feeding the darkness inside him along the way.

"His desire to use his powers freely complemented Queen Lamiobra's ultimate desire to rule rather than serve – a desire he, too, became seduced by. These desires made him more and more indifferent to the suffering his planned revolution would cause. But his genuine belief that it may benefit others apart from Queen Lamiobra and himself – however small that number in the end – has also played some part in the indifference he now feels."

"Is there any hope that he might – somehow – go back to the way he was before he met Lamiobra?"

As soon as he had asked the question, Al regretted it. He felt foolish for having entertained what he now perceived to be a ludicrous thought, even though it seemed quite plausible for a split second.

"It might be too late," Clemerc said simply.

"I think you're right. Shall we carry on with our journey?"

◆ ◆ ◆

"We're nearly there!" Clemerc yelled over the sound of his own beating wings.

They were flying over the glassy blue surface of a tranquil ocean. Al found it astonishing that the outstanding beauty beneath him would soon be tarnished. And then he heard it. At first, he thought it was the wind, but it quickly became apparent that it was the muffled sound of wailing that was filling the air. It was getting louder and louder and clearer and clearer as they moved closer and closer to its source: a black speck, surrounded by pure blueness, getting larger and larger in the distance.

They were there. Clemerc began to descend gingerly as the wails turned into anguished pleas for help. Epis Islet was a flat, oval-shaped rock, no bigger than a barge and surmounted by a small, partially ruined stone tower. It looked like a tiny lighthouse and was painted brightly with images of fountains. A dozen Spirits were slumped all around this tower and tethered to it with chains. These were long and thick and wrapped around each Spirit's arms, legs and waist – every single link of every single chain was burning a bright, ferocious orange.

Clemerc landed as far away as he could from the tower on the very edge of the Islet. As Al dismounted, the Hawkanine let out a cry that momentarily drowned the anguished pleas – a dormant chain had lunged at him like a snake, missing his beak by mere inches.

Al did not hesitate. He withdrew the powerful weapon from his pocket, and it turned from a copper-tipped dagger into a copper-tipped sword once again. The burning chain had fallen onto the rocky ground with a great metallic clatter, but it was now rising again ... Al struck it with the sword as hard as he could. The chain froze in mid-air and burnt a little brighter than before. It then fell, charred and broken.

"Yes!" cried Al, punching the air.

The pleas for help intensified.

"Best if you stay here, Clemerc," said Al, edging towards the Spirits, his sword aloft and his blue eyes fixed on the twelve fiends of fiery metal he was about to vanquish.

Clemerc gladly obliged and stayed rooted to the spot.

Al struck the chains one by one with the sword, destroying each of them and liberating the prisoners from their torment. He had not felt gladder to have the ability to wield Marshal's sword. If hundreds of such chains sprang out of Epis Islet, he would have happily cut those down too. He held the sword up like a trophy, his thin fingers wrapped tightly around the golden hilt, determined to never part with it until the dark times were over.

But Al's ecstasy soon diminished. Now that his task had been fulfilled, he was able to focus his attention fully on those he had just freed. Despite their eagerness to express their gratitude, the Spirits were all in a terrible state. Their clothing was heavily singed, and they were covered in dark gashes from head to toe. These looked incredibly painful and were emitting what looked like white vapour, which seemed to be becoming gradually less dense.

"What *is* that?" Al asked a tall male Spirit with some trepidation, pointing at the wisps of vapour escaping from a huge gash on his hand with Marshal's sword.

"The damaged part of us, Sir," he replied weakly. "It's beyond repair, so we're letting it go. It'll be gone soon. We'll never be whole again, and nor will our powers."

"So – it's true ..." said an old female Spirit with gnarled features, who kept flinching with pain. "You – Chief Alfred's grandson – are as p-powerful as they say. Luxfons is lucky to – have you."

"Let me take you all back to Sundomum," implored Al. "You need Mistress Magistery's help. She'll be able to give you something to make you better and get rid of your pain."

A high-pitched wail rang out, making Al jump. It had come from a bulky male Spirit, who was standing closest to Al and whose rugged face was wet with tears. For a moment, Al thought he had been recaptured by a chain that had somehow lain hidden and escaped annihilation, but this was not the case.

"We're not worthy of such kindness," cried the bulky Spirit before letting out another wail. "We betrayed Her Nobleness. And we betrayed ourselves. We're not even worthy enough to help those that we love – this must be our ultimate punishment!"

"No," Al said kindly, "it's okay—NO!"

The bulky Spirit dived towards Marshal's sword, making Al leap backwards. He fell onto the hard rock and broken chains, painfully grazing both his hands. And then he heard an almighty splash behind him. The pain that was making him scowl seemed to vanish all of a sudden as he realised what had happened. Al sprang up to his feet.

"Why did you make me do *that for*?!" He spat at the bulky spirit, who was now sobbing into his huge hands. "If I can't get that sword back, they may never be defeated! Everything will then be over – for my world *and* yours!"

"I wouldn't have b-been able to b-bring myself to Depart otherwise," the bulky Spirit lamented without lowering his hands.

Al yelled out in frustration. Before any idea of what to do next had arisen in his mind, there was another almighty splash behind him. Clemerc and the Spirits gasped as Al spun round. And then he, too, gasped.

A figure – perfectly dry – had emerged out of the Ocean and was now floating in the air above the Islet, though it was wingless. It was the figure of a small, putto-like boy clothed in a simple blue-and-white garment. His hair was curly and golden and had a strange luminous quality to it, and his cheeks and lips were of the deepest crimson. The smile on his bulbous face was radiating absolute contentment and serenity.

"What ... I mean ... who are you?" asked Al.

The Spirit-boy giggled shyly and with a sweet voice, said, "My name is Epis." He pointed at the tower. "That's where I used to live!"

"*You're* Epis?" piped up Clemerc. "The mentor of Raja Nawab himself?"

Epis giggled even more shyly and nodded.

The confusion fogging Al's mind did not become any less dense as those around him gasped yet again.

"What were you doing in the Ocean?" Al probed further.

"I was put in horrible chains and thrown in by Raja Nawab's consort," said Epis, his jolly countenance faltering for a moment. "But they were cut away by the shiny sword! I was able to finally break through the surface – after ages and ages!"

"Why did Lamiobra do this to you?" Al felt disgusted.

"To stop me from telling Raja Nawab what she'd asked me," replied Epis. "She came to see me once without him. And ..." Epis hesitated and giggled shyly yet again. "And because I know everything there is to know about Luxfons, she asked me how the Unsighted Gates could be kept open forever. And I gave her the answer, even though I thought it was a bit of an odd question. What was even more odd was when she tried to make me promise not to tell Raja Nawab. I said that I was really sorry, but I couldn't keep any secrets from the Spirit-noblest of Luxfons. She then became angry – I was so frightened!" Epis shuddered as he finished.

Although Al had no intention of causing Epis any more distress, he proceeded to tell him in great detail about the crisis they were all facing at present because of the evil Spirit who had imprisoned him such a long time ago. Al was hoping that the all-knowing Spirit-boy would be able to help: to give them a swift and simple way to bring the dark times to an end ...

"You're not telling the truth!" Epis looked scared and confused. "I don't know why you're lying, but please stop it!"

Al was dumbstruck, but Clemerc and the Spirits emphatically stated that what he was saying was, indeed, the absolute truth.

"No, no, I won't believe it!" persisted Epis, shaking his head and on the verge of tears. "Raja Nawab would not let such darkness stay in Luxfons. Never ever."

"But he's not here!" Al finally blurted out.

"Even if he has Departed Luxfons," said Epis, "as the

first Spirit-noblest, he can return if his legacy is at risk. If things are as bad as you say they are, he would've come back by now to put them right!"

"He hasn't come back, though!" Al said desperately. "And things *are* as bad as we say – you have to believe us! Please – tell us how to bring him back."

Epis shook his head again, placing his fat palms against his ears, and floated upwards.

"I have to go now," he said. "The Ocean wouldn't let me. I've been waiting ages to be at peace."

And with a final look of distrust and fear, Epis became smoky and shapeless and was engulfed by the air.

The sword! Al had been staring at the spot of nothingness where Epis had been floating moments earlier, trying to digest what he had been told, when he suddenly remembered that the greatest weapon they had against Queen Lamiobra and Metanos and their army was now buried deep inside the Ocean. *I have to get it back at any cost.*

"Clemerc – can you help me? Need you to use your sight to find Marshal's sword."

"I'll try," said Clemerc. "My eyes are not nearly as powerful as they used to be, but I will try."

He and Al stood right on the edge of the Islet, and Clemerc's yellow eyes scanned the blueness beneath him.

"I see it!" he said after a little while before taking off and touching an inconspicuous part of the blueness with one of his great talons. "It's here."

"How deep is it?" Al asked without taking his unblinking eyes off the spot Clemerc had indicated as he flew back to his side.

"It's quite a long way down now – and still going."

Al focussed as hard as he could on the glassy spot in his

sights.

"It's stopped!" said Clemerc. "And now it's moving up towards us very fast, indeed! Nearly there ..."

The image of the golden hilt bursting out of the blueness was burning into Al's mind, and his excitement was growing. He did not doubt that, in a mere moment or two, he would be beholding that image in reality. But he was wrong –

"Oh no," sighed Clemerc.

"*What?!*"

"It won't break through the surface. It's just beneath it – but trapped. Don't let it fall again!"

Al was beginning to feel fatigued, but not even a shadow of the idea of resting crossed his mind. Without averting his eyes from the spot they had been glued to for what seemed like a very long time to him now, he asked the Spirits to come to his aid. They rushed over to him, in spite of their unhealed injuries. But all their efforts were in vain: the sword remained where it was, and the surface of the Ocean remained as smooth and glassy and impenetrable as ever.

Al realised that he only had one option left. Without looking at it, he lifted the small silver bugle hanging close to his rapidly beating heart and blew into it as hard as he could. The glorious sound it made was still ringing in Al's ears when the beam of white light hit the Islet like a bolt of lightning, finally making him avert his eyes.

"The sword's trapped in the Ocean!" he cried as soon as Mistress Magistery had morphed into her true form.

She was clutching a much larger version of the vial that contained the healing concoction, and she unstopped it as she approached them. The Spirits, bowing, scrambled out of the way to let her pass, and each of them was showered generously with the concoction before the vial and stopper vanished. She came to stand beside Al and Clemerc in silence, her narrowed eyes piercing the Ocean with unfaltering fierceness.

The surface of the Ocean cowered under her gaze: it began to bubble and froth ... And then, at last, yielded Marshal's sword, which did, indeed, burst out as Al had envisioned – like a torpedo. It hurtled towards him, and he caught it by its golden hilt with ease. As soon as it had shrunk down to a dagger again, Al placed it safely in his pocket, sighing with relief.

"The Ocean probably thought it was full of too much darkness to be released," said Mistress Magistery. "What actually happened?"

"Well ..."

Mistress Magistery was shocked to hear about Epis's emergence from the Ocean and the circumstances of his entrapment. She became a little emotional and told Al she always believed Epis had Departed prematurely, as did Raja Nawab, who was devastated –

"He loved and respected Epis. They emerged out of the River together—"

"Epis said Raja Nawab's able to come back and should've done so by now because of what's happening! He didn't tell us how or anything but said he definitely could!"

Mistress Magistery looked sceptical and said, "Were this to be the case, Raja Nawab would've told me during the Noble Succession: when, just before Departing, he handed the Noble Powers over to me. He told me no such thing, however."

Al's heart sank; *Epis seemed so sure.*

Mistress Magistery turned round to face the newly

healed Spirits, who fell to their knees, pleading for her forgiveness and vowing to stand with her in the fight against Queen Lamiobra and Metanos.

"I welcome your declarations of loyalty," Mistress Magistery told them, smiling and nodding. "Kindly accompany us to Sundomum, where you'll be questioned thoroughly on the activities of your former masters. It's important to gather as much information—ah, the Unsighted Gates are open again."

"May we first continue with our task in the Domain of the Living, Your Nobleness?" the bulky Spirit asked gingerly.

"You may," Mistress Magistery replied after a few moments of contemplation.

The twelve Spirits' enthusiastic cries of gratitude filled the air as they got to their feet. Each sprouted angel-like wings and, one by one, flew off the Islet towards their respective Unsighted Gates.

"It's about time I resumed *my* tasks in the Domain of the Living too," Mistress Magistery said to Al. "I'll take you and Clemerc to Sundomum: you both deserve to have a long rest. Miss Iceni, Mister Weston and Miss Walsingham will be making their way to your family as I speak, and I'm sure we'll know whether they'll be joining you in Sundomum before long. Right – shall we go?"

Al and Clemerc nodded. They were then blinded by white light, and the rollercoaster ride commenced.

When Al's feet hit solid ground once more, he found that he was not standing on a carpet of Oculus Plume beneath Sundomum. He was back in Ancient Gates Wood and facing the two tree trunks where Mistress Magistery and Metanos's Unsighted Gate was located.

"Thought we were going to Sundomum ..." he said,

frowning.

Mistress Magistery's pearly face was stony and looked particularly ghost-like in the dusky light of this part of the Wood, which was darker than Al remembered.

"It seems we have been betrayed, Al."

"*Betrayed?!* How?!"

"I've just heard the trumpets that I asked Lord Havelock to leave in your family's possession: they were only to be sounded if our enemies discovered the location of the hideout. It's evidently been revealed to them."

"But they have the lock of hair!" cried Al, battling with the suffocating grip of panic tightening round him. "They should be fine!"

"Yes, yes, the lock of hair will protect them indefinitely," Mistress Magistery reassured him. "I'm just finding it difficult to come to terms with the fact that at least one of *the Spirit-nobles and Future Spirit-nobles* – apart obviously from Mister Weston and Miss Walsingham – has betrayed us. It's only they who knew the location." She looked heartbroken.

Al's panic was rapidly replaced by a mixture of anger and disgust. A moment later, he was holding Marshal's sword aloft once more.

"Let's end this." The fierceness in his voice surprised even him.

Mistress Magistery looked at the sword and then at Al before nodding resolutely.

"Might I be of any assistance?" piped up Clemerc.

"I cannot ask any more of you, Clemerc," Mistress Magistery told him. "You have already performed with valour and selflessness so soon after your horrific ordeal. You truly do deserve to rest. Go to Sundomum, and forgive me for not being able to take you there directly."

Clemerc bowed his copper-coloured head, spread his great wings and shot up out of sight over the leafless, grey branches.

Mistress Magistery closed her eyes and murmured inaudibly under her breath for a short while as Al had seen her do before.

"I had to enlighten my Spirits-liminal on why you're present in Luxfons and why you'll be accompanying me to the Domain of the Living," she explained once she had finished. "Right – let's go."

18

A Chance to Say Goodbye

The beam of light Al and Mistress Magistery were travelling as seemed to leave most of its brightness behind in Luxfons as it zoomed across the divide. When it finally reached its destination, Al soon discovered that he was accompanied by a figure that looked nothing like Mistress Magistery as he knew her. She was smoky, shapeless and phantom-like.

"We cannot take our true forms in the Domain of the Living," she reminded him as he stared at her, open-mouthed.

It was cold, crisp and bright, and they were standing beside an enormous stone fountain in the shape of a rose. It was in the shadow of a country house with numerous tall and elaborately shaped brick chimneys and almost as many windows as Sundomum. There was a cottage a short distance away next to a small grove of oak tress – its walls and roof were almost entirely covered in ivy. A black cloud was hovering over the compact building, almost touching its roof, and a number of figures were gathered immediately outside it.

As he and Mistress Magistery raced towards them, it quickly became apparent to Al who some of the figures were. He was not able to ascertain the identity of four of them as they were in the same form as Mistress Magistery. Edward, who was holding Ivar's cane, seemed to be having a conversation with one of these featureless Spirits. Karen, Helen and Margaret – all grasping silver, old-fashioned trumpets – were standing a few feet behind Edward with the other three Spirits. Al was utterly perplexed by what was going on. Yet, the sudden surge of dread at the mere sight of such a scene made him feel nauseous.

"Al!" cried Karen, Helen and Margaret in unison.

Al was not sure whether he detected relief in their voices or dread – or a mixture of both.

"What's going on?" he demanded, his eyes darting from his father to the Spirit he had been conversing with as he raised Marshal's sword a little higher into the air.

It was the Spirit who answered – in a familiar deep voice:

"You speak with such authority and wield that sword with such confidence. You keep forgetting that *you* are a Non-Spirit – not even a fully grown one. In fact—"

"Al is the Future Spirit-noblest of Luxfons, Metanos," Mistress Magistery said emphatically. "It would be wise for you and Queen Lamiobra to never forget that!"

With his narrowed eyes fixed upon Metanos, Al raised Marshal's sword yet higher. There were only a few feet between them. All he had to do was go forth and strike, and Queen Lamiobra's consort would be no more. *Just a few feet.*

"Lower that thing, Al," Edward said sternly.

"But—"

"Look – we're talking," Edward sighed. "It's important."

"What?!" blurted out Al, reddening. "*Do you know who*

this is?!"

"Yes, I do. Al – you're still only fourteen! There are some things you don't understand!" Edward was shaking.

Al had never seen him like this before, nor had he ever heard such desperation in his voice. He did as he was told and lowered the sword.

"Mister Baba," Mistress Magistery said gently, floating a little closer, "don't do anything you might regret."

Edward ignored her and turned back to Metanos.

"So you're absolutely sure you can do that?" he asked him.

"Now, now, Mister Baba," Metanos sneered, "there's no need to insult me by underestimating my powers. I've already told you that I can."

"Right ..." said Edward, sounding relieved. "Right. There you go."

And he gave the cane to Metanos. The knobbly stick disappeared inside the smoky figure, along with its rose-shaped finial.

Al wanted to believe with all his might that what he had just witnessed was a mere hallucination of some sort, but the cries of horror around him (the loudest of which were being uttered by Mistress Magistery) convinced him beyond any doubt that his frozen eyes had not been deceived. *How could he have done this?*

With a triumphant cackle, Metanos began to ascend towards the black cloud still hovering over the cottage. At the same time, another smoky and shapeless figure emerged from it.

"I have great pleasure in returning Your Highness's rightful possession!" Metanos declared with glee as he came to a halt opposite them. "One of the Non-Spirits was, indeed, foolish enough to believe me just as you'd predicted!"

"You've done well, my noble Consort," Queen Lamiobra said in her brash voice.

Ivar's cane shot out of Metanos like a striking serpent and was caught by a scaly, scarlet hand with long claws that had materialised where Queen Lamiobra's hand would have been in her true form. And then another hand appeared – just as grotesque as the first. This one, fingers outstretched, detached itself from Queen Lamiobra as though it had a mind of its own – and hurtled down towards Al.

"GIVE ME THAT SWORD!" screamed Queen Lamiobra.

Al ducked and fell onto the ground, tightening his grip on the golden hilt. The very next moment, he was blinded by white light, and the usual rollercoaster ride recommenced.

But it was extremely short on this occasion. Mistress Magistery had brought him, the other Babas and the three Spirits (who Al now assumed to be Kerr, Virginia and Cloelia) to the inner bailey of a partially ruined castle.

"This is a calamity," she told them, sounding resigned. "An absolute calamity. I cannot emphasise enough how weak our position has been rendered."

"We can't stop fighting, though, *can we*?" asked Kerr. "How can we lose hope when so many depend on us to save them?" Surely not, Your Nobleness?"

"Kerr's right, Your Nobleness," said Virginia. "We still need to make it as difficult as possible for them to get the power they desire, however disadvantaged we may now be. We still have to try."

Cloelia seemed to be weeping but still managed to say something that, though inaudible, sounded like an endorsement of what her fellow Future Spirit-nobles had just said.

"Your resilience is extraordinary," said Mistress Magistery. "It gives me much hope – thank you. Mister Weston and Miss Walsingham, kindly join me for a stroll to the keep."

Al stared at the three Spirits as they drifted off towards the gigantic stone structure on the other side of the vast bailey. He had no idea why Mistress Magistery had decided that now was the right moment for a stroll in the company of Kerr and Virginia. But however great his puzzlement was, it was not able to displace the thick fog that had been tormenting his mind since his father's actions. He stowed the weapon that had nearly been snatched out of his hand mere moments ago into his pocket. And then Al turned to Edward. He and Helen were standing side by side against the heavily weathered curtain wall. Edward was grasping her hand – he looked crestfallen, and his head was bowed.

"*Why?*" was the only word that Al allowed to escape from his lips with great restraint.

Edward lifted his head and removed his spectacles to rub his eyes, which were bright red.

"I was offered something I had no choice but to accept," he said in little more than a whisper. "I'm sorry."

"What were you offered?" probed Al, reddening. "Did he say your life would be normal again? That you'd be able to go back home? What did he offer that is worth *more* than the lives of millions of people?!"

"Don't be too hard on your dad, darling," pleaded Helen. "You don't understand …"

Al's eyes remained fixed on Edward.

"What were you offered?!" he repeated.

"He was offered a chance to say goodbye!"

Helen had finally managed to avert Al's eyes from her husband.

"What?"

Helen tightened her grip on Edward's hand; she then sighed and said, "Metanos told your dad that, in return for the cane, he'd be able to bring Alfred back temporarily, allowing us to meet him. He was so persuasive, darling – he used your dad's emotions against him."

"I wanted to see him again so much," said Edward. "Not only to say goodbye, because I never had the opportunity to do so when he passed away, but also to thank him for everything he did for us – to tell him how grateful we are ... and how much we love him. I always thought that our strange luck every Christmas had something to do with him ... Just an instinct. And it ... it made me love him even more, which I didn't think was possible."

"Oh, Edward," lamented Margaret, who was holding Karen's arm for support. "We must accept that our Alfred is gone. I miss him terribly every single day, and if I had the power to bring him back, I would. But the fact is: we can't – nothing can."

"He just made a mistake," Helen said a little defensively. "Metanos almost had me convinced he was telling the truth too."

"I'm so sorry for being selfish," muttered Edward, a small tear rolling down his thin face. "I really am."

Al immediately went and hugged him. Even though they loved each other dearly, Al could not remember the last time he had hugged his father. But it felt right, and he could tell that Edward appreciated it.

"It's my fault too," Karen said tearfully. "I've been going on and on about Grandad and my time with him in Luxfons and—"

"What's done is done."

It was Mistress Magistery who had spoken. She had joined them again, but Kerr and Virginia were no longer with her.

"Mister Weston and Miss Walsingham have been given a task to undertake in Luxfons," she told them. "Miss Iceni – kindly await my return in Sundomum."

Cloelia drifted away up into the air, as if caught by a powerful gust of wind.

"And now, Al," said Mistress Magistery, "the time has come for us to part."

"What? Why?"

"You're now in the most danger you've ever been, Al. You need to go into hiding with your family."

"I want to help! You *need* help!"

"Do I really need to remind you of Queen Lamiobra's first act when she took possession of Lord Havelock's cane?" Mistress Magistery's pearly face was etched with uneasiness. "She has everything she needs now to launch an attack on Sundomum in a most cowardly manner, but she won't forgo taking the sword and capturing the one who can wield it."

Helen gasped and said, "Perhaps you should listen this time, Al."

"I'm not the same boy I was a few weeks ago, Mum," Al sighed. "I can look after myself now, and I know my limitations."

"I know, my darling," said Helen. "And we're very proud of you, but I can't stop being your mum."

Al nodded and turned back to Mistress Magistery.

"You told Metanos that he and Lamiobra should never forget that I'm the Future Spirit-noblest of Luxfons. So let me defend my future home. My grandad would never have gone into hiding, knowing that he was able to help. You knew him better than I did. Do you think he would?"

"No," Mistress Magistery conceded after a moment or two.

Al smiled and said, "I could disguise myself, and I don't even have to use the sword on those not protected by the cane, so she'll never know it's me!"

"Very well, Al. You're a truly noble individual. Although I'm still not wholly at ease with the idea, I'll take you back to Luxfons with me."

"Thank you," said Al, feeling relieved. "What about my family?"

"They obviously can't go back to the cottage on Lord Havelock's estate ..." said Mistress Magistery, frowning. "And they certainly can't stay here – it's not as comfortable and unexposed as it was when I grew up here ... It'll be a case of finding somewhere else. I hope you're all in agreement ..."

All the Babas nodded.

"Actually, I know just the place," said Mistress Magistery.

She had brought them to the burnt-out shell of a Tudor mansion enclosed by a very high spiked fence. Although what was left of its blackened timbers, steeply pitched roof and redbrick chimneys reminded Al of his family home, the derelict building could not have looked more uninhabitable in comparison. He was surprised that Mistress Magistery thought otherwise.

"A little refurbishment wouldn't go amiss before we

move in," Margaret said a little tartly, coughing; the air was heavy with the stench of ash and decay.

Karen, Edward and Helen murmured in agreement.

"I think you'll *all* be pleasantly surprised when you step inside," said Mistress Magistery, sounding amused.

"What is this place?" asked Al.

"This was the home of the last of my descendants. She died many years ago after reaching a grand old age but was not destined for Luxfons. It's been unoccupied ever since and, as you can see, has faced a number of misfortunes in that time. Kindly follow me inside."

As they all made their way along a pebbled path towards the mansion's charred door, which was almost off its hinges, Al noticed that the air was becoming cleaner. When they finally reached it, Mistress Magistery simply floated through. It flew open with a bang to let the others pass into the darkness and then slammed shut behind them. There was a flash of white light, and every Baba gasped, including Al.

They had found themselves in a magnificent entrance hall. It was completely undamaged – there was no indication anywhere that even a single ember had dared to undermine its grandness. The room was brightly lit with candles sticking out of ornate iron candelabra; its oak wall panels, beams and heavy furniture were all of the richest browns, and the portraits and tapestries adorning its walls had a vibrancy that looked as though it would last an eternity.

"All the rooms here are now as they used to be when the house was first built, with a few modern additions you might appreciate," said Mistress Magistery. "I hope you'll be very happy here – however long this house ends up being your abode."

Karen, Edward, Helen and Margaret all thanked her and remarked that they were sure they would be. At Mistress Magistery's invitation, they went off to explore the other rooms, leaving her and Al alone in the entrance hall.

"I haven't yet seen anything through the eyes of my Spirit-creature that causes me alarm," she told him. "But it's only a matter of time now before our enemies launch their attack. We must return to Sundomum very soon. Have you thought about what kind of disguise you'll adopt?"

"Um ... no."

As he started to ponder, Al's eyes came to rest on a large portrait hanging above an elaborately carved settle. The subject was an elderly nobleman with a curly, chestnut-brown beard.

Al smiled, and the very next moment, he sported an identical beard. He then looked round quickly in turn at the other portraits surrounding him ... When his family returned to the entrance hall, they found that the smoky, shapeless figure of Mistress Magistery was now accompanied by a rotund, bearded individual with an aquiline nose, who was wearing an ankle-length overgown of green velvet and a large Tudor bonnet of the same hue.

Karen laughed and said, "You may not be recognised, Al, but you'll definitely stand out!"

"How can you say that after having been to Luxfons?" Al chuckled.

"You're right – I take it back!"

After a tearful farewell to those he loved most, Al had been brought back to Luxfons by Mistress Magistery (who was now, once again, in her true form). They were about to ascend the newly constructed stairs to Sundomum when a familiar voice gleefully exclaiming "Greetings! Greetings! Greetings!" made them spin round.

Hermit the Apothecary was zooming towards them in an enormous sleigh flying of its own accord and laden with an almighty brown sack the size of a small elephant. The sleigh came to a halt directly in front of them, though it continued to hover. Hermit jumped out with a swish of his purple toga and landed with tremendous agility onto the Oculus Plume.

"I've done it, Your Nobleness!" he cried after bowing to Mistress Magistery. "I've managed to do exactly as you asked! I'm now the proud owner of gallons and *gallons* of the Dormshield Concoction. Gallons of it!"

"You bring great news, indeed, Hermit!" said Mistress Magistery, eyeing the sack on the sleigh.

"Yes! Yes, that's right!" Hermit was becoming more and more elated. "That's some of it. Split into hundreds and hundreds of vials – each containing precisely twelve drops. Another request from Your Nobleness fulfilled!"

"You've truly done Luxfons a great service."

"Thought you couldn't make some more ..." Al said to Hermit. He remembered how disappointed the Spirit was at being unable to recall the recipe he had worked on for centuries.

Hermit's glee vanished. It was replaced by bemusement as he observed Al with narrowed eyes from head to toe.

"How would *you* be aware of such significant

intelligence concerning *me*? You're a stranger. I've never seen you before in either Luxfons or the Domain of the Living. Explain yourself!"

Having been abruptly reminded that he was in disguise, Al felt glad it was having the desired effect.

"Now, now, Hermit," said Mistress Magistery. "Let me assure you that this *Spirit* isn't our enemy. I told him the details about your noble endeavour."

Hermit's glee reappeared as quickly as it had vanished.

"Let me tell you what happened then, Stranger. Her Nobleness asked me whether I'd permit her to peer into my mind, and I agreed. Instantly! I was adamant that she should even after she explained the dangers of doing so. I couldn't deny her the opportunity of having the greatest adventure she's ever had! I couldn't do *that*, Stranger – definitely not! When the thrill she'd experienced was over, she reminded me of how I'd ended up creating the Dormshield Concoction as a token of her gratitude!"

Al gave Mistress Magistery a look of the utmost admiration and received a warm smile in return.

Hermit's attention was then caught by the sack of vials he had brought, and his face fell once more as he muttered, "Perhaps I'm handing over too much." And then his demeanour changed again. "I could always make some more!" He turned to Mistress Magistery. "Take it. Take it all!"

Mistress Magistery did not give him another opportunity to question his own generosity. Her eyes darted towards the gigantic peacock dutifully circling the silver spire of Sundomum, and the handsome Spirit-creature swooped down in a flash of blue and green. He snatched the sack up in his talons, making the vials inside clink loudly, and then returned to the spire to resume his task. Hermit broke into a hearty round of applause. He, too, then rose up into the air and leapt into the sleigh.

"Time to go!" he announced. "I can't wait to make some more. Then again, perhaps I should have a long rest first. What do you think, Stranger? You must've had to make important decisions before now. What do *you* think I should do?"

"Um ..." began Al.

"Too late!"

The sleigh zoomed off into the distance.

Mistress Magistery began to climb the stairs, but Al remained where he was.

"Is something the matter, Al?"

"He's right."

"Who? Hermit?"

"Yes."

"What's he right about?"

"I *have* made important decisions," Al said bitterly. "Leaving the cane with my family was one of them. And it was a bad one. If the cane hadn't been there, then Lamiobra wouldn't have it right now. Dad and Karen may think they were to blame, but if you think about it, I'm responsible for what happened."

"No, Al," Mistress Magistery said firmly. "Unlike some of the decisions I've made of late, yours was steeped in wisdom. Certain circumstances, which are beyond our control and which cannot be foreseen, can sometimes make the wisest decision seem like a foolish one."

She turned round and resumed her ascension. Al soon followed.

19

The Witness

Mistress Magistery was greeted immediately by Cloelia and Clemerc as the gold portcullis crashed down behind her and Al and glowed bright orange again in its usual manner. The anxiousness etched on Cloelia's skeletal face was more profound than ever.

"I will shortly descend and summon all those who have so far vowed to help defend the Laws of Luxfons, along with the other Spirit-nobles and Future Spirit-nobles," Mistress Magistery told Cloelia before she had the chance to allow any of the questions she was clearly brimming with to burst out. "However, it's imperative that I first show this particular Spirit – an acquaintance of mine – that which, alas, I can show no other at this present time."

Unlike Al, Cloelia and Clemerc did not exhibit any signs of bewilderment. They nodded, and Mistress Magistery stepped aside to let them pass. As the sound of the portcullis crashing down tore through the vast space once more, Mistress Magistery told Al to stay close by her side and then began to stride up the hall.

When they reached the two disappearing-and-reappearing archways, she turned towards the one leading into the east wing – the very archway that Al had seen her emerge from when Alfred brought him to Sundomum for the first time. As Al approached it, he could make out nothing but pure darkness beyond in the split second that the archway ceased to be thick, impenetrable stone.

"At my command, this archway will remain in place only a moment longer that it usually does," Mistress Magistery said once they had come to a halt before it. "You must step through without hesitation. Otherwise, you'll be entrapped in stone. I won't be able to release you if that happens. Now!"

They leapt into the darkness in unison. But then the darkness was gone, and Al was even more enthralled than he was a short while ago, when he first laid eyes on the magnificent entrance hall inside the derelict Tudor mansion.

He and Mistress Magistery were in a huge, squared room that was as bright as the hall they had just left behind. It was full of countless wooden boxes – of all sizes, colours and designs imaginable. Every single one, though, had a keyhole. The larger ones – great coffers and chests – cluttered the ermine-patterned floor, leaving only a narrow path across the room to the oak door on the other side. The smaller ones were on dozens of stone shelves snaking around the room all the way up to the fan vaulting. Some of these, no bigger than trinket boxes, were decorated with brass, silver and enamels and gleamed gloriously in the light streaming through the many round windows.

As Mistress Magistery led him to the oak door, Al looked over his shoulder: the darkness they had emerged from was somehow contained within the archway, unaffected by the brightness on either side.

The next room was almost identical, and so was the one after that, and the one after that. Mistress Magistery strode in silence through all of them without stopping. Al had now guessed what he was about to be shown and was feeling a little daunted as he followed closely behind. They had almost reached the oak door of the fifth room when Mistress Magistery stopped and turned round.

"The Power to Kill is kept here."

"Where exactly?" whispered Al, looking round.

Mistress Magistery lifted her trembling hand with the palm facing upwards, and a small box fell onto it from one of the top shelves. It was no bigger than a matchbox and crudely painted with blue, green and yellow stripes; its miniscule brass keyhole was grimy and almost blended in with the blue paint around it.

"Here," said Mistress Magistery.

Al stared at the box for a few moments, struggling to digest the fact that the darkest power in existence, sought by the evillest Spirits in existence, was housed in something so unremarkable.

"What does it look like?" Al gulped without averting his eyes from the box.

"Like a wisp of the blackest and thickest smoke you can imagine."

Al looked up. "Why are you showing me this?"

"Because if our enemies obtain this tiny little vessel even without its key and I'm incapacitated for whatever reason, you must do everything in your power to get it back – *without* using your sword and revealing your identity."

"But—"

"You cannot take being captured by Queen Lamiobra and risking the future of Luxfons so lightly!" Anger flashed across Mistress Magistery's face.

Al, somewhat taken aback, nodded.

"I'm sorry you're being burdened with such a big responsibility," she said softly, "but I can only share it with you. I had intended to bring the Spirit-nobles and Future Spirit-nobles here for the same purpose but ..." Her voice faded away as her face fell.

Al remembered with a nauseating jolt that they had been betrayed.

"I'm of the hope that Mister Weston and Miss Walsingham will be returning soon," she continued. "I have every confidence that they'll succeed in the task I've given them: discovering the traitor amongst us. And now it's time to summon the greatest gathering of Spirits that Sundomum has ever witnessed."

The little box in her hand rose high into the air and disappeared amongst the hundreds of others.

When Al and Mistress Magistery rejoined Cloelia and Clemerc beneath Sundomum, the mighty stairs began to dismantle as usual – but this time, the resultant fragments did not fall in a shower all round them. Instead, they rose as a mass along with the surplus jagged rocks dotted around on the Oculus Plume in the distance. Mistress Magistery glanced up in their direction, and a few moments later, a great floating wall had been constructed directly in front of the burning portcullis, obscuring it entirely. She then began to walk briskly away from Sundomum, with Al, Cloelia and Clemerc following in her wake. When Al could finally make out the houses of the little village he and Frederick had traversed on Kiang in some detail, she stopped and turned to look at the colossal mass of glass and lustrous ochre directly behind them in the sky.

"Here will do," she told them. "The Unsighted Gates have closed just in time."

The little silver bell materialised in her hand, and she brought it close to her lips. "Your Spirit-noblest humbly requests your assistance in defending the Laws of Luxfons!"

The peal that followed her words was like the sound of dozens of church bells being heard in close proximity. It was soon replaced, though, by a crescendo of howls, screeches, growls, trumpets and roars mingled with passionate cries of loyalty to Luxfons and its leader. The vast space covered by Oculus Plume in front of Al, Mistress Magistery, Cloelia and Clemerc was rapidly filling up with a sea of Spirits and Spirit-creatures, and Al found himself being utterly overwhelmed by the sight.

When the other Spirit-nobles and Future Spirit-nobles began arriving, they did not join the ever-growing throng of hundreds, but those facing it instead. All of them, apart from Frederick and Alcea (who arrived with Morfox in the chariot flown by Kiang), sported their angel-like wings, which shrank away soon after they landed. Kerr and Virginia were the last Spirits to arrive. They, like the other Spirit-nobles and Future Spirit-nobles, failed to recognise Al but did not probe his identity.

Virginia, beaming, bowed deeply in front of Mistress Magistery and said, "It gives me great pleasure to inform Your Nobleness that Mister Weston and I succeeded."

Mistress Magistery stepped forward and the noise subsided.

"Spirits and Spirit-creatures of Luxfons," she began; her voice was not amplified, but Al was sure those she was addressing were able to hear her as clearly as he could, "I cannot express how grateful I am for your presence here. I'm moved by your loyalty to our Laws and to me. However, it grieves me to say that there's at least one here amongst us who's been exhibiting only a facade of loyalty. They have betrayed us to our enemies – those who want to use Luxfons and the Domain of the Living for their own evil ends."

The great rumble of disquiet that had arisen subdued as Mistress Magistery continued a touch louder:

"Because of the actions of this traitor or these *traitors*, our enemies are now in possession of a relic that elevates them to a very advantaged position, indeed. Their attack is imminent. I now invite Mister Weston and Miss Walsingham to enlighten us all – even me – on what they've discovered."

The two young Spirits took Mistress Magistery's place in the intense spotlight of hundreds and hundreds of staring eyes. Both seemed nervous all of a sudden – perhaps because of the sheer significance of what they were about to reveal. It was Virginia who quickly overcame her hesitancy and began to speak, though she continued to fidget with her lace ruff.

"Before Her Nobleness honoured Mister Weston and me with the task of finding out who'd betrayed us, she shared some invaluable knowledge. She told us that every creation in Luxfons – however inanimate – holds a residue of the creator's powers. This is why we can't simply pass through any of the objects here as we do in the Domain of the Living. Sometimes, that residue is so potent that the creation possessing it may be able to see, hear or even speak. Her Nobleness thought there was a chance that one of these creations could have witnessed the act of betrayal, and, unsurprisingly, she was right.

"Sadly, the Spirits she suspected happened to be our fellow Spirit-nobles and Future Spirit-nobles. And so we decided to visit each of their abodes in turn until we found the witness we were looking for."

A small glass orb materialised between Kerr and Virginia. It grew larger and larger as it floated upwards; when it finally came to a halt far above their heads, it was the size of a hot air balloon. Al, like every other being in his midst, observed with astonishment as the huge figures of Kerr and Virginia suddenly appeared inside it.

They were walking up to a brick house that Al was extremely familiar with – Vulcanest. Kerr rapped its red door with his fist, but there was no answer. They then poked their heads into the storage building and the forge, but these, too, seemed to be deserted.

"They must all still be in the Domain of the Living," said Virginia, sighing with relief. "It's better this way."

"How so?" asked Kerr.

"It avoids the need for an explanation – one which is bound to offend any loyal Spirit of Luxfons to the core."

Kerr nodded vigorously, making the tassel on his mortar board bob round like a fish out of water.

"Speak if you can!" Virginia said as her eyes swept the bright surroundings.

But nothing did.

The two Spirits positioned themselves back to back and raised their arms as though they were embracing the air. The brightness around them seemed to intensify for a few moments before subsiding.

"Is there anything in our midst that can at least see or

hear?!" cried Kerr as he and Virginia lowered their arms.

"I can do both, and now I can speak too," said a voice. It was loud but laboured, and the speaker sounded bored.

Kerr and Virginia shot off in its direction – towards the hillock. They stood in front of it, seeming unsure how to proceed.

"What are you?" asked Kerr.

"Isn't it obvious what I am? A meagre knoll. You're welcome to have my sight if you're in need of it. I don't have much use for it – being stuck in one place."

"Could you tell us whether you've seen anything suspicious?" continued Kerr. "Anything at all being done or said in secret?"

"I have, yes," replied the hillock. "On a few occasions. Quite recently, in fact. It made a blissful change to witnessing nothingness again and again and again."

"What did you witness?" probed Kerr.

"I don't see how revealing it will benefit me," the hillock said nonchalantly. "It won't take away my boredom – simply repeating what I witnessed."

"What you tell us may benefit Luxfons in a way I can't even begin to describe!" enthused Virginia.

"How will it benefit *me*, though?" the hillock asked in the same stubborn vein.

"We'll allow you to keep the voice we've given you!" Virginia fired back. "That should help get rid of your boredom for a while!"

"You're right. It will."

"Well ...?" pressed Kerr.

"Yes, yes," said the hillock. "Listen closely because I won't repeat anything. The first interesting event I witnessed was when two Spirits in red appeared next to me – they emerged out of mist. One had a crown, was in scaly attire and looked very anxious, whilst the other was in metallic attire and looked very weak.

"When the mistress of the house – Alcea – came over to us, I discovered their names: Queen Lamiobra and Metanos. They tried to persuade her to join their cause, and she agreed. She told them that her husband, Frederick, was a Future Spirit-noble and would forever remain loyal to a Mistress Magistery so she would keep this alliance a secret from him. She also told them that their Spirit-creature, Morfox, accompanied her husband to a place called Sundomum and she was sure that this Spirit-creature would reveal everything he heard there to her. She would then pass this information on to them. In return, she wanted the chance to plunder the riches of the Domain of the Living when their so-called revolution had taken place.

"Queen Lamiobra and Metanos agreed and told her that something called a Hawkanine would always be watching her abode from the sky and would come down at her signal to receive any messages. They then turned back into mist and drifted away.

"Soon after, I witnessed another interesting event. Alcea carried Morfox in her arms up onto my back and told him to create a ring of fire. He did so without question and scalded my back in the process. A great hawk-like Spirit-creature fell out of the sky and landed next to Alcea. She told this Spirit-creature about a plan Mistress Magistery had for finding the soldiers of Queen Lamiobra and Metanos ...

"I'm sure I was about to witness a similar event when Alcea and Morfox were interrupted by the arrival of a beam of light that turned into two Spirits ... I think. Later on, a very happy-looking Alcea returned with Morfox, and my back was scalded once more by another ring of fire. When the Hawkanine came down, she told it to inform its master that a cane of some sort was in the Domain of the Living with the Baba family, who lived in an ivy-covered cottage near a large house with many chimneys and a fountain shaped like a rose."

The gigantic orb in the sky vanished. The stunned silence it left behind seemed to endure long after it had gone, however. Although Frederick, Alcea and Morfox were near him, Al was struggling to look in their direction. He did not feel any anger towards Alcea or Morfox, but the revelations had broken his heart – even though it had not yet fully mended since his grandfather's Departure. His unwillingness to see the effect of the revelations on Frederick – his friend – kept his eyes firmly on the Oculus Plume. But then the sound of rapid movement in the chariot made him look up instinctively.

Frederick had scrambled out of it. His horrified face was drenched with tears, and it seemed like he wanted to get as far away as possible from the chariot and its occupants, but he stumbled, disorientated. Alcea and Morfox jumped out and sprinted towards him.

"Forgive me, dearest," cried Alcea, attempting to get a hold of Frederick's hands, which he jerked out of her reach. "I was wrong – so – so wrong. Greedy and foolish! You have no idea of the weight of my guilt! I was going to tell you everything – believe me – dearest – *please* believe me!"

She began to sob uncontrollably and crumpled to the ground.

Morfox, meanwhile, was yowling, his handsome red head bowed. He kept repeating "Forgive" at regular intervals.

Al could not help but be moved by their plight and – somehow – found himself becoming certain that their show of repentance was genuine. And it sounded like others agreed: he was surrounded by the sound of stifled sniffs and sobs.

Frederick hesitated, but then bent down and brought his wife to her feet in a loving embrace and gently patted Morfox on the head, managing to console both of them a little.

"In spite of how much I've been hurt by what you've done," he told them, fresh tears leaking out of his eyes, "I can't bear to see you like this. I forgive both of you. But it's more important for you to ask Her Nobleness for forgiveness – your fate is now in her hands."

Alcea and Morfox did as they were told at once – with sincerity, Al felt – and kept their heads bowed reverently in front of Mistress Magistery. She looked torn.

"I cannot simply ignore the scale of your actions," she sighed. "Nor the darkness that was inside you, which drove you to carry them out. How can I be sure it won't grow again to smother the light you now clearly exhibit?"

"The fears of Your Nobleness are justified," said Alcea. "I'll accept whatever form of punishment you hand out. But please don't deprive me of this chance to atone for what I've done – to defend the Laws of Luxfons with the one I love most."

"The situation you're in is very similar to that of another Spirit, who I came across not so very long ago: Agrius Poley-Babington. He currently has no choice but to remain entrapped in his abode. I'll only release him when our enemies have been vanquished once and for all – and we'll then pass judgement on his character and fate in Luxfons. It would be grossly unfair to treat you and Morfox any different."

Alcea nodded, looking resigned.

"Your Nobleness," piped up Hexa, her pretty face full of concern, "we're on the brink of the biggest battle Luxfons has ever seen, and our position is tenuous to say the least. Forgive me for disagreeing, but I firmly believe Missus Hancock should have her wish: we need all the help we can get."

"Miss Parr is right, Your Nobleness," said Lady Tyto. She hesitated before gingerly adding, "This is one of those occasions when a wise principle should be set aside in light of the situation."

"I'm very grateful to you, Lady Tyto, for reminding me of my own words," Mistress Magistery said after a while, nodding. "I have reconsidered and do now agree with both of you." She turned to Alcea. "Very well, Missus Hancock. You and Morfox may remain with Frederick – with us all – to defend our Laws. I wish you every success."

Alcea and Morfox thanked her numerous times before making their way back to the chariot with Frederick. Before they reached it, though, the air was struck with what sounded like a high-pitched siren, and every head turned towards Sundomum. The peacock had left his station. He was now flying over the Spirits and Spirit-creatures and distributing vial upon vial of the Dormshield Concoction in a glittering shower from the great sack in its talons.

"They're coming!" cried Mistress Magistery. "Drink the contents of the vial in its entirety at once!"

The amalgamation of noise and movement that followed was tantamount to an earthquake. Without thinking, Al reached into his pocket –

"No, Al," barked Mistress Magistery. "You mustn't remove the sword! Keep close to me!"

"Yes, yes, of course – sorry."

Any nervousness Al felt rapidly evaporated. He was gripped by a sensation of being at one with those around him *and* his future world. He was determined to defend its Laws against the oncoming dark forces with every ounce of strength he possessed.

The peacock landed in front of Al and Mistress Magistery with the ferocity of a gale, the last few vials in the sack tinkling onto the Oculus Plume. Mistress Magistery climbed onto his back and beckoned Al to do the same. Once he had done so, the peacock rose to hover directly in front of the tumultuous sea of Spirits and Spirit-creatures.

"A tower formation up to the very dome of Sundomum!" roared Mistress Magistery.

It was a seamless operation. And the result made the tears flow readily from Al's astonished eyes. Standing before him *was* an actual tower – made of Spirits and Spirit-creatures. Al tried to spot all those he was familiar with dotted around in the colossal formation: Hamelin and Kerr were at the bottom, sitting on gigantic black rats (Fickle had not only grown, but duplicated herself); Hexa and Cloelia were next to them, each grasping a golden trident; Frederick, Alcea, Morfox and Kiang were at the apex – the two Spirits carrying dozens of chains over their shoulders; Lady Tyto and Virginia were directly beneath them on gigantic, vicious-looking eagle-owls; and in the very heart of the tower, in a flying galleon with dozens of canons, were Admiral Keel and Polemus.

Al also noticed the presence of many of the Spirits he

had visited with Mistress Magistery such as Alisha and Jay Khan; those he had witnessed becoming Spirits of Luxfons such as Stephen Brown; and all the Spirits he and Clemerc had rescued on Epis Islet.

As the cries of loyalty became louder and more passionate, the peacock's siren-like call sounded out once more, and the tower fell silent, allowing Mistress Magistery to speak:

"Our aim will be to defend and capture – not to harm! But let me assure you – if you're left with no choice but to break this particular Law, you'll face no repercussions. May victory be ours!"

The peacock rose up in harmony with the wave of cheers and flew over the tower. He returned to his station, bringing Al and Mistress Magistery with him. This time, though, he did not circle the silver spire but hovered next to it and stared into the distance in anticipation of what was coming.

Al noticed a tiny sliver of gold embedded in the silver. "Is that the key to the box?" he whispered. "The box that contains the Power to Kill?"

"Indeed." Mistress Magistery glanced at it and with unmistakable trepidation in her voice, said, "I have a feeling our enemies won't have a need for it to get what they're coming for."

Al suddenly found he had the same feeling too.

And then – what looked like a shimmering sandstorm descended upon them.

20

Gains and Losses

The Spiritsnuff, shining ever brightly, was forced to settle down on whatever it could, having failed its task. As visibility was restored, Al was surprised to find that the Hawkanines still loyal to Metanos were nowhere to be seen. But the glittering particles of gold now sprinkled all over him and his surroundings had brought something else with them – the black cloud that had hovered over the Babas' cottage.

It was now hovering high above the ground in front of the tower of Spirits and Spirit-creatures, almost level with the top of the spire. After a few moments of silent stillness all around, the cloud flinched violently. And out of it burst the screaming army of Queen Lamiobra and Metanos.

Al knew immediately that they were outnumbered. Their foes were fully armoured in red steel and were carrying an array of weapons – swords, spears, clubs, pikes, halberds, axes and flails. Each soldier was also wearing a fluttering red cape that had somehow given them the ability to fly without wings. Together, in one red mass, they launched themselves at the portion of the tower directly in front of the floating wall. And chaos ensued.

The top of the tower collapsed onto the oncoming tsunami of scarlet steel. The explosion of sound was such that Al was sure it had shaken Luxfons to the very core. The next moment, he and Mistress Magistery had been flown directly into the heart of the battle, which was raging with a volcanic intensity. The soldiers hacked away mercilessly at the defenders of the Laws of Luxfons, who were trying ferociously to capture them. None more so than the Spirit-nobles and Future Spirit-nobles and their Spirit-creatures –

Hamelin and Kerr's gigantic rats were leaping into the air and snatching soldiers out of it with their gnashing teeth. Hexa and Cloelia were shooting jets of water at them with their tridents, freezing them in blocks of ice. Frederick and Alcea, zooming round in their chariot, were bombarding them with their chains, which turned into cages of fire; Morfox, meanwhile, was protecting his master and mistress by turning himself into *shields* of fire. Lady Tyto and Virginia's gigantic eagle-owls were seizing them in their talons, ripping off their capes and dropping them from a great height. And Admiral Keel and Polemus's galleon was spinning on the spot, shooting canons at them that turned into thick nets of rope.

The peacock was crisscrossing round the plethora of attacks and counterattacks. Mistress Magistery was making the Oculus Plume rise up in waves round the soldiers, entrapping them. And Al was busy protecting his allies from their vicious attacks – which had destroyed so many already, leaving them no choice but to Depart. He was creating shield after shield and flinging them between the array of melee weapons and the ones they were about to strike.

He was particularly relieved after saving a gallant golden elephant that had its ever-extending trunk wrapped around a dozen soldiers at once from being hacked to pieces. The culprits were quickly pierced to the ground by the spear-like stingers of gigantic honeybees and were then entangled in a mesh of vines conjured by three identical Spirit-youths.

Al was soon exhausted, but the battle was showing no sign whatsoever of ending, or even abating. And Queen Lamiobra, Metanos and his Hawkanines had not yet even made an appearance. Al knew they were somewhere high, high above them, though – watching the battle closely and waiting ... perhaps for their enemies to tire or diminish further in number before they made their move.

And sure enough, when the battle *finally* began to lose some of its intensity, a familiar screeching rang out. It was mingled with a loud hissing. Al's heart sank when he looked up. Queen Lamiobra was torpedoing down towards them on a monstrous gold cobra with each wing as long as its body. She was carrying a huge iron mace in one hand and Ivar's cane in the other. Metanos, on one of his Hawkanines, was directly behind them, flanked by the other two. And behind them were dozens of soldiers – identical to those battling below but with black plumes sticking out of their helmets.

The cobra (and those that followed it) headed straight for the floating wall. It now lay undefended.

Kiang got there first, though. Every single one of the chains Frederick and Alcea catapulted at the cobra missed. Queen Lamiobra's shrill cackle tore across the sounds of battle as she struck the chariot with her mace. Frederick and Alcea leapt out as it shattered, the angel-like wings erupting out of their backs, whilst Morfox fluttered away in the form of a robin.

The next moment, the wall, too, was in pieces. But the defenders of the Laws of Luxfons were still determined to hinder their foes ... Lady Tyto and Virginia's eagle-owls tried their utmost to tear at the cobra's head. But it was all in vain. Queen Lamiobra's mace soon disposed of them, too, forcing their distraught mistresses to hurtle away like the Hancocks.

And then it was the turn of Admiral Keel and Polemus to put themselves in front of the burning portcullis, making Queen Lamiobra shriek with rage.

As canon after canon bounced off the invisible dome of protection around her and her Spirit-creature, they tried their utmost to vanquish their opponents and get past. But every time the cobra got anywhere near the galleon, it would start spinning in rapid fashion, pushing it back to its original position.

"HELP ME!" Queen Lamiobra screamed at Metanos.

And he did. At his command, the Hawkanines and the soldiers charged at the galleon. They tore through it like a colossal red cannonball, obliterating it entirely. Admiral Keel and Polemus, having just managed to fly out in time, could do nothing more than observe its remains raining down onto those still battling fiercely below.

Queen Lamiobra cheered manically. She raised her mace aloft, and the cobra stormed through the burning portcullis like it was a mere veil – which was then ripped and discarded, leaving nothing more than a gaping hole behind in the ochre-coloured stone. Queen Lamiobra was inside Sundomum.

The peacock had been trying for some time to fly Al and Mistress Magistery up to the palace, but they had been surrounded by a ring of soldiers. Mistress Magistery buried the last few of these in the Oculus Plume as the Hawkanines and the soldiers with black plumes in their helmets poured into Sundomum. The Spirit-nobles and Future Spirit-nobles rallied round their leader as quickly as they could, their surviving Spirit-creatures remaining locked in battle. And in the following moments, the peacock had led them all through the gaping hole after their foes. They were waiting for them.

The sight inside abhorred Al and almost made him yell out. Queen Lamiobra was sitting on the Grand Throne. Her flying cobra had now lost its body and wings and shrunk back to a head adorning her circlet, but she was still holding her mace and Ivar's cane. And sitting next to her – on his former throne – was Metanos, his three Hawkanines hovering above them. The soldiers, meanwhile, had split themselves into two groups: one was standing directly in front of the disappearing-and-reappearing archway leading into the west wing and the other – in front of the one leading into the east wing. The smugness on Queen Lamiobra's face overshadowed even that which was being exhibited by Metanos.

"It's almost over!" she cried as Mistress Magistery and Al dismounted the peacock. "When I have the Power to Kill in my arsenal and have destroyed you, Mistress Magistery, and all your ... minions, I'll destroy this abomination of a place too. I cannot wait!" She gritted her teeth and looked round the hall in disgust before adding, "I now *kindly* invite you to get on your knees and beg for mercy."

"I concede you have many powers, Queen Lamiobra" retorted Mistress Magistery, "but you don't have the power to peer into the future."

Queen Lamiobra threw her head back and cackled manically. "So you still believe that you have a chance of defeating me?" She sighed exaggeratedly. "How foolish. I almost pity you for being so weak-minded! Anyway, here's a taste of what's to come. You may proceed, my elites!"

Before their very eyes, the soldiers in the two groups began to melt into one another. Soon, an armoured Spirit-giant, almost as tall as the pillars, was standing in front of each of the disappearing-and-reappearing archways. They simply turned and smashed through them, destroying much of the stone walls.

"Go after them!" Mistress Magistery pleaded to those around her as Queen Lamiobra, Metanos and his Hawkanines lunged towards her like they had each imbibed the Spirit of the gold cobra head itself.

The Spirit-nobles and the peacock refused to leave Mistress Magistery's side. Meanwhile, Kerr, Virginia and Cloelia flew in the direction of the west wing, and Alcea and Polemus flew in the direction of the east wing – Al following closely behind.

With a speed Al could not have imagined possible, the Spirit-giant was trampling on each wooden box – whether big or small – with its shield-sized solleret, scooping it up in its gauntleted hands, peering inside through its visor and dropping it on the ermine-patterned floor. The din was deafening. Every kind of rope, net, chain and vine Al, Alcea and Polemus bombarded it with whilst trying their utmost to dodge the falling boxes was flung aside by the Spirit-giant with ease. And soon, it had destroyed every single box in the room. The stone shelves lay empty, and a mountain of wood littered the floor. It kicked the debris aside and smashed through the oak door into the next room.

Al and the two Future Spirit-nobles pursued it doggedly. But they failed to entrap it in that room too. And the one after that. *And* the one after that. As it smashed its way into the fifth room, cold dread wrapped itself round Al, almost numbing him. *It's going to find the box containing the Power to Kill. It's only a matter of time.*

"COME ON!" bellowed Polemus, looking back as he and Alcea burst into the room whose turn it was to be ransacked with unabated ferocity.

Al did as he was told. He leapt like an acrobat over the debris in front of him and sprinted after them along the wide path made by the Spirit-giant.

Polemus's big, oily face looked as though it was about to explode with rage. He flapped his angel-like wings and flew up to the very helmet of the Spirit-giant, which he then began to batter with cannonballs almost as large as himself. Al and Alcea scrambled out of the way as they came crashing to the ground. Polemus finally managed what the three of them had failed to achieve thus far: the Spirit-giant halted its task. But not for very long. It flung the enormous coffer it was holding at Polemus and sent him hurtling into the shelves on the other side of the room. Polemus disappeared into a pile of wood and stone and did not re-emerge.

And then Al's worst fear came true. The Spirit-giant had just picked up a small box from one of the shelves near the fan vaulting, thrown it down and trampled upon it. When the broken vessel was scooped up, Al caught a glimpse of it – blue, green and yellow stripes. The Spirit-giant brought the remains up to its visor –

"WE HAVE IT!" jubilantly yelled what sounded like fifty voices at once.

It turned round and thundered towards the hall.

"We can still stop it!" cried Al, turning to Alcea. "When we've caught up with it, follow my lead!"

And they were both off again. Al leapt and sprinted as fast as he could back through the debris-strewn rooms, and Alcea zoomed alongside him. The Spirit-giant came to a standstill as soon it had crossed the threshold into the hall, and it was only then that they caught up with it.

Although the sounds of battle beyond Sundomum had now died, the hall itself was bursting with them. The peacock was using his tail like a whip to defend himself against the stabbing beaks of two of the Hawkanines near the dome, having entrapped one of them in a blue-and-green cloud of his own feathers. The Spirit-nobles were trying to capture Metanos with monstrously thick iron chains as they dodged his daggers and spears of reddish energy. And Mistress Magistery, wielding a golden sword shining even more brightly than the crystals on her gown, was locked in fierce combat with Queen Lamiobra and her mace.

"WE HAVE IT!" the Spirit-giant repeated with increased jubilation, holding out its gauntleted hand to show its master and mistress the broken box.

Al narrowed his eyes and directed his gaze at one of the pillars near him. The entire, colossal stone structure broke away and launched itself at the Spirit-giant. It let out a deafening howl before falling to the floor, which shook like a leaf. And then, as it lay there trapped underneath one pillar with its hand still outstretched, another one crashed down on top of it at Alcea's behest.

Queen Lamiobra, abandoning the battle, tried to sprint towards it ... but Mistress Magistery spun into the air with a great swish of her gown and landed in front of her opponent, leaving a furious Queen Lamiobra no choice but to re-engage. Both of them looked exhausted. As Al made a move to retrieve the box, he was confronted by the terrifying sight of the gold cobra head whizzing towards the Spirit-giant's outstretched hand, its mouth open. It was nearly there when Alcea flung one of her chains at it, entrapping it in a floating cage of fire.

"METANOS!" screamed Queen Lamiobra. "*GET IT!*"

He, like her, had been prevented from getting near the Spirit-giant. But then, in an imitation of Al and Alcea's actions, he caused a pillar to launch itself at his five opponents, defeating them. With a great sigh of relief, he raised his hand towards a racing Al, who was inches away from the broken box, and sent him flying backwards into the stone debris. Al struggled to his feet, wincing in pain, just in time to see Metanos bend down and simply take the broken box out of the Spirit-giant's hand. *It's over – all is lost.*

He ripped apart the little lid and tipped the contents of the box into his mouth.

Laughing victoriously, his bloodshot eyes wide with joy, Metanos turned towards Queen Lamiobra. "The Power to Kill is mine, Your Highness!" he cried. "It's *mine!* And it'll soon be yours too!"

Queen Lamiobra shrieked with unadulterated ecstasy. Mistress Magistery crumpled to the floor, and her sword fell to her side with a clatter. She had succumbed to her exhaustion. Queen Lamiobra raised the mace aloft to strike her. But then – she, too, crumpled with exhaustion. Her mace rolled away. And so did Ivar's cane.

The peacock, now having entrapped all three Hawkanines in his feathers, swooped down by his mistress's side. Al was about to do the same when – with a jolt – he realised that he now had a perfect opportunity to destroy an unprotected Queen Lamiobra *and* Metanos with Marshal's sword. *They can still be defeated.* But something inside him prevented him from reaching into his pocket. Something was telling him that he should not intervene. He was contemplating whether to overrule it when Metanos discarded the empty box he was holding and quickly scooped up both the mace and the cane. He handed the cane back to Queen Lamiobra. Al remained where he was, confused and angry.

"Destroy her," Queen Lamiobra commanded Metanos. "Once and for all."

"No!" yelled Al. "You can't! She saved your life!"

Metanos spun round – the glee on his taut face had disappeared in its entirety.

"What do you mean?!" he spat. "*Who are you?!*"

"Never mind who I am," said Al, moving closer to him. "It's true! When you were a baby, your mother was about to kill you, but Mistress Magistery intervened! She used the Power to Kill on your mother and saved your life! And then ... then she looked after you all your life – she made sure you had everything you needed – and more! And when you died, you weren't meant to come *here* – to Luxfons – but Mistress Magistery brought you here by force and then ignored the darkness she saw inside you! She loved you like a mother in life and in death. Probably still does!" Al was panting hard by the time he finished.

"Don't listen to him," said Queen Lamiobra, her voice getting louder. "Just destroy her!"

Metanos ignored her. He turned and looked down at Mistress Magistery, whose head was bowed.

"Is this true?" he asked her. His deep voice was no longer tinged with pride or mockery.

Mistress Magistery raised her head slowly, her face streaming with tears. She nodded.

Metanos observed her expressionlessly for a few seconds. And then – flung the mace across the hall.

"What are you doing?" demanded Queen Lamiobra. "Get it back! Give me the Power to Kill!"

"She fears Taurbrum," Metanos told Mistress Magistery. His eyes seemed to lose their bloodshot appearance as they became dewy. "I'm sorry," he added before giving her a bow.

And then he became smoky and shapeless ... Metanos Departed, taking his three entrapped Hawkanines and the Power to Kill with him.

21

Taurbrum's Task

Before Al could fully digest what had just happened, Queen Lamiobra rose to her feet. She looked demonic. Her bout of weakness seemed to have evaporated, and she raised her hand in the direction of the fallen mace, which came spinning back to her. Mistress Magistery remained where she was. Her head was bowed again, and the peacock had his tail around her shoulders like a comforting arm.

Queen Lamiobra observed her for a moment or two. "Don't be foolish enough to think that you're now victorious," she seethed. "I can still rule this world for now. Without any hindrance! All I have to do is obliterate you – that won't be too difficult." Her smile made her look even more demonic. "And mark my words: I will find another way to keep the Unsighted Gates open! And I will conquer the Domain of the Living *and* any other realms out there when I've created the most powerful army in existence! It's only a matter of time!"

"We made the giant Depart!" announced an excited voice.

It belonged to Kerr, who came flying into the hall out of the west wing, closely followed by Virginia and Cloelia.

All three of them flinched at the sight of Queen Lamiobra towering over Mistress Magistery as they landed next to the still-entrapped Spirit-nobles.

Their looks of fear intensified a great deal more when Queen Lamiobra let out a piercing scream and raised her mace at the same time –

"Taurbrum!" cried Mistress Magistery.

The enormous, golden-horned black bull materialised beside her at once, and it was Queen Lamiobra's turn to look fearful. Instead of Mistress Magistery, she struck *him* with the mace – squarely on the head. Taurbrum remained as he was, though, and looked unharmed. Queen Lamiobra edged backwards, raising Ivar's cane in front of her. She then turned into red mist and drifted out of the hall through the gaping hole she had triumphantly created earlier. She had abandoned the entrapped cobra head and Spirit-giant.

Mistress Magistery sprang to her feet and lifted the pillar off the Spirit-nobles with a wave of her wrinkly hand.

"I wish I knew why she fears you so much, Taurbrum," she said before sighing heavily.

"Where does he disappear off to?" asked Al.

"The same place us Spirits will end up when we Depart," said Mistress Magistery.

"What?! How come he has the power to come back to Luxfons?!"

"Because the Sceptre is the only tool that allows me to Accept Newly Departed Spirits, and it can *only* be fashioned from his horns. Taurbrum was the first Spirit-creature of Luxfons, and no other Spirit-creature will be more powerful than he is. He emerged out of the River together with Raja Nawab and Epis."

"Epis!" cried Al. He had just been reminded of what the putto-like Spirit had told him. "Mistress Magistery ..." he said, his heart beginning to race, "please tell Taurbrum that Raja Nawab's legacy is at risk."

Mistress Magistery looked taken aback, but she did not argue and did as she was told. Taurbrum disappeared. There was complete silence in the heavily damaged hall for a few moments. And then Taurbrum reappeared. And all the Spirits gasped. And Al felt like cheering.

Taurbrum was now accompanied by a majestic figure. He was tall and handsome and had a small goatee of the purest white. From neck to toe, he was wrapped loosely in a long and heavy-looking mantle of green velvet, which was lined with ermine and embroidered with suns and peacocks in gold thread. A huge crown of emeralds and sapphires was resting on his head of long white hair.

"Raja Nawab!" Mistress Magistery sobbed, bowing.

All the other Spirits, the peacock *and* Al bowed too.

Raja Nawab smiled appreciatively, but the look of concern on his face did not diminish.

"So, she's back ..." he said, his eyes lingering on the cobra head caged in fire.

Al had never heard a softer voice, nor a more authoritative one.

A moment later, both the cobra head and the Spirit-giant had Departed.

"She was never gone," Mistress Magistery told him. "She wasn't entombed in stone as we thought ..."

"Yes," said Raja Nawab. "She managed to trick me at my weakest point." A sliver of indignation passed over his face, which was enough to make all the Spirit-nobles and Future Spirit-nobles flinch. "But she will get her comeuppance now. I know exactly where she's hiding."

"Why didn't you make me aware of the fact that Taurbrum could bring you back?" demanded Mistress Magistery, sounding hurt.

"Because, at the time, I didn't want to come back. It *was* selfish, I admit. But you must remember, I was betrayed by the one I loved most – I had suffered too much in Luxfons to want to come back. It was a mistake not to tell you, though. How did you work it out?"

"I didn't. Al did."

"Al?"

Raja Nawab was not the only one who was confused by Mistress Magistery's revelation. Al morphed back into his true form to the delight of the Spirit-nobles and Future Spirit-nobles.

"I sense you're not a part of this world ..." Raja Nawab said to him, frowning and observing his peacock-feather sash, "but I see Mistress Magistery has already chosen you as her eventual successor."

Before Al or Mistress Magistery could respond, Raja Nawab smiled and said kindly, "I now know everything that I needed to know about you, Al. And I wholeheartedly agree with Mistress Magistery's decision. The future of Luxfons looks very bright, indeed.

"It's now time for me to go and bring it out of the darkness. I want the Spirit-noblest of Luxfons *and* the Future Spirit-noblest of Luxfons to accompany me."

Raja Nawab turned into a bolt of lightning. It struck Mistress Magistery in the chest, immediately absorbing her into itself. And then it struck Al. It was over in a split second: being blinded by golden light, his feet leaving solid ground and the dizziness.

Raja Nawab had brought them to the riverbank, which was brimming with tall, gloriously yellow dandelions.

After asking Al and Mistress Magistery to remain where they were, he glided to the very edge of the bank, bent down and touched the perfectly still surface of the water with the tip of his finger. He then quickly made his way back to join them. Al expected the River to outshine the stormiest of seas almost instantly, and he was not disappointed. As watery sea creatures danced together high in the air, splashing the banks with great droplets of water, the River ejected a soaking Spirit from its depths.

Queen Lamiobra landed on her feet in front of her foes and found herself unable to move. She no longer had her mace, but was still grasping Ivar's cane in her hand.

"That's enough," said Raja Nawab, looking up at the watery sea creatures, and tranquillity was restored at once.

His eyes then came to rest on his former consort. The fear on her face was gone – it had not been replaced with remorse of any kind, but with smug indifference. She stared directly back at him.

"I'll take back what's mine first of all," said Raja Nawab, snatching the cane out of her hand. "You've gone unpunished for hundreds of years, Lamiobra, but not any longer. Luxfons will finally be free of the abhorrent darkness inside you."

Queen Lamiobra remained silent.

"Al ..." Raja Nawab held out his hand.

Al removed the dagger from his pocket – it became Marshal's sword once more as he handed it to its creator.

"That sword will *never* touch me," Queen Lamiobra scoffed as Raja Nawab raised it aloft.

She became smoky and shapeless and faded into nothingness. The sword burst into flames, making Al and Mistress Magistery jump back, and then it, too, was gone.

"Did you make it do that?!" Al asked Raja Nawab.

He shook his head. "I'd just designed it that way. The sword also contained a great deal of darkness. I didn't want such a weapon lingering in Luxfons once its purpose was over: once Queen Lamiobra Departed."

"So if *I* had used it on her, I would've been engulfed too?"

"Yes," Raja Nawab said simply. "Marshal wore armour for that very reason, and I am lucky enough to be immune to the flames. Did you have an opportunity to use it on her at any point?" he added, looking curious.

Al nodded.

"Why didn't you?"

Al hesitated. "It's like ... something was telling me not to," he said finally.

"What an extraordinary young man you are," said Raja Nawab, smiling.

Al and Mistress Magistery exchanged looks of bemusement.

"There are many secrets concerning Luxfons that I wasn't able to share with you, Mistress Magistery, before I Departed," said Raja Nawab. "I'm glad I now have an opportunity to share one of the most significant ones with *both* of you – Luxfons itself speaks to us from time to time, providing guidance when we need it most. Not all of us have the power to listen, though. The fact that you, Al, as a Non-Spirit, can hear what this world – this mysterious world rooted in goodness – is telling you truly does make you extraordinary.

"It's a precious power to have, but one that can easily be clouded. I now know that my devastation at Lamiobra's betrayal was such that it prevented me from listening to what Luxfons was telling me at the time: that I'd been tricked by her in the Orangery. But it doesn't matter anymore – she's gone. And we're entitled to feel jubilant!"

The three of them beamed at each other for a few moments. But then Raja Nawab's face betrayed a hint of sadness.

"There's a particular reason why you wanted us to accompany you, isn't there?" asked Mistress Magistery.

"There is," replied Raja Nawab. "I want to tell you both something that you must keep secret in order to maintain this peace. When I Depart Luxfons again, I won't be able to return. This is because Taurbrum needs to Depart fully now, for good. Since he won't be returning, he can't bring me back." He sighed heavily. "The blow that struck him earlier injured him so significantly that even I can't heal him. He's powerful enough to hide his injuries from us and control his excruciating pain, but only temporarily. He must remain with me in the place where there's no suffering."

Mistress Magistery nodded but looked concerned. "How will I Accept Newly Departed Spirits if I can no longer fashion the Sceptre out of his horns?"

"I know that Taurbrum will be noble enough to leave his horns behind in the form of the Sceptre," Raja Nawab assured her. "And now" – he hesitated – "I must visit a small part of Luxfons that I tarnished in my despair. I'm ashamed about what I did and wish to make amends. You're more than welcome to join me."

◆ ◆ ◆

Raja Nawab had brought them to the Orangery. The colossal, fortified wall was the first to go, followed closely by the rotting vegetation and its stench. The Orangery was now surrounded by a beautiful meadow of daisies, dandelions and buttercups. And then the building itself was transformed into a little piece of bliss. It was unshackled from the thorny vines, glittering glass appeared in every window and the heavy wooden door vanished. Inside, the gloomy reddish glow had been replaced by a warm golden one, the pillars carved with grotesques had turned into pretty fountains and the now perfectly intact pots and urns were bursting with a breath-taking array of exotic and pleasant-smelling plants.

"The tunnel leading to this place will never cease to exist," Raja Nawab told Al and Mistress Magistery as they looked round in awe. "Hermit's skills are to be commended! The Spirit-creature I placed inside it Departed a while ago, though."

He let water from the fountain he was standing next to trickle onto his hand before sighing and saying, "I could've stayed here for an eternity."

"You still can!" said Al, feeling hopeful.

"I don't belong to this world anymore, Al. My time in Luxfons runs out the moment Taurbrum decides to Depart again; I'm depending entirely upon him to be here. Even though he's gracious enough to allow me to stay for as long as I see fit, we need to Depart soon in light of what's happened to him."

He placed Ivar's cane gently against the fountain and then turned to Mistress Magistery. "Is there anything else I could aid you with before we return to Sundomum?"

Mistress Magistery pondered for a few moments and then nodded.

◆ ◆ ◆

She had brought them to another place Al was familiar with: the desolate moor where Agrius Poley-Babington lay buried in his abode. She made the moor relinquish the rusty cabin, which had the chain of white light still wrapped around it. With a flick of her finger, the chain disappeared and the lopsided corrugated door creaked open, allowing the Spirit-youth to gingerly step out. He looked petrified.

"Greetings, Mister Poley-Babington," said Mistress Magistery. "I'm glad to inform you that the darkness that threatened our world has been vanquished. And it is now time to honour my word. However, it won't be the Spirit-nobles and Future Spirit-nobles and I who will determine whether you can continue with your task. It will be Raja Nawab himself."

Agrius froze. He then turned his head slowly towards Raja Nawab, bowed deeply, swooned and fell to the ground in a heap.

"You may rejoice, Mister Poley-Babington," said Raja Nawab, gliding over to him. He bent down and brought Agrius to his feet. "I declare that you may continue to help those that you love most."

◆ ◆ ◆

Raja Nawab had brought Al and Mistress Magistery back to the battlefield in Sundomum's shadow. It was still strewn with weapons and debris, but the cages of fire, the blocks of ice, the nets of rope, the giant stings, the vine meshes, the mounds of Spiritsnuff-sprinkled Oculus Plume and everything else that had entrapped the armoured soldiers had disappeared – their prisoners had Departed. But none of the defenders of the Laws of Luxfons who had remained behind in the battle outside were anywhere to be seen either.

Once the carpet of Oculus Plume was restored to its untarnished glory, Raja Nawab turned his attention towards the rock fragments hanging in the air around Sundomum. In a matter of moments, the mighty stairs had been constructed once more, the surplus rocks falling to the ground, and Raja Nawab began to ascend, with Al and Mistress Magistery following in his wake. When they reached the top, they did not find a gaping hole *or* the portcullis, but the great golden doors, which were standing open to let them process into the palace. And when they stepped into the hall after him, Al was not at all surprised to see that its battle scars had vanished. The wide archways leading to the two wings now remained firmly in place, full of bright, golden light.

The Spirit-nobles and Future Spirit-nobles (including a delighted and unharmed Polemus), Taurbrum and the peacock were gathered by the thrones. Accompanying them were – Morfox, Fickle, Kiang and Clemerc. Al felt pure joy rush through him; *they* had survived the battle outside Sundomum.

"I'd like us all to honour those who have sacrificed their tenure in Luxfons in defending its Laws," announced Raja Nawab. "But before we do, we need to spend a moment or two acknowledging how integral Mister Al Baba – the Future Spirit-noblest of Luxfons – was to our victory!"

Al's reddening ears rang with the glorious sound of

applause and cheers.

Raja Nawab then led them all to the threshold of Sundomum. He raised his hands, and a tower made of bluebells erected itself in the clearing before toppling onto the jagged rocks now strewn all around.

"They shall remain here forever," said Raja Nawab, bowing.

The Spirit-nobles and Future Spirit-nobles, keen to rejoice in their own abodes, bade their farewells and left soon afterwards. Clemerc and the peacock were the only two Spirit-creatures left behind (apart from Taurbrum). Mistress Magistery suggested that the two of them join Io and spend some time recuperating in what she declared was the most beautiful place in Luxfons: the Meadow. As they flew off into the distance, Al, Mistress Magistery, Raja Nawab and Taurbrum made their way back to the thrones.

"It's almost time for me to return to my own world," said Raja Nawab as he came to a halt in front of the Great Throne.

Something appeared in his hand: three single bluebells. He placed one on Alfred's throne and the other two on the throne that was now Frederick's – but once belonged to Ivar *and* Metanos.

He then turned to Taurbrum and observed him in silence for a short while. The black bull nodded, and there was a flash of light: Taurbrum was now hornless, and Raja Nawab was holding the Sceptre. He handed it to Mistress Magistery.

"You're now in the twilight of your tenure as Spirit-noblest," Raja Nawab told her. "I'd say you only have a century or so remaining in Luxfons before you feel it's time to Depart."

Chuckling, he became smoky and shapeless and faded into nothingness, as did Taurbrum.

Al looked down at the bluebell on his grandfather's throne. "I wish he and Robin were here to celebrate with us," he said, his voice breaking.

"Me too, Al. Me too."

Looking up, Al saw Mistress Magistery steal a glance at the two bluebells on the other mahogany throne.

"Did you ever think that Metanos would change once he knew the truth?" he asked her, feeling curious.

"When Karen revealed what Clemerc had done for her, a very, very small part of me started to believe that if one of his Spirit-creatures could retain some of their light, so could he. But when I discovered that he was in league with Queen Lamiobra, I concluded that it was impossible for him to have retained any. Clearly, I was wrong. It seems you're far better skilled than I am at listening to Luxfons when it's trying to guide us," she added, her voice brimming with pride.

Al went red again. "It feels so weird not having anything to worry about anymore."

Mistress Magistery laughed. "Come, Al," she said, "let's go and inform Hermit that there's no need for him to make any more of the Dormshield Concoction. And then maybe we can have a nice, long stroll in the Meadow ..."

"What great idea!" enthused Al.

22

A Parting Promise

It was time for Al to finally go home. He had spent a great deal of time leisurely exploring the beauty of Luxfons, which he had enjoyed immensely. Many of the Spirits he met along the way had been kind enough to invite him into their abodes and thank him heartily for everything he had done to help save their world from tyranny. Their love and gratitude moved him a great deal, and he could have happily stayed in Luxfons for a very long time ... But there was no place in that world he could definitively call home – yet. And he missed his family.

Mistress Magistery brought Al to the site of Alfred's Unsighted Gate. They were accompanied by Frederick, who had sometimes taken Al on little excursions in his new chariot to places he himself loved and thought Al would enjoy too.

"Although your life will never fully go back to the way it was, Al, knowing what you now know," said Mistress Magistery, "it's important that it should be as close as possible to the happy life you were leading before the events of Christmas Day. You and your family are entitled to that.

"The Non-Spirits in your lives will not enquire where

you've been for the past couple of months – they're of the belief that none of you ever left. Your lives will resume seamlessly."

"And ... um ... my powers?"

"Once you leave Luxfons, they'll gradually be absorbed back into your Spirit and remain there, locked."

Al smiled and nodded.

"Will you let me help you and your family to normalise your lives?" Frederick humbly asked him.

"Of course!" said Al, feeling curious. "How exactly?"

"I'll personally take on Chief Alfred's task of bringing whatever light I can into your lives," Frederick declared, his voice bursting with pride. "Your Christmases will be as joyous as before for as long as I'm a Chief Spirit-noble. That's a promise!"

"Thank you, Frederick," said Al, beaming.

"I know you're more than capable of dealing with any problems you might face in the future," said Frederick, "but there's no harm in getting a little help now and again!"

Al chuckled before embracing his friend in farewell.

Mistress Magistery turned into the sphere of dazzling white light, which engulfed Al for the last time ...

And he was back in his very own garden. It was night-time, and Al began to shiver almost immediately. He and the smoky, shapeless figure of Mistress Magistery remained in front of the mighty oak tree for a few moments, however, looking at the large Tudor house. Its lattice windows were aglow with golden light, and Al knew it was warm and cosy inside; Mistress Magistery had already delivered the good news to his family and brought them home a while ago. As the pair made their way up to the house, Al noticed something glinting in the grass. The Spiritsnuff from Christmas Day was still there! Then it disappeared.

"You'll find that your bedroom won't have any either now," Mistress Magistery told him. She laughed and said, "It probably brightened the place up somewhat, though!"

"Are you coming in?" Al asked her when they reached the garden door.

"I think not, Al. Thank you. Thank you so much for helping us defend the Laws of Luxfons – the Laws of your future home. Farewell!"

Al bowed.

The phantom-like figure turned into a beam of light, which zoomed off into the dark branches of the oak tree and vanished.

It was early December, and Al, now fifteen, was sitting in the library, surrounded by a stack of books. He had had sleepless nights in the past few days due to sheer worry. No matter how hard he tried, he simply could not grasp a topic he had been introduced to in his physics class. He had read and read, and his teacher had explained and explained, but to no avail. And the books he currently had his head buried in may as well have been written in a language that was completely alien to him.

He was getting tired and thought it was now probably a good idea to head home for a good rest and some turkey sandwiches. But he was still determined not to give up altogether. Even though every part of him was telling him it was futile to do so, he took out two of the books that looked a touch friendlier than the others, planning to grapple with them later.

He discovered that it was snowing heavily as he left the library and felt glad he had brought his big green coat, hat and scarf along. As he made his way carefully down the iced high street, his heavy satchel swinging by his side, Al's mind fluttered back to his woe. *What will happen if I don't ever understand? Will I fall behind? What if I fail the exam? Will I be kept behind a whole year?* Every one of these stabbing thoughts made his heart sink, but his attention had been wholly captured by them. He did not even notice the merriment all around him.

In spite of the weather, many families had decided to spend their Saturday afternoon doing some Christmas shopping. The children – and many of the adults – were enthusing about the presents they had just purchased, or the festive decorations adorning every shop window, or the snow itself.

A very loud thud behind Al managed to rouse him, and he turned round. A red-haired man in a coat lined with reddish fur was crouched on the ground gathering up books lying in the snow and replacing them in the large cardboard box he had clearly just dropped. He was struggling to get them all in quickly and looked round for assistance ... but nobody provided any. Even though he was now exhausted and extremely hungry, Al decided to help him. He smiled at the pale-looking man as he approached him before bending down to pick up some of the snow-covered books.

"Thanks," the man said in a growly voice.

"No problem. Donating all these to the charity shop?"

The man nodded.

Al brushed the snow off one of the books he was holding and was about to add it to the box with the others when it caught his eye. The cover was metallic green, and the title pertained to the exact topic Al was struggling with. He flicked through it and squealed with delight: it seemed a great deal friendlier than the ones he had in his satchel.

"Could I have this please?" asked Al, his excitement mounting.

"Yes," replied the man.

"Brilliant! Thank you!"

The man picked up the last few books remaining on the ground, quickly placed them in the box, sprang up and walked away in the opposite direction to the one Al was heading in. Al placed the book in his satchel and headed off again. He looked back almost immediately, but the man seemed to have become lost in the crowd of merry shoppers.

He did notice a small robin sitting on top of a distant pillar box, though. It fluttered away as Al began to chuckle.

ABOUT THE AUTHOR

Junaid Ashraf

I am a pharmacist from Birmingham, UK, and this is my debut novel. I first got the idea for it at university, inspired largely by my love of the supernatural and Dickens' A Christmas Carol! Soon after I qualified, I started working on a part time basis in order to get the idea I'd allowed to bloom in my mind on paper. Building a whole fantasy world with an array of quirky characters has been more exhilarating than I can put into words! I will be writing a sequel in due course.

Concerning my other interests, I have a passion for history (especially the Tudors) and feel most at home in castles and cathedrals!

AUTHOR WEBSITE

junaidashrafauthor.co.uk

ACKNOWLEDGEMENT

Family, friends, colleagues, editors, beta readers, artists, social media family AND you! Thank you all so much.

Cover Illustration: Jacqueline Abromeit

www.ingramcontent.com/pod-product-compliance
Lightning Source LLC
LaVergne TN
LVHW041015150826
845672LV00001B/88
* 9 7 9 8 8 3 8 0 6 6 5 2 7 *